Jeanne Whitmee originally trained as an actress and later taught speech and drama before taking up writing full time. She has written many novels including her last, *All That I Am*.

THE HAPPY HIGHWAYS

Although from opposite ends of the social spectrum, Sally and Fiona become firm friends whilst working together in an aircraft factory during the Second World War. After the war ends neither can settle down, and then Fiona has the idea of the pair opening a catering business together. Whilst their new venture gets off to a good start in spite of rationing and transport problems, their personal lives are not so successful. Fiona, whose fiancé died during the war, is sure she can never love again. Meanwhile, cockney Sally falls for Fiona's RAF pilot brother who she feels is socially superior. But secrets lie uncovered in both Fiona and Sally's pasts that will shape their own futures and the lives of those they love.

Books by Jeanne Whitmee
Published by The House of Ulverscroft:

ORANGES AND LEMONS
THE LOST DAUGHTERS
THURSDAY'S CHILD
EVE'S DAUGHTER
BELLADONNA
KING'S WALK
PRIDE OF PEACOCKS
ALL THAT I AM

JEANNE WHITMEE

THE HAPPY HIGHWAYS

Complete and Unabridged

CHARNWOOD
Leicester

First published in Great Britain in 2005 by
Robert Hale Limited
London

First Charnwood Edition
published 2005
by arrangement with
Robert Hale Limited
London

British Library CIP Data

Whitmee, Jeanne
   The happy highways.—Large print ed.—
Charnwood library series
1. Female friendship—Fiction
2. Great Britain—Social life and customs—Fiction
3. Large type books
I. Title
823.9′14 [F]

ISBN 1–84617–049–4

Published by
F. A. Thorpe (Publishing)
Anstey, Leicestershire

Set by Words & Graphics Ltd.
Anstey, Leicestershire
Printed and bound in Great Britain by
T. J. International Ltd., Padstow, Cornwall

This book is printed on acid-free paper

1

'I still can't quite believe it's over at last.'

Fiona had to raise her voice to be heard above the noise in the market square. It seemed as though the whole of Northbridge was here, tightly pressed together to celebrate the Allies' victory over Japan, bringing the long, weary years of war to an end.

As Fiona excitedly squeezed Sally's arm a cloud of stars burst overhead accompanied by a collective 'oooh' from the upturned faces of the crowd. In the silvery light the girls looked at each other.

'Going to change things though, isn't it?' Sally said.

She was voicing the thought that had been on both their minds ever since last May when the war in Europe had officially ended. Already the demobbed servicemen were beginning to drift back on the promise that their jobs at the factory would be waiting for them. The female workforce was well aware that its days were numbered.

Fiona looked at her friend. 'Afraid so,' she said.

A man behind her cannoned forward almost knocking her off her feet. 'Sorry, duck,' he mumbled. 'Not me, it's them behind.'

Fiona said, 'Look, Sall, shall we try and find a drink somewhere before this mob invades the pubs?'

Nodding agreement, Sally grasped the back of Fiona's jacket and they began to elbow their way towards the fringe of the crowd.

The Rose and Crown was already packed with revellers in varying stages of good humoured inebriation and, after jostling for attention at the bar, they held their half pints aloft and struggled through the crush to where Sally had spotted a couple of vacant seats in the corner, mercifully well away from a rather inept pianist who was pounding out wartime favourites.

Subsiding gratefully on to chairs they grinned at each other. 'It's good to sit down,' Sally said, taking a sip of her beer. 'God knows what it'll be like an hour from now when everyone starts to pile in.'

'You're right. What do you say we drink up and make tracks for home?' Fiona suggested. 'I've got half a bottle of gin and some lemonade in my locker. We could celebrate in comfort.'

The factory hostel had been home to the two girls ever since they had been assigned to Northbridge's Webber Marshall aircraft factory in 1940.

Sally Joy had been dismayed on the day she arrived to find she was sharing a room with Fiona Crowther. 'Toffee-nosed' had been her initial impression of the willowy blonde with the snobby accent and posh name. She couldn't see that this upper class vision could possibly have anything in common with a Lyons Corner House 'nippy' with a cockney accent as broad as the River Thames.

At their first meeting she was almost

aggressively defensive. 'Where're you from then?' she asked as they unpacked their cases. 'Kensington, or would it be St John's Wood?'

Fiona glanced at the diminutive figure with the bright, intelligent eyes and dark curly hair. Did she sense an air of resentment? 'Suffolk actually,' she said. 'And you?'

Sally laughed. 'Obvious, innit? East End, *actually*. Bethnal Green!' She sat down with a bump on her bed and looked up at Fiona, a challenge in her brown eyes. 'Cockney through an' through, me! An' while I'm at it I might as well come clean about meself. Me mum weren't married. Took off when I were six months and left me with me gran and grandpa. Never set eyes on her from that day to this and good riddance too, if you ask me! Grandpa's got a greengrocer's shop — corner of Fish Lane — and Gran goes out cleanin'. I ain't been to secondary school nor nothing so I'm dead ignorant. Left the local elementary when I were fourteen and went to work in the kitchens at Joe Lyons. I got to be a waitress later though,' she added, thrusting her chin out proudly. 'At Leicester Square Corner 'ouse. So no one can't say I didn't try to get on.' She stood up and began to put her underclothes away in a drawer. 'That's me an' all about me, like it or not. So there!'

Fiona sat down on her own bed opposite. 'Thanks for telling me all that, Sally,' she said gently. 'There was no need, but thanks anyway. I don't know about you, but I tend to take people as I find them. Birth and background don't have

3

much to do with anything, I find. It's what's inside that matters.' She took a packet of jelly babies from her handbag and offered Sally one. 'But as you've volunteered all that, I suppose I'd better do the same. My parents live in the Manor House at Saltmere St Peter in Suffolk. It's a nice village, if you like the country. I went to a boarding school, which I hated by the way, and when it came to exams I was a dead loss, unlike my brother Stephen who won a scholarship to Cambridge. When I left, my father paid for me to go to a cordon bleu cookery school in London, as that seemed to be the only thing I was any good at.' She grinned disarmingly. 'So you see, we have more in common than you think.'

'Oh, don't get me wrong. I'm good at lots of things!' Sally protested. 'I can stand up for myself for one thing. No one don't put nothing over on me.' She paused. 'I can reckon up pretty quick too and . . . ' she paused. 'And I can sing.'

'Sing?' Fiona's eyes widened. 'Gosh! Can you? I've always wished I had a voice. Do you do much singing — in public, I mean?'

'Believe it or not I used to sing with the church choir.' Sally grinned. She was beginning to relax now, warming to the other girl who was quite different from what she'd thought. 'Only way Gran could get me to go to church.'

'So — you enjoyed it?'

'Yeah, it was OK. The vicar used to sing too, so he was interested — got me singin' solos an' all that. Christmas time we used to go all over with the carols and that. His wife taught music

4

and she took me on and gave me some lessons — for free.'

'What luck!'

'Yeah.' Sally leaned forward. 'So this cookery — cordon what's-its-name — when you left, did you get a job cooking?'

'There wasn't time. I'd only just finished the course when the war started. My brother Stephen is in the RAF. I wanted to join the WAAF but my parents wouldn't agree. They wanted me to stay at home and knit socks for sailors, but I wanted to do some proper war work.' She looked at Sally. 'I wanted to leave home if the truth is known,' she confessed. 'I hate the kind of life my folks live. I wanted to get away from all that and meet people — *real* people.'

Sally regarded her new room-mate thoughtfully. 'I never fancied the services somehow,' she said. 'All that marchin' about an' everyone wearin' the same clobber. I thought if I came here they'd let me work in the canteen like I'm used to, but they keep them jobs for the older women.' She frowned. 'I'm a bit worried about making aeroplanes.'

'Worried — why?'

'I wonder if I'm gonna be able to do it right. I mean — blokes is gonna have to *fly* them things.'

Fiona laughed. 'I don't suppose they'll expect us to make whole ones,' she said. 'Just little bits for someone else to fit together.'

'Oh, do you reckon?' Sally looked relieved. 'That's OK then.'

★ ★ ★

5

Without realizing it the two girls learned a great deal from one another during the months that followed. Sally soon realized that the way Fiona spoke wasn't affected at all but natural with rhythms and inflections that were almost musical. She listened to her carefully, hardly aware that as she did so her own speech underwent subtle changes. She learned to correct her own grammar and sound her previously dropped aitches. Fiona in her turn learned from Sally's cheerful, easy manner how to blend in and get along with the many kinds of women she found herself working with. She learned to relax — to laugh off the ribald jokes and casual swearing and to let herself go. Sometimes, when they were off duty on Saturday afternoons they took the bus into Northbridge to look at the shops, have tea in a café and go to the cinema. Simple pleasures enjoyed together. Occasionally they went along to the dances at the army camp at nearby Strapford. Some of the boys they met were nice and in the ordinary way they might have been tempted to see them again. But Strapford was a transit camp and most of the young soldiers were bound for undisclosed overseas postings and were unlikely to pass that way again.

As they got to know one another better Sally learned that Fiona was deeply in love with her brother's friend, Mark Fenner.

'We're going to be married someday, after the war,' Fiona said dreamily. 'My parents don't approve, of course. Mark's father is manager of a gents' outfitters in Hull and they think that's quite beyond the pale, but we're determined that we'll be together some day.' She turned her head to look at Sally. 'It makes me so angry, Sall. Father's great-grandfather made his money out of a cotton mill up north during the industrial revolution, yet to hear them you'd think they were landed gentry.'

Sally was silent. Money was money in her eyes, however you came by it. And, as her gran always said, *money talks*.

'One of these days you'll have to meet my nanny, Joan,' Fiona said.

'Is that your gran?' Sally asked.

'No, she was my nanny. She brought Stephen and me up until we went to boarding school. She's always been more like a mother to me than my real one.'

'You had a *nanny*? I thought that was only in books and on the pictures!' Sally could not imagine what it must have been like, growing up in Fiona's home with acres of green fields to play in and her own pony to ride. It was a different world.

'Yes. We hardly saw anything of our parents when we were little,' Fiona went on. 'They were always out socializing up in London or abroad, Monte Carlo or Paris. Nanny Joan lives in Kent now. Her parents left her their smallholding when they died and she still runs it. You'd love it down there, Sally.'

'Oh, I know Kent,' Sally said proudly. 'Gran and me used to go hop picking down there when I was little. We always had a smashing time. Do you go and stay with her then?'

'Yes. I used to take Mark there. Nanny Joan loves him. I know she'll be pleased to see us married. Next time he gets leave we thought we might go and spend it with her.' Fiona turned to look at Sally. 'Is there anyone you love, back home?'

Sally laughed. '*Love?* The fellers I used to know were only interested in one thing and it wasn't love!' She sighed. 'I hate all that. I want a feller who'll show me some respect. One of these days when I meet a really decent bloke like that, *then* I'll fall in love. Trouble is, knowing my luck, he probably won't fall for me.'

★   ★   ★

The work they did was repetitive and boring, but the girls enjoyed the twice-daily diversion of Music While You Work, which was relayed from the wireless over the public address system. Fiona soon learned to sing her heart out along with all the other girls, and, working alongside Sally, she heard the other girl's voice for the first time and was impressed by its strength and sweetness.

'You should take it up professionally,' Fiona said. 'You're certainly good enough.'

But Sally shook her head. 'I'm happy where I am,' she said. 'I like singing but only for fun. I wouldn't want to swap my pals for it.'

It was late one evening towards the end of 1941 that Fiona received a devastating telephone call from her brother. Mark Fenner's plane had been shot down in a raid over Germany. Fiona

8

was heartbroken and it was Sally who held her while she wept inconsolably long into the night, rocking her gently and weeping with her in silent sympathy. In the face of tragedy the differences in their upbringing were irrelevant.

Sally had seen her grandparents very few times during the war, but each time she visited she was appalled at the toll the bombing had taken of her beloved East End. Each time it seemed that the landscape had changed. Familiar landmarks were disappearing rapidly — the Prince Albert pub, the little Baptist chapel at the end of Fish Lane; the pawnbrokers and the eel and pie shop. Great craters and gaps scarred the beloved streets — sometimes whole rows of houses had vanished, replaced by piles of rubble. Familiar faces were missing too. Either evacuated to safer parts of the country or dead under the heaps of debris that had once been their homes. But perhaps the worst part was the lack of children. No cheeky little dirty faces. No childish voices ringing out at play. No games of street football, skipping or hopscotch. It was frightening and disturbing.

When Sally's grandpa was killed serving at his ARP post during the blitz she returned to London for the funeral. It was then that Gran told her that she had decided to go and live in Southend with an old friend who had also been widowed. Edna had inherited a house from an elderly relative and together they hoped to turn it into a boarding house after the war when folks started having holidays again. The little greengrocer's shop in Fish Lane with the flat above had been badly damaged and was now boarded up for the duration.

'If it's still standin' after the war, maybe I'll be able to sell it,' Gran said without much hope. 'But I've got me savin's an' what your grandpa left. Edna's got a bit put by as well as the house, so between us we'll make a go of it.'

It was typical of her stoical character to be planning for the future, but Sally felt a secret pang of sadness for the only home she had ever known and now would never return to.

★   ★   ★

Every time Fiona visited Saltmere St Peter she was shocked at how unaffected the village seemed by the war. Apart from the local branch of the Women's Institute where her mother presided over the annual jam making and knitting for the troops they all seemed to her to be quite detached from it all. When she was foolish enough to voice this thought her mother bristled indignantly.

'A German plane came down on Gresham's Farm last month,' she said. 'It landed in one of Arthur Gresham's fields and killed a *sheep*!'

When Fiona laughed Marcia's face reddened. 'Mrs Bray at the post office lost her son at Dieppe,' she said stiffly. 'And you seem to have forgotten that your brother is an RAF pilot. Your father and I are in constant dread of losing him. Every time we hear on the news how many of our planes are missing or I see a telegram boy in the village my knees turn to water.'

Fiona was instantly contrite. '*Mother*! I'm sorry,' she said. 'It's just that Stephen writes me such funny letters, full of all the things he and his friends have been up to and . . . '

'Surely you realize that is all bravado.' Marcia said. 'I would have thought that Mark Fenner's death would have given you a better understanding of the reality of life in wartime.'

'Yes, I know all about bravado — and reality, Mother,' Fiona said quietly. The remark was a blow below the belt and Fiona's throat tightened painfully. Her mother had neatly turned the tables on her as she so often did. So many of the girls at the factory had lost husbands, fiancés and brothers, but they learned to put on a brave face and shed their tears in private just as she had. She turned and went up to her room to hide her hurt and humiliation. Only Sally knew just how much Mark's death had meant to her. She couldn't hope to make her mother understand and it was pointless to try.

Stephen had always been her mother's favourite. Ever since they were children Marcia had shown a transparent preference for her son and now that they were grown up she lost no opportunity to press the point that Fiona was proving her right. If she hadn't loved her brother so much Fiona might have resented it. Stephen succeeded where she had failed at school. Stephen was brave and handsome and his mother was confident that he would marry well and have a great future. Fiona on the other hand, she clearly despaired of. She simply would not conform, refusing to attend hunt balls and

11

parties given by the local elite on the grounds that they were boring. She preferred to spend time with her pony instead. Marcia had all but given up on her. The last straw was when the war came and she chose to work in 'that dreadful factory place' instead of doing useful voluntary work at the local hospital. In her mother's eyes she was a misfit.

★　★　★

The hostel was deserted when they got back, but as they turned the corner of the corridor they saw the familiar portly figure of Annie, the middle-aged canteen manageress coming towards them. Sally had always liked Annie; as fellow Londoners they often swapped reminiscences and news about their families back home.

'Not out celebrating, Annie?' she called. 'Come and have a drink with us.'

The older woman smiled. 'Thanks. Don't mind if I do.'

'So what are we going to do now it's all over?' Fiona asked as the three of them sat on her bed, sipping gin and lemonade.

Sally shrugged. 'I haven't even thought about it. Go back to Lyons and ask for my old job back perhaps. What about you, Annie?'

The older woman pursed her lips. 'I'll have to take what I can find,' she said. 'I used to be parlour maid for the Frobisher family in Eaton Square but I was too long in the tooth for that kind of work before the war. I've done some waitressing but what with all the gels comin' out of the services I doubt they'll take me on for that either. I'll be lucky to get a cleanin' job, I reckon.' She drew down the corners of her mouth in a rueful grin. 'It ain't no joke gettin' old when you 'ave to earn your own livin'.'

Both girls were silent for a moment then Fiona asked, 'If you had the choice what would you like to do?'

'I reckon women like Annie and me are not going to have that much choice,' Sally said. 'Apart from working here all I've ever done is waitressing. There's already a rumour that we'll be getting our notice with the next wage packet, so we'd better start thinking.'

Annie looked at Fiona enquiringly. 'I suppose you'll be going back to the Manor. I bet your mum is planning to have you presented at Court and all that.'

Fiona's look of abject horror made them laugh. 'I'm not even going to *think* about it!' she said. 'Getting decked out in a frilly white frock and being hauled around all those awful coming out balls — *ugh*! It's like a cattle market! Besides, it's for eighteen-year-olds. I'm too old for all that rubbish now.'

'That's a shame. Don't you want a nice rich husband?' Sally teased.

'Some chinless wonder with a crumbling pile in the wilds of Yorkshire? No thank you!'

Annie chuckled. 'You wouln't 'ave to ask me twice. Sounds a bit of all right to me!'

Fiona was silent and Sally knew that she was thinking of Mark. A moment later the other girl confirmed her guess.

13

'I wish you could have met Mark,' she said. 'He was so lovely. Handsome and kind and thoughtful. We had so much in common — so many plans. There'll never be anyone like him.' She gave her shoulders a little shake. 'Oh, let's not get maudlin tonight of all nights.' She looked up. 'Tell you what — you must both come and visit me sometime.'

'What, to the Manor 'ouse?' Annie laughed. 'Not me darlin'. I know my place and that's *below* stairs.'

Sally pulled a face. 'God knows what your folks'd think of me, Fee.'

Fiona knew exactly what her mother would think of Sally, though she didn't say so. Maybe it wasn't such a good idea after all. She wouldn't want her friend to suffer her mother's disapproving scrutiny and heavy sarcasm. Maybe she could take her friends down to Nanny Joan's in Kent sometime instead. She was sure they'd get along.

'So if you're not gonna let your ma find you a rich 'usband what will you do?' Annie asked.

'I might see if I can get some kind of clerical job in London,' Fiona said thoughtfully. 'Only one thing's certain. I'm sure as hell not going back home to live.'

'Chance'd be a fine thing,' Sally said. 'My home's gone and so have Gran and Grandpa.'

'Mine was bombed to blazes in '42,' Annie said. 'Looks like I'll be movin' in with me sister Ada in Islington, at least till her old man gets out of the Navy.'

'Well let's at least make a pact not to lose

14

touch with each other,' Sally said. 'Somehow or other we'll have to meet up again.'

After Annie had gone off to her own room and they were getting ready for bed Fiona asked, 'Where will you go, Sally? Have you got any plans?'

'I've still got a few friends in Bethnal Green and Hackney,' Sally assured her. 'I'll find something, don't worry.' She spoke with a confidence she didn't feel. In truth she dreaded the uncertainty of the future, the life that was coming to an end. The war had been terrible of course, but she had to admit that she'd been happy here in Northbridge these five years, working at the factory. Maybe the happiest she'd ever been. She would miss all of it; the job and the other girls. But most of all, Fiona. It was odd, they were so far apart in class, education and background that they would never have met if it hadn't been for the war, yet Fiona was the nicest, the very best friend she had ever had.

'But we won't lose touch, will we, Fee?' she asked, her eyes wistful. 'I couldn't bear it if we did after all this time.'

'*Lose touch?*' Fiona's eyes widened. 'You bet your sweet life we won't! You're my best friend *ever*, Sall. We'll always be friends — I promise.'

They hugged each other to confirm the pledge but Sally was doubtful. Once they both returned to their own environment — whatever Fiona said, life would fall back into the old patterns. Nothing would be as it recently had been.

2

Sally could hardly wait for her day off.

Sometimes it seemed to her that she spent her whole life looking forward to the time she spent away from the *Cosy Café*. Mostly she spent it trying to make her dismal bed-sit look more homely or catching up on the sleep she lost because of the endless roar of traffic under her window and the noise the other tenants made. Living in the quiet of a small town she had become accustomed to undisturbed nights, and since returning to Bethnal Green in September of 1945 the noise, dirt and smells of London were things she was having trouble getting used to again.

Nothing was the same. The East End she'd grown up in was gone. There were great yawning gaps where familiar landmarks had been. Bomb sites everywhere.

The only room she could find where she could afford the rent was a shambles. Furnished with the bare minimum, it was at the top of the three-storey house, dark and cheerless. Perowne Street had been badly bombed during the blitz. Number 64 was one of only a handful left standing, but the destruction had taken its toll. When it rained the wet came in round the window frames and through the ceiling. What it would be like when the winter came Sally dared not think.

She had been in the job at the *Cosy Café* for just over a month but she hated it. It had been the only work she could find and she had tried hard to make the best of what was literally a bad job. It was half past two and the lunchtime rush was over. Sally piled the used crockery on to the counter and wiped down the oilcloth-covered tables with a damp cloth. She opened the street door to let out the steam and tobacco smoke that pervaded the small crowded space and took a moment to take in a breath of air.

At the counter Alf Chandler stood refilling the tea urn. He was a huge man with greasy black hair that flopped over his shifty eyes. He wore a stained white apron over his collarless shirt, and the rolled up sleeves revealed heavily tattooed arms.

'Shut the bleedin' door, Sall,' he shouted. 'Parky enough in 'ere without you lettin' the cold in.' His small black eyes took in the back view of the neat little figure and he grinned lecherously. Did she realize that when she bent down he could see right up to her shapely thighs or did she do it on purpose?

Aware of his eyes burning into her back, Sally turned, reluctantly closing the door. 'Just thought I'd let the pong out,' she said. 'All that stale food and fag smoke!' She began to wipe the condensation off the uncurtained top half of the window. 'This net could do with a wash too,' she said, fingering the nicotine-stained material with distaste.

'You want it washin' — you can take it 'ome and do it yerself,' Alf said. 'My customers got

17

better things to think about. So've you, come to that. There's sandwiches needs cuttin' an' all the washin' up. After that there's a pile o'spuds to be peeled an' chipped in the kitchen.'

'All right, all right, I know. Can't be everywhere at once, can I?' As Sally ducked under the counter flap and edged past him to get to the back kitchen he reached out a large hand to squeeze her bottom painfully. She spun round, her face scarlet.

'*Ow!* Leave off!'

'Why? You know you like it.' He moved in closer trapping her against the wall. 'Give us a kiss, Sall — go on.' His huge ham-like hands were suddenly everywhere and Sally ducked under his arm and slipped through the kitchen door slamming it behind her, her heart pounding with revulsion.

Alf Chandler had been a stoker in the Merchant Navy. He'd served on the Atlantic convoys until an accident in the engine room had left him with an injured leg. He walked with a slight limp, but apart from that his other faculties seemed unimpaired, Sally told herself ironically. She was constantly on her guard against his wandering hands, trying to ignore his suggestive remarks and leering looks. His slack mouth with the stained cigarette butt constantly hanging from one corner made her flesh crawl.

The ping of the doorbell heralded a customer and Sally heaved a sigh of relief. With someone to see to in the caff Alf would be less likely to follow her through to the kitchen and renew his unwanted pursuit. 'Roll on tomorrow,' she told

18

herself as she rolled up her sleeves and began to tackle the pile of potatoes beside the sink. Alf's pregnant and down-trodden wife, Milly, would come in and cover for her on her day off tomorrow. How the poor woman stood him, she couldn't imagine.

Sally had arranged to meet Fiona at Oxford Circus outside the tube station and she was really looking forward to it. It was almost two months since they had left Northbridge and the two hadn't seen each other since. Fiona had found a job in the Food Office in Kensington. She wrote regular letters, describing the job and the women's hostel where she lived.

There are lots of other girls here, she wrote. *It's almost like the hostel at the factory, but not as friendly and certainly not the same without you. The job is almost as boring as making aircraft components, but without the fun and the companionship we had at Northbridge.*

Sally privately thought it sounded like a doddle compared to working for Alf at the *Cosy Café*. She wondered how Fiona would cope with Alf's groping and his one-track mind. He probably wouldn't dare try anything on with a girl as classy looking as Fee. She caught an early train and was there first, waiting near the flower barrow outside the Tube entrance and searching the faces of all the passers-by for her friend. In the end Fiona surprised her by coming out of the underground behind her and tapping her on the shoulder.

'Hello stranger.'

Sally spun round, a wide grin of delight on her

face as she threw her arms around her friend. 'Fee! Oh, I've missed you something chronic!'

'I've missed you something chronic too,' Fiona laughed. 'Come on, let's treat ourselves to coffee and a delicious sticky cake.'

Seated at a corner table in a nearby milk bar the girls looked one another over.

'You look smashing,' Sally said as she took in her friend's smart navy blue jacket and skirt. 'Is that a new suit?'

Fiona nodded. 'Thought I'd splash out my coupons and some of the cash I'd saved. Do you like it?'

'It's lovely. You've had your hair done too.' Fiona's hair had grown to shoulder length and she wore it with one lock sweeping forward in the popular Veronica Lake style. 'It really suits you.'

'It's nice to be able to wear it loose again after tucking it under those awful snoods we had to wear at the factory,' Fiona said. She noticed that Sally sounded wistful. Her washed out appearance hadn't escaped Fiona's notice either. 'Are you all right, Sally?' she asked. 'I mean, you look wonderful of course, but just a little . . . '

'Clapped out,' Sally finished for her. She knew she'd lost weight since they last met. The waistbands of her skirts were loose and even she could see the dark circles under her eyes when she looked in the mirror. 'I'm not used to the traffic yet so I wake up a lot in the night. But I'll get used to it,' she said.

'Have you picked up with any of your old friends since you've been back?'

'One or two,' Sally told her. 'It's not the same though, somehow. Quite a few of them have got married or moved away but Jenny Gifford who I went to school with is still there. Trouble is she's a nurse and works all kinds of funny shifts. Her off-duties and mine don't often come together.'

Fiona looked concerned. 'How do you pass the time then?'

'Sleeping mostly. You know, catching up. I'm always so tired.'

'That's awful. Why stay on? Leave and get something better.'

'Easier said than done. I'm not brainy like you. All I know is waitressing apart from making aeroplane components and there's no call for that any more.'

'I'm sure you could do what I do,' Fiona said. 'All I do all day is dish out emergency ration cards to ex-servicemen waiting for their civilian ration books to come through. And the hostel isn't the height of luxury but it's not bad.' She leaned across the table to touch Sally's red and roughened hand. 'Look at you, Sall. You're worth better than this.'

Sally didn't tell her about Alf Chandler's constant groping and suggestive remarks. She knew she'd be appalled if she knew about the odour of chip fat and cabbage water that permeated all her clothes — the mice and cockroaches that infested the kitchen. Such things were beyond her comprehension and it was best they stayed that way.

'Why don't you leave? There must be better jobs for a bright girl like you.'

Sally smiled ruefully. 'I couldn't just walk out,' she said. 'Alf's wife is expecting a baby soon and it'd mean she'd have to do my job till he found some other mug. He's got no consideration. I'll have to stay on a while for Milly's sake.'

'Well, I admire your loyalty,' Fiona said. 'I hope he deserves it. Think about it though. I'm sure you could find a better job near me. And you could share my room until another comes vacant.'

Sally smiled and shook her head. 'It's lovely of you to offer, Fee, but I couldn't really afford to — not without any money coming in.'

'Well, don't worry, we'll think of something.' Fiona sighed. 'Between you and me, I certainly can't see myself staying on in my job permanently. Wouldn't it be fun if we could get something together?' Her eyes brightened. 'Cook and housemaid with living-in accommodation. How about that?'

Sally pulled a face. 'I know you're a qualified cook and everything but I can't see your mum and dad being very happy about that.'

'I'm a big girl now,' Fiona said. 'I don't need their approval.'

But Sally still looked doubtful. 'To be honest, I don't think 'service' is my cup of tea. I've never been all that good at taking orders and toeing lines.' A grin tugged at the corners of her mouth. 'I'd probably get the sack the first week for answering back and being cheeky.'

Fiona smiled. 'Mmm, I know what you mean.'

'Have you been home lately, by the way?' Sally asked.

'Not since my mother and I fell out. Daddy came up last week though and we met for lunch. They have a house in Gower Street. It got a bit damaged in the blitz and he came up to see the builders about the repairs. He's rather an old dear really. I think you'd like him. He's just a bit under Mother's thumb, that's all. He tried to talk me into going home the weekend after next.'

'So — are you going then?'

'It's tempting.' Fiona shook her head. 'Stephen's going to be there apparently. It'll be his last leave before demob and I haven't seen him for ages. He's bringing a friend with him.' Her face brightened. 'Daddy suggested I bring a friend too so why not come with me, Sall? I'd definitely go if you were coming too.'

'I couldn't get the time off. I have to work weekends. That's how I get a day off in the week. Anyway they'd disapprove of me.'

'Of *course* they wouldn't.'

'Your mum would. A waitress who works in an East End greasy spoon caff. She'd think you'd taken leave of your senses.'

Fiona shook her head. 'Look, you're my best friend. We come as a package as they say, and frankly I don't give a damn what anyone says.' She reached across the table to squeeze Sally's hand 'Come on, let's go and buy you something nice to wear and we'll get your hair done — my treat. That'll perk you up no end.'

By four o'clock that afternoon the two girls were exhausted. Together they had searched the shops and used up the last of Sally's clothing coupons and most of the money she had saved

23

on a stylish winter coat and a pretty wool dress in a rich shade of red. Fiona had taken her along to her favourite hairdresser for a restyling afterwards. The stylist had looked at Sally's pert features from every angle and suggested a 'bubble cut'. As the scissors snipped at Sally's jawlength bob, the natural curl sprang up until her small piquant face was framed by a halo of dark curls.

'You look marvellous!' Fiona exclaimed. 'So much better than when I first saw you this morning.' She looked at her friend, her head on one side. 'So — are you going to do as I suggested — give in your notice and move in with me?

Sally smiled ruefully. 'I can't, Fee. I'm an East End kid at heart — even if things have changed, it's where I belong. I'll just keep on looking out for a better job.'

★ ★ ★

As the weeks passed and autumn turned into winter things got no better at the *Cosy Café*. Milly had a little girl in mid November, but the baby was sickly and had died when she was two days old. Poor Milly came home from the hospital washed out and depressed and Alf was more bad-tempered than ever.

'Can't do nothing bloody right,' he complained to Sally. 'She don't wanna do nothing these days, don't like the pictures no more, don't wanna go shopping. I get 'ome after a hard day at the caff and she ain't even *started* cooking the

24

meal. Just sits starin' at the wall. I tell you, Sall. I'm bleedin' sick of it.'

'I expect it's losing the baby,' Sally said. 'It must be awful, going through all that and no baby at the end of it.'

'Yeah — well — not likely to be no more kids, the way things is goin',' Alf muttered. 'Won't let me anywhere near her these days. You'd think I was poison!'

Sally said nothing. All her sympathy was with Milly. She couldn't imagine having to share a bed with a man like Alf. The thought sent shudders of revulsion through her.

Fiona wrote regular letters. She was still at Kensington Food Office and still looking in vain for a better job. She wrote that she had been home for the weekend after their last meeting. She and Stephen had had a great time. He'd brought his friend Ian with him and she wrote amusingly about the spree the three of them had enjoyed on the Saturday evening when — much to her mother's disapproval — they made a tour of the local pubs.

Every other week a post card would arrive from Gran. She'd never been one for writing and the few scribbled words on the backs of the cards were meant only to keep in touch and let Sally know she was well. Fiona's, on the other hand, were funny and expressive and full of news. Sally kept them all in an old chocolate box, reading them over and over to herself in the evenings. She missed her friend so much and was often swamped with nostalgia for the happy times they had spent together at the factory in Northbridge.

Although she replied to the letters she knew her efforts couldn't compare with Fiona's easy-to-read style and she often suspected sadly that they would lose touch eventually. Since they'd been apart the differences in their background had become more apparent. Now that the war was over she supposed that people would drift back into their own classes and environments. And maybe that was as it should be, she told herself.

Christmas was approaching fast and Sally had begun to wonder what she would do over the holiday. The caff was closing for Christmas and Boxing days and the thought of spending two whole days and nights alone in her bleak little bed-sit was something she preferred not to think about.

One evening in early December she and Jenny managed to meet and go to the cinema. They treated themselves to a trip up West to see *Blithe Spirit*. Apart from the day she had gone to meet Fee it was the first outing Sally had had since moving back to London.

Later as they sat over a cup of coffee Sally wanted to discuss the film, but all Jenny could talk about was her boyfriend, Gerry, who also worked at the Royal London Hospital.

'He's training to be a theatre technician,' she told Sally proudly. 'And as soon as he gets promoted we're going to get engaged. I've been a staff nurse for a year now so I'll soon start applying for a sister's post.' She looked at Sally across the table.

'You know, *you* could do worse than start nursing training,' she said. 'It'd get you out of that awful job at the caff, *and* out of that bed-sit. You'd get a room at the nurse's home. It's not posh but at least it's warm and dry.'

'Can't see myself kow-towing to some starchy old matron.' Sally mumbled, making patterns in the sugar with her spoon. 'I'd soon be telling her where to get off and I'd be out on my ear before you could say knife.'

'Not if you knew what was good for you, you wouldn't. Look, Sall, you've got to pull yourself together and do something about your life,' Jenny said sternly. 'You look *terrible*.'

'Thanks! Always could rely on my old mate for compliments!'

'Well, you *do* — worn out and really pinched.' Jenny looked accusingly at her friend. 'Are you eating properly?'

Sally shrugged. 'I get most of my meals at the caff.'

'At the *caff*?' Jenny looked shocked. 'After what you've told me about that place I'm surprised you haven't gone down with food poisoning before this. If you're not careful you're going to get ill.'

'You haven't seen the state of the kitchen where I live,' Sally said. 'No one ever bothers to wash up or clean the place. I can't face trying to cook anything in there.'

'What are you doing for Christmas?' Jenny asked.

Sally was getting a little tired of Jenny's cross-questioning. She'd always been a little bossy-boots even at school, and being a nurse just seemed to have made her worse. 'Not sure

27

yet,' she said noncommittally. 'I expect something will turn up. Might even get invited to Suffolk to stay at Fiona's place.'

Jenny had heard all about Fiona and her upper class family. 'Oh well, if you'd rather be with your posh new friends at the Manor House,' she said.

'I never said that. And anyway, Fee's not a new friend. She and I shared a room at the hostel for four years!'

'All right. Keep your hair on! Well, it's up to you, but you know you'd be welcome to come to us if you want,' Jenny said.

Sally thought with longing of Jenny's large extended family, brothers and sisters, cousins, aunts and uncles, grannies and grandpas. It would be fun to be round at the Giffords' house for Christmas. 'You sure?' she asked. 'Hadn't you better ask your mum first?'

Jenny laughed. 'You know Mum. There's so many of us that one more won't make any difference.'

'OK then,' Sally said, cheering up. 'P'raps I will.'

'Just turn up Christmas morning. We don't stand on ceremony at our house,' Jenny said.

⋆　⋆　⋆

The changing of the seasons was hardly noticeable in the East End. The weather was either hot or cold — wet or dry. But as winter deepened the cold became intense. The wind threw rain at the windows and howled down the chimneys and the passing traffic threw up dirty water from the puddles to splatter the shoes and legs of pedestrians.

Sally's little room was almost impossible to heat in spite of the endless shillings the voracious gas meter gobbled up. Rain dripped through the ceiling and she had to move her bed to avoid it. She complained to the landlord, but all he did was supply a bucket in which to catch the drips. She spent most of her evenings huddled in front of the hissing gas fire, shivering miserably.

There was no bathroom at 64 Perowne Road. An all over wash entailed boiling a kettle downstairs in the freezing kitchen, carrying it up two flights to her room and pouring it into the enamel bowl, provided for the purpose. Then, as there was always someone downstairs yelling for the kettle, it had to be returned before starting her toilet, by which time the water was usually stone cold.

Fiona sent a Christmas card with a picture of a Spitfire aeroplane on it. Inside she had written an invitation to Sally to join her at Saltmere St Peter for Christmas. But Sally wrote back to say thanks, but she had already accepted Jenny's invitation.

Alf Chandler's moods grew worse as the festive season approached. He'd taken to keeping a bottle of whisky under the counter and Sally soon learned that boozing made him prone to sudden and unpredictable mood swings. Sometimes he would take out his spleen on Sally, shouting at her all day long. At other times he would be full of maudlin self-pity, pouring his grievances into her unwilling ears in the hope of a little sympathy.

'Milly's bleedin' ma's coming tomorrow,' he told her late one afternoon as she was washing up in the kitchen after the café closed. 'It's the last bloody straw, 'avin' 'er to stay for Christmas. Proper old battleaxe, she is, built like a brick shit 'ouse an' about as friendly. She 'ates me. Reckon I'll be in for some real ear-ache.'

'Not that you don't deserve it,' Sally muttered under her breath.

'What's that?' Alf said sharply, turning to look at her.

'I said you don't deserve it,' Sally amended, reaching up to the shelf for a dry cloth. She didn't care for the look in his eyes. He'd been swigging from the whisky bottle again all afternoon and she could tell from his eyes that he was three parts cut.

'Too right, I bloody don't!' He hung up his apron and lurched towards her. 'What I've 'ad to put up with these past months! It's more than any normal man should be expected to stand.' He took a step closer, his bloodshot eyes peering, slightly unfocussed into hers. 'An' 'avin' to watch *you* all day don't 'elp, neither,' he said, a meaty hand reaching for her arm.

'Why, what have I done?' she asked, trying to extricate her wrist from his iron grip.

'What've *you* done?' He leered at her. 'As if you don't bloody know! Dinxin' up an' down with your tight little bum in them short skirts. Showin' off yer figure in them tight sweaters.

30

You've been askin' for it, Sall, that's what you've done.'

'No! I haven't! It's not — ow!' She gasped as he pushed her hard up against the draining board and thrust himself against her.

'What with me not getting' any at 'ome and you flauntin' yerself all day — it's enough to drive a man mad, Sall. But that's what you like, don't you?' He pushed his face close to hers. 'A right little tease, you are. Well, let's see if you can deliver the goods.'

Before she could avert her face his mouth came down sickeningly on hers, wet and slack, his breath whisky laden, making her stomach heave. She pushed at his chest with all her might but it only seemed to inflame him even more.

'Proper little tiger, eh?' he panted, pushing one leg between hers. 'Come on, Sall, relax and enjoy it. You been askin' for it long enough.' His hand was under her skirt, clawing at her thigh, creeping higher whilst the other, in the small of her back, pressed her so hard against him that she could scarcely breathe. She tried to scream but she hadn't enough breath.

'*Let me go!*'

'All in good time.' He was panting hard, holding her fast with the bulk of his body as he unbuckled his belt.

Sally twisted and turned in an effort to free herself. 'If you don't stop right now I'm going straight to the police!'

'Oh yeah?' He laughed. 'Think they'd believe a common little tart like you? Only gotta look at the way you dress!'

31

Managing to get one hand free she raked her fingernails down his cheek.

'*Christ*! You little . . . ' His hand flew to his face, giving her just long enough to wriggle free from his grasp and head for the door. Reaching it, she turned, her heart pounding in her chest.

'You can bloody well find someone else to do all your donkey work from now on, Alf Chandler!' she shouted.

'Don't be so bloody stupid!' Suddenly sober, he was dabbing at the scratches on his cheek with a tea towel, staring in bewilderment at the spots of blood on it. 'It was only a bit of fun.'

'You want to think yourself lucky I'm not going to the police station right now! But I won't be coming back here to work again. Not after tonight!'

'You're throwin' in a good job — just 'cause I tried to have a bit of a laugh with you?'

'*A laugh*?' Sally said, tearing off her apron. 'I'm sick of being a skivvy here for next to no money. But I'm even sicker of being mauled and slobbered over by an ugly great gorilla like you!'

'You lippy little cow!' he exclaimed, throwing the teacloth into a corner. 'You flaunt yerself under me nose for weeks — just beggin' for it — then you turn all nasty when you get what you was askin' for. Well, you c'n sling yer 'ook right now this minute. No more'n a little slut, that's what you are. Go on, bugger off!'

Anger had sent the adrenalin coursing through Sally's veins as she faced him from the other side of the kitchen. Why should she scuttle away in disgrace when *he* was the guilty one?

'I will do — *gladly* — when you pay me a week's wages in lieu of notice!'

'*A week's wages?*' The colour left his face as he stared at her disbelievingly. 'Your bleedin' cheek! I should bloody coco! You got another think comin' darlin'.'

'Right. If you're chuckin' me out maybe I'd better go round and explain why to poor Milly, seeing that she'll be the one doing all the work from now on! I wonder what your ma-in-law will have to say about that!'

For a moment she thought he was going to cross the kitchen and land her a fourp'ny one but although her knees were knocking she stood her ground. Her eyes blazing, she stared him out until finally, his face ashen he went to his jacket and opened his wallet, taking out some notes and slamming them down on the table.

''Ere! Take this and clear off, you little bitch,' he shouted. 'An' bloody good riddance!'

She picked up the money and grabbed her coat from the back of the door.

'An' don't show yer bleedin' face in 'ere again if you know what's good for you!' Alf shouted.

Determined to have the last word Sally looked over her shoulder as she slipped through the door. 'Oh, that's one thing you *can* rely on!'

★   ★   ★

It had felt like a triumph at the time, but by the time she had trudged back to Perowne Street in the rain the triumph had turned to despair. Shut away in her damp and chilly little room she sat on the bed and gave way to the tears that had been welling up inside her ever since the incident with Alf at the caff. Although she would never have let it show, the physical attack and the horrible names he had called her left her shocked and humiliated. Lying face down on the hard little bed she sobbed till her whole body ached. Now she was out of work and without a decent place to live. Surely life couldn't get much worse than this.

But the next day she was to find out that the worst was still to come.

* * *

She wakened with a dull ache in her head and a throat that felt like sandpaper. Lifting her head from the pillow she felt as though a ton of sand had fallen on it and fell back again with a groan. Her only consolation was that she didn't have to go to work. She could never have dragged herself there anyhow.

Somehow, clutching the banister with both hands, she made her way dizzily down to the kitchen and made herself a hot drink, but almost as soon as she'd drunk it she was violently sick. After that she crept back upstairs and collapsed into bed. She slept on and off for the rest of the day, rousing only when a painful, racking cough threatened to tear her chest apart and left her weak and trembling.

She had no idea how long she lay there, hot and perspiring one minute, chilled and shivering the next. Day became night, and night, day. She slept restlessly, wakening only to make the essential faltering trips down to the freezing outside lavatory that left her exhausted and frail. She neither ate nor felt like eating. At first she worried about it, but in the end she welcomed the light-headed feeling that emptiness gave her, sinking into a dream-like state where the crazy clairvoyant. Madame Arcarti from *Blithe Spirit* visited her, inviting her to put on one of the filmy costumes worn in the film by Kay Hammond and play the part of a ghost for her.

She neither knew nor cared how much time had passed when she became dimly aware of the door opening. Then a voice — a familiar voice — shouting — telling people off. Vaguely she wondered what was going on but she had neither the will nor energy to open her eyes and find out. She was aware of being lifted, carried — bumping painfully along in some kind of vehicle — of bright, white lights and probing fingers. Then a merciful black void.

When she opened her eyes next she saw that Madame Arcarti was wearing a starched white apron and cap. And oddly her face had become the face of Jenny Gifford. 'What — what d'you want?' she muttered.

'Welcome back to the land of the living, Sally,' Madame — Jenny — Arcarti said.

Alarmed, Sally struggled to sit up. Where was she? The familiar stained wallpaper and tatty curtains had gone and there were screens round her bed. Jenny's hands on her shoulders pressed her gently back against the pillow.

'No, don't try to sit up. How do you feel?'

'I — don't know. Weak as a kitten, I think. How long have I been here?'

'You've been very ill, Sall,' Jenny told her. 'You're here in hospital. You scared the living daylights out of us.'

'But why — how did I get here?'

Looking round to make sure the sister wasn't looking, Jenny seated herself carefully on the edge of the bed. 'When you didn't turn up at ours on Christmas morning I thought you were being awkward so I came round to fetch you. And found you in this terrible state — rambling and burning up with fever.' Her mouth hardened. 'I had a word or two to say to the other tenants of that place, I can tell you. Clueless lot of morons! No one had seen you for days but not one of them had the gumption to check on you.'

Sally nodded, dimly remembering someone shouting.

'I sent one of them down to the call box in the street to ring for an ambulance and we got you in here straight away. It's a good job I turned up when I did, Sall. It was pneumonia — touch and go. You were in an oxygen tent for three days.'

'But — I don't remember any of it.'

'Just as well. It was bad enough for us. Doctor says you're on the mend now though.' Jenny grinned. 'A tough little customer, he called you, and I reckon he's right.'

'You said it was bad enough for *us*,' Sally said. 'Who do you mean?'

'Well, all of us on the ward have been worried about you,' Jenny explained. 'But there's one person who's been here to see you every day, even though you were too out of it to know.'

'Who?'

'Can't you guess?' Jenny stood up. 'I found the box with her letters in when I went back to your room to pack some things for you, so I let her know you were ill. She's here now. Feel up to seeing her?' Jenny moved one of the screens aside and a familiar figure appeared. Sally's eyes filled with tears.

'*Fee*! Oh, Fee.'

Fiona laid a bunch of chrysanthemums on the locker beside the bed and bent to kiss Sally's cheek. 'I can't tell you how good it is to see you awake again,' she said. 'We've all been so frantic about you. How could you let yourself get into a state like that?'

Weakness had set the tears flowing again and Sally dabbed angrily at her cheeks with a corner of the sheet. 'I don't know what happened. I thought it was flu. I can't remember much about it.' She looked at Fiona. 'How long have I been in here?'

'Almost three weeks. January is half over.'

Sally looked alarmed. 'But — my room. I haven't paid the rent and I'll lose it.'

Fiona shook her head. 'Jenny and I have seen to all that. I was horrified when I saw how you were living, Sally. We persuaded the landlord to waive the rent, pointing out a few of the shortcomings to him and the fact that you were probably ill because of them. I've packed up all your things and taken them back to the hostel with me and I'll be taking you there when the hospital discharges you.'

'But I couldn't afford it! Or the fares back here to work ... ' She groaned as another painful memory filtered back into her mind. 'Oh no! I lost my job, Fee. At least, I chucked it in — that day before I got ill. Alf Chandler ... '

'I know. We went to see him too.' Fiona shook her head. 'That café, Sally! Why didn't you tell me how awful it was? And that unspeakable man!'

'What did he say?'

'He was very sheepish — worried about what he *thought* you might have said. So much so that he more or less gave himself away. I assume that he overstepped the mark and you gave him what for.' She grinned. 'Am I right?'

Sally nodded. 'What am I going to do, Fee?' she whispered, tears trickling down her cheeks. 'I've made such a mess of everything, haven't I?'

Fiona took out her handkerchief and wiped them away. 'You're going to let me look after you until you're well again.'

'But how can you?'

'It's all arranged. I'm taking you to Kent to Nanny Joan's. Country air and Nanny's home cooking. It's just what you need to put you on your feet again.'

'But I ... '

'No arguments. It's ages since she's had anyone to fuss over and she's really looking forward to it,' Fiona said firmly. 'So — from now on all you have to think about is getting better. And you're not to worry about a thing. Right?'

3

It was February before Sally was finally discharged from hospital. Before she left she was given a chest x-ray to make sure her lungs had not been damaged through the pneumonia and the doctors had given her a thorough check up and a clean bill of health.

Fiona's brother, Stephen, had lent her his car for the weekend so that she could drive Sally down to Fairfield to stay with Nanny Joan and the two set off mid-morning to avoid the worst of the traffic.

'Don't look so worried,' Fiona said, casting a sidelong glance at Sally as she sat beside her in the passenger seat. 'You'll love Nanny and she'll love you. She likes nothing better than to have someone to look after.'

* * *

Moon Cottage stood on its own at the end of a lane, surrounded by about three acres of land. It was sturdily built of mellow brick and shingle and the ground floor boasted two bow windows, one on either side of the blue painted front door, which stood welcomingly open as Fiona drew up outside. She smiled encouragingly at Sally as she hauled her suitcase out of the back of the car.

'Come on, I can smell the newly baked bread from here. Nanny's been busy.'

As they walked up the herringbone brick path Joan Harvey came to the door to greet them, beaming and wiping her hands on her apron. She was tall and strongly built, with high cheekbones and twinkling blue eyes. Her face had the healthy glow of someone who worked out of doors and her greying fair hair hung in a long thick plait down her back. She was not what Sally had imagined at all.

'So this is the little invalid,' she said, holding out both hands to Sally. 'Come on in my loves and sit you down. I've got the kettle on. I know you must be gasping for a cup of tea.'

The kitchen was warm and cosy. Opposite the door a range sat in an alcove, a rail above it for airing clothes. The quarry-tiled floor was scattered with bright rugs and the bow window that looked out over the front garden had a window seat and bright yellow curtains. A large table took up the centre of the room and on it were wire trays filled with fragrant newly baked loaves and small buns. Four wheelback chairs were tucked under the table, and drawn up close to the range stood a rocking chair filled with patchwork cushions, on which sat the largest and blackest cat that Sally had ever seen.

Nanny Joan evicted him with a sweep of her hand. 'Get you off there, Barney, and let the young woman sit down.' She chatted as she busied herself at the range with kettle and pot. 'Had a good journey then, did you? I don't know how you dare drive that old rattle trap of young Stephen's. I know my old truck is past it but it doesn't shake you up like that thing does. Last time he was here he took me into Maidstone in it.' She laughed and flapped one hand. 'Never again! Bless you, no!' She poured three cups of tea and took a seat at the table. 'Now then,' she said, looking from one to the other. 'I want to hear all about this young woman and what she's been up to.'

Fiona looked at Sally. 'I told you about Sally in my letter,' she said. 'She's had a bad time since moving back to London. Then she caught pneumonia at Christmas. She's in need of some of the special Nanny Joan cosseting to get her back on her feet.'

'I'm not used to being waited on,' Sally put in quickly. 'I like to do my bit to help.'

'Oh, you'll get your chance to do that, my love,' Nanny told her. 'But all in good time. I want to see the roses back in your cheeks first. Now, drink up your tea and help yourself to a bun. I'll show you up to your room when you're rested. It's going to be nice, having another woman to natter to and I can see right off that you and me'll get along a treat.'

The cottage was neat and compact, with a living room on the other side of the central hallway. It was clear that Nanny didn't use it much, preferring the cosiness of the kitchen.

'Tell you what,' she said as they stood in the doorway. 'I'll move one of the easy chairs through so we'll both have a comfy chair to sit in,' She closed the door and Fiona winked at Sally as they followed Nanny up the narrow staircase.

'The parlour is only for high days and

holidays,' she whispered.

There were two bedrooms on the upper floor. 'There used to be three but I had one made into a bathroom when I had the piped water laid on,' Nanny said. 'In my parents' day there were only oil lamps and a well in the garden. Thank heaven we've got the electric now — and the telephone. Don't know what I'd do without that. Need it for my business, you see. Oh, and the wireless of course. I hope you like the wireless, Sally. I.T.M.A's my favourite. A real scream, that Tommy Handley is. We'll listen together, eh?'

She opened the door to the back bedroom. 'I've put you in here, my love.'

Sally gasped with delight. The big feather bed was covered by a pristine white bedspread and the polished boards of the floor scattered with rose-pink, hand-pegged rugs.

'I like to have something to do with my hands of a winter's night,' Nanny explained. 'Either the rugs or the patchwork. I don't like to be idle.'

The dormer window with its rose-sprigged curtains looked out over Moon Cottage small-holding. Sally could see the well-kept vegetable garden and beyond it a large fruit cage. Apple, pear and plum trees, as yet devoid of leaves made up an orchard where chickens clucked and pecked among the grass. To the left the winter sun was reflected in the glass roofs of two large greenhouses, and beyond it all, fields and hedges stretched as far as Sally could see. It was even better than Northbridge.

'Oh, it's lovely,' she said, turning to Fiona. 'After what I've left it's like heaven.'

'Well you just unpack your things and take your time,' Nanny said. 'Fiona and I will go down and leave you to it. Just come down when you're ready. This is your home while you're here so just do as you like.'

In the kitchen Fiona and her old nanny looked at each other. 'Poor little scrap,' Nanny said. 'There isn't two-pennorth of her. Looks as if a puff of wind'd blow her away.'

'She's had a really tough time since the end of the war, Nanny,' Fiona said. 'She needs building up, her confidence as well as her physical strength and I can't think of anyone better than you to do it for her.'

Nanny beamed. 'Well, you know how I love to look after folk. Don't you worry, I've a feeling that she and I are going to get on like a house on fire.' She looked closely at Fiona. 'But what about you, my lovely? Anyone spoiling you these days?'

Fiona laughed. 'Not that you'd notice.'

'Been home lately?'

'At Christmas. Only for a couple of days. I wanted to get back to Sally. She was in hospital and so ill at the time and she's got no family.'

'Everything all right with you and the folks?'

'Fine — with Daddy and Stevie at least.'

'And your mother?'

Fiona shrugged. 'You know how we are, Nanny. We've never seen eye to eye about anything. I gave up trying to please her years ago.'

'I daresay she'd like you to go home and do the rounds,' Nanny said, referring to the

43

debutante circuit. 'Maybe you'd like that if you gave it a try. Never know, you might meet someone nice.'

But Fiona was shaking her head. 'You know how I felt about Mark, Nanny. There'll never be another man like him. I don't want anyone else.'

Nanny sighed. 'You must move on, my love. You've got a lot more years to live yet and a lot of love to give. It'd be a sin to waste it all.'

'I don't intend to. I want to have a career of some sort — maybe some kind of business. I want to be independent.'

'Well, you know best.' Nanny reached across the table to cover Fiona's hand with her own. 'And you know your old Nanny Joan is here when ever you need her, don't you?'

Fiona squeezed the strong capable hand. 'Of course I do. What would we do without you, Nanny?' They smiled at each other for a moment then Nanny glanced up at the darkening window.

'I really think you should start back, my love. The light's fading and I don't like to think of you driving in the dark.'

'Right. I'll just say goodbye to Sally.' Fiona stood up. 'And I'll come down as often as I can at weekends to see how she's getting on.'

'You do that. You know you're always welcome. And don't worry about little Sally. I'll have her built up again in no time.'

★ ★ ★

44

As the weeks passed Sally's strength slowly returned. For the first few days Nanny made her stay in bed until after breakfast, but gradually she was allowed to get up and help around the house. She'd heard all about Nanny Joan's legendary cooking from Fiona and now she was enjoying it to the full. It seemed there were few food shortages in the countryside. There were always new-laid eggs for breakfast and home-cured bacon from the farm. Nanny made wonderfully tasty soups and her larder was full of home-made jams and bottled fruit. In one of the outbuildings big shiny green Bramley apples were stored, their rich fragrance assailing the nostrils every time the door was opened. Sally soon learned that there was nothing quite as good as Nanny Joan's apple dumplings, full of spicy juice and swimming in creamy custard.

She learned a lot as the days went by, helping Nanny gather eggs and round up the hens into their coop for the night. Clad in wellington boots and the overalls that Nanny provided for her she helped dig out potatoes and carrots from the big earth clamp behind the greenhouses and cut cabbages and sprouts to take into Fairfield for the market twice a week, accompanying Nanny in her battered old pick-up truck. At the end of February she helped to spray the fruit trees and sterilize the greenhouses ready for spring. She even learned how to handle the rotivator when the time came to till the ground ready for planting.

She learned a lot about cooking too. 'Plenty of time for cooking in the winter months when there's not much to do outside,' Nanny Joan told her. 'And what could be a nicer occupation in the warmth of the kitchen on a winter's afternoon?'

Sally couldn't have agreed more.

★   ★   ★

Fiona came as often as she could at weekends, taking Sally to the *Dog and Duck* on Saturday evenings for a gossip and a drink. Nanny Joan didn't drink, but she had no objection to anyone else drinking.

'What's the point?' she said philosophically. 'No one's going to stop because I don't like it! Why should they?'

Fiona was delighted at the change that took place in Sally over the weeks. Every weekend saw a new improvement. She was steadily putting back the weight she had lost and her skin and eyes grew clear and healthy again. She congratulated Nanny Joan on doing a good job. The older woman shook her head.

'It's so easy. She's so appreciative of everything,' Nanny said. 'And such good company too. I've enjoyed having her here.' She smiled reminiscently. 'D'you know, she came to church with me last Sunday and I was amazed at her beautiful voice when we sang the hymns.'

'Yes. She often sang at factory concerts,' Fiona told her. 'She even had a chance to turn professional once but she wouldn't take it.'

'She told me she'd been afraid her voice might have suffered because of the pneumonia,' Nanny

46

said. 'But I can tell you it hasn't. Folk were turning round to see where it was coming from. I felt quite proud.'

'I knew Nanny would put you right,' Fiona said as she and Sally sipped shandies in the bar parlour of the pub one Saturday evening in mid-March.

'I keep thinking I really should leave though,' Sally said. 'I've been here more than six weeks now. I can't impose on Nanny's hospitality much longer.'

'She loves having you,' Fiona said. 'And as for imposing — she's been telling me what a help you are and how you've taken to country life.'

'I really enjoy it and it's the least I can do,' Sally protested. 'But I'll have to come back and start looking for a job soon.'

Fiona gave her a rueful look. 'You're missing London, aren't you?'

Sally smiled. 'Well — yes, I am — a bit. Trouble is, I've got nowhere to live. I'm not going back to the East End. Nothing's the same there any more.'

'All your things are at the hostel. You might as well come and stay with me there till you find something. But there's no rush, why don't you leave it another week or two?' Her face brightened. 'I know! I'll be going home to Saltmere St Peter for Easter. Why don't you come with me?'

Sally stared at her. 'Fee — I couldn't.'

'Yes, you could. It's only two weeks away. Oh do say yes. Stevie will be there and I can't wait for you to meet him. Then we can travel back to London together.'

'But — what about your mum and dad?

'They know you've been ill and that you've been staying with Nanny. I'm sure they'll be happy to see you.'

Sally looked at her friend's expectant face and knew she could not refuse. It would be an ordeal, but she owed Fiona so much. It seemed a small thing. And after all, it was only for a few days.

'OK then,' she said. 'I'll come.'

Later, after Fiona had gone she confided her fears to Nanny. 'I said I'd go because I know Fee wants it so much but I don't belong in that kind of place,' she said as they sat at the kitchen table with mugs of bedtime cocoa. 'I'm still a cockney kid at heart. I'm not used to all that upper class stuff. I won't know how to behave and I'll let Fee down. I know I will.'

'That you won't!' Nanny reassured. 'You've got really nice manners. Anyone can see you were properly brought up.'

'Gran was always very strict about manners.'

'Of course she was. She's from a generation that believed things like that mattered, whatever class you were.' She peered at Sally. 'There's more than that worrying you though, isn't there?'

Sally sighed. 'I love Fee. She's the best friend I've ever had, but I can't help feeling that I'm not — not good enough for her. It was all right when the war was on and we were working

48

together at the factory, but now — well, it's all changed somehow.'

'Why? You're the same two people.'

'Going back to Bethnal Green — doing that job at the caff — it reminded me of who I am.'

Nanny reached across the table for the hand that picked nervously at the table cloth. 'Sally — that man you worked for. There was some kind of — incident, wasn't there? Fiona hinted but she didn't tell me anything.' Sally nodded, her head down.

Nanny persisted gently, 'Want to talk about it? You know it'll go no further, don't you? Sally — how much did he hurt you? He — didn't . . . ?'

'*No!*' Sally's head came up, her eyes meeting Nanny's. 'I scratched his face — got away before he . . . He didn't hurt me — not physically. It was more the things he said. The names he called me. Afterwards I felt so dirty and ashamed. As if it had been my fault.'

'*That* it wasn't!' Nanny said stoutly. 'That was just his cowardly way of trying to put the blame on you. You must try to forget it, my love.'

'I don't know if I can. I still hear those names when I'm alone in bed at night. They're still there, inside my head, like sores that won't heal up.' She looked up into Nanny's compassionate eyes. 'I blackmailed him too. I threatened to tell his wife what he'd done if he didn't give me a week's wages in lieu of notice.'

Nanny burst out laughing. 'Bless you love! That's not blackmail. It's the least he could give you. He's lucky you didn't ask for a lot more!'

49

She got up from her chair and fetched the milk saucepan from the range, refilling Sally's mug. 'Now, you listen to me,' she said. 'You're a good girl. You're as good as the next woman and don't you dare ever let anyone say any different. You go to Saltmere St Peter with Fiona. And you hold your head up high. Just you show them you're as good as the best of them.' She wagged a finger at Sally. 'Don't you dare let me down, girl, 'cause I shall be asking Fiona all about you afterwards. All right?'

Sally grinned. 'All right.'

4

Fiona nudged her. 'Ipswich is the next stop,' she said. 'We'll be there in a minute.'

Sally turned to smile at her friend, but the butterflies that had been active in her stomach ever since they had boarded the train were doing back flips as she stood up and reached for her case.

At Saltmere St Peter the bus stopped conveniently outside the gates of the Manor House. The girls alighted and Sally stood looking up at the wrought iron gates set in the high brick wall. The solid gate pillars were surmounted by a pair of stone lions and through the gates she could see an avenue of chestnut trees, their new leaves spreading a lush green canopy over the gravel drive. In the distance she glimpsed a house built of honey-coloured stone. It looked very grand and she instinctively held back. Fiona took her arm.

'Come on,' she said as she unlatched the gate. 'Don't be scared. Just be yourself and everyone will love you.'

It was Donald Crowther, Fiona's father, who opened the door to them. He was a tall, spare man in his late fifties with silver hair and bright blue eyes like Fiona's. He wore corduroy trousers and a brown cardigan.

He kissed his daughter. 'Welcome home, darling.' He peered short-sightedly at Sally. 'And this must be your friend, er, Selina, isn't it — or Cynthia?'

Fiona laughed. '*Sally*. You are priceless Daddy!'

Donald laughed with her and held out his hand to Sally. 'Of course, forgive me, Sally. Memory's not too good these days — well, it never was really. Welcome to Saltmere St Peter. I hope you enjoy your weekend with us my dear.' He led the way through the hall.

The stone flagged floor was partly covered by a large Turkey carpet patterned in rich reds and blues. Sally took in the oak-panelled walls and the vase of yellow daffodils on a highly polished antique table flanked by two carved Queen Anne chairs.

'Your mother has prepared the blue room for your friend, Fiona,' Donald was saying. 'You are in your old room of course. I'll leave you to unpack. Tea in the drawing room in ten minutes, eh?'

The blue room overlooked the garden and Sally looked out of the window, overawed by the sight that met her eyes. Green lawns swept away towards a high beech hedge behind which daffodils nodded under the trees. She could just see a wall of mellow red brick and a stately cedar tree standing guard beside a wrought iron gate set in an archway.

'Behind the wall is the kitchen garden,' Fiona told her. 'Plenty of vegetables all through the war. The gardener was called up though, so poor Daddy had to do most of it himself, with the help of an old chap from the village. Then, beyond that are the stables. Daddy kept Bunter and Maisy, our two ponies all through the war, bless him, though I doubt that Stephen or I will ride them again.'

Sally looked down on it all with wonder. She had only read in books about people living like this and she hardly believed it to be true even then. 'Oh, Fee,' she said. 'It's beautiful!'

'It's an anachronism,' Fiona said. 'It belongs to a bygone age.'

Sally stared at her. 'All the same, it's really lovely. Fancy growing up in a place like this! It's like something out of those Enid Blyton Sunny Stories we used to read at school.' She turned to look at her friend. 'You had all this to play in. All I had was the street and a back yard, mostly full of the rotting veg and fruit that grandpa hadn't sold. I can still smell it now if I close my eyes. We had no bathroom either. We used to have a dip in the tin tub on a Friday night — all three of us used the same water 'cause Gran had to heat it up in the copper. Either that or we went to the public baths. And the only horses I ever saw were the dray horses from the brewery and the nag that pulled the coalman's cart.'

'Well, I hope all that belongs to a bygone age too,' Fiona said. 'The war has changed a lot of things, Sally, some of them for the worse, I know. But perhaps a lot of good changes will come out of it too.'

'Oh, I wasn't complaining,' Sally protested. 'I had a happy childhood. It was all I knew. Gran and Grandpa did their best. I never went without good food and clothes and I knew they loved me.'

'Then maybe you had more than me in some ways.' Just for a moment Sally saw the shadow of wistfulness in her friend's eyes, but it was only momentary. Fiona turned to her with a smile. 'Come on, we'd better go down or they'll be wondering where we are.'

Fiona's mother, Marcia Crowther was waiting for them in the drawing room. It too looked out on to the garden with two long windows reaching almost to floor level, curtained and swagged in blue velvet. A log fire burned in the large marble fireplace where two blue plush sofas faced each other. On a low table between them stood a tray bearing a silver tea service and delicate porcelain cups and saucers.

Marcia came forward and kissed her daughter on both cheeks. 'Fiona. How good to see you. It's been far too long.'

She was a tall woman with grey-streaked dark hair worn in a chignon. She wore an elegant skirt of grey wool and a pale blue twin set, pearls at her neck and ears.

'Mother, this is Sally Joy,' Fiona said.

Marcia turned her attention to Sally, her sharp eyes sweeping over the diminutive figure. She held out a long white hand. 'How do you do. I hope you are quite well again now.'

'Yes, thank you.'

'And you had a comfortable journey?'

'Oh yes. It was fine.' Sally's voice sounded strange to her, coarse and squeaky after Marcia's cultured tones.

It was clear by her expression that it sounded odd to Marcia too. Her eyebrows rose slightly and she cleared her throat. 'Good. And your room — have you everything you need?'

'Oh yes. It's smash — er — lovely, thank you.'

Donald joined them, lightening the atmosphere with his easy manner, and for the twenty minutes that followed Sally was fully occupied with balancing her cup and saucer and a plate holding a buttered scone without disgracing herself by dropping crumbs on the carpet.

'Have you any plans for the weekend?' Donald asked his daughter.

She shook her head. 'I'd like to show Sally Framlingham Castle,' she said. 'And introduce her to Bunter and Maisy, but apart from that nothing.'

'There's a concert in the church tomorrow evening,' Marcia put in. 'I've promised the vicar that we'll support it. He's worked so hard with the choir and the youth orchestra. There's a young soprano coming over from Colchester. She's supposed to be very good.'

'Sally sings, don't you, Sally?'

Embarrassed, Sally nodded, her mouth full of scone. 'A bit, yes.'

Marcia glanced at her. 'Really?' she said coolly. She turned to her husband. 'Did Stephen ring?'

Donald shook his head. 'No, but I'm sure he'll be here soon. Probably had trouble with that old car of his.'

After tea Fiona took Sally out to the stables to see the horses. 'Bunter's the black one. He was Stephen's, Maisy's mine, aren't you old girl?'

Fiona stroked the grey pony's velvet nose and held a sugar lump out on the palm of her hand for the pony to crunch. 'Daddy let some of the local children come and ride them through the war so that they got enough exercise,' she went on. 'But I think he'll have to sell them to the local riding stables now that we've both definitely left home.'

'Don't you mind?' Sally asked, fascinated by the pony's gentle brown eyes and soft mane.

Fiona shook her head. 'It's all in the past now,' she said. 'We have to move on, don't we?' She moved away from the pony and closed the lower door of the stall. 'War changes everything. I've never felt I fitted in here. I'd have left home years ago if it hadn't been for Daddy. Since I've been away I'm not the same person. I think I've found the courage at last to be who I really am and I'm not about to give that up. I daresay you feel the same, don't you?'

'Funny, I never gave any thought to who I was till after the war,' Sally said. 'Before that life seemed pretty much mapped out for people like me. Now, I'm not so sure.'

'You could do anything you liked,' Fiona said.

Sally looked doubtful. 'Mmm. Easier said than done.' She could see instinctively that Fiona's outlook on their change of circumstance was very different from her own. She missed her grandparents and would have given anything to go back to the simple life she'd had before.

Suddenly Fiona held up her hand. 'Listen! I can hear a car. Come on!' She took off at a run, Sally following — across the stable yard and through a gate — along a path until they emerged on to the forecourt of the house. The old car that Fiona had driven Sally to Fairfield in had pulled up outside the front door and a tall young man in air force uniform was getting out of it. Fiona gave a whoop and launched herself into his arms.

'*Stevie!*'

He lifted her off her feet and swung her round. 'Well! If it isn't my little sister! Didn't know you'd be here too this weekend.' Laughing, he put her down and looked over her shoulder. 'Hello, bet I can guess who this is.'

Sally found herself looking into the dark grey eyes of quite the best looking young man she had ever seen. She'd seen snapshots of Fiona's brother but none of them had done him justice.

'This is Sally Joy, my best friend,' Fiona said, her eyes shining. 'Sally, this is my big brother, Stephen.'

He held out his hand and took hers, pressing it warmly as the grey eyes smiled down into hers. 'Sally Joy,' he repeated. 'What a wonderful name. And how very appropriate.'

To her horror Sally felt a hot flush suffuse her face. What was the matter with her? She never blushed. 'Hello,' she said. 'I've heard a lot about you.'

He laughed. 'Oh dear. That sounds ominous. So you've heard all about my chequered past, have you?'

'Oh no — I . . . '

Sally got no further. Marcia Crowther had opened the front door and was bearing down on them, running down the steps, her arms outstretched.

'Stephen, *darling*!' She kissed him then held him at arms' length, shaking her head. 'I'm sure you've lost weight since last time you were home. We shall have to do our best to feed you up. Now . . . ' She linked her arm through his and began to steer him up the steps, away from the girls and into the house. 'How much longer do they intend to keep you in the RAF?'

Stephen gave his sister a conspiratorial wink over his shoulder as they disappeared inside the house.

Fiona shrugged resignedly. 'See what I mean?' she said. 'I've always been the odd one out.'

           ★   ★   ★

They ate dinner in the dining room. Sally was impressed by the long oak table and high backed chairs, the silver cutlery, crystal glasses and fine linen napkins. The food however, was quite another matter. The soup was thin and half cold, the main course was some kind of casserole in which the vegetables had disintegrated and the unidentifiable meat burned. It was accompanied by lumpy mashed potato and cabbage, stewed to a slimy greyness. When the taciturn woman who had served them eventually arrived with the rice pudding it was watery and covered by a brown skin the consistency of leather.

Marcia sighed, looking round the table apologetically. 'I'm sorry, we're between cooks at the moment. We have to make our own breakfast and lunch and Mrs Hobbs comes in from the village every evening and I'm sure the does her best but . . . ' Her voice trailed off as she pushed her plate away from her. 'It's a terrible problem, trying to find good staff nowadays. We're not going to feed you up much like this, Stephen, are we?'

Fiona cleared her throat. 'Daddy grows so many good things in the garden,' she said. 'It's a pity you can't eat better than this. I'll tell you what.' She looked across the table at Sally, raising an eyebrow. 'Sally and I will cook dinner for you tomorrow evening if you like. I'm sure we can do better than your Mrs Hobbs, can't we. Sall?'

Sally smiled noncommittally. Marcia looked from one to the other. 'I suppose you may as well, if you want to,' she said ungraciously. 'I don't suppose you can produce anything much worse than we've eaten tonight.'

Donald cleared his throat. 'I think you forget, Marcia, that Fiona qualified at the Epicure School of Cordon Bleu Cookery before the war.'

'I should think she's forgotten everything she learned by now,' Marcia said dismissively. 'But you may as well try if it amuses you.'

Stephen laughed. 'Oh come on, Ma. They're bound to do better than old mother Hobbs's burnt offerings.'

'Thank you all so *much* for your votes of confidence,' Fiona said, her cheeks pink. 'I will cook and Sally can help me. She's been getting expert training from Nanny Joan so I think you're in for a pleasant surprise!'

Marcia failed to put in an appearance at breakfast next morning. Donald prepared coffee and toast in the kitchen and when Stephen, Fiona and Sally came down they were invited to help themselves. Sally much preferred the informal atmosphere to that at dinner the previous evening. Secretly she was relieved not to have to face Fiona's mother over the breakfast table. She found the woman austere and intimidating.

Fiona repeated her plan to take Sally to Framlingham Castle and at once Stephen offered to take them in his car. 'It's a glorious morning. We could have lunch at the pub,' he suggested.

Fiona looked thoughtful. 'I don't really see how I'll have time this morning,' she said. 'Daddy's going to get the vegetables for me from the garden. There are plenty of onions so we'll have French onion soup. And for pudding we can have apple sponge. It's the meat that's the trouble. All I can find in the fridge is some tough looking stewing steak. It seems it's all Mrs Hobbs knows how to cook. I can't think of anything sophisticated I can do with that.'

'Nanny Joan has a way with tough steak,' Sally put in. 'She cooks it really slowly in the bottom of the oven then pops a lovely suet crust on it to make a smashing meat pudding. I couldn't get enough of it.'

Fiona looked doubtful. 'It's hardly gourmet,'

she said. But the two men gave a whoop of approval.

'Who needs gourmet?' Donald said. 'I haven't had a decent steak and kidney pudding for ages. Let's have that. Tell you what, while you're out sight-seeing I'll go out and see if I can find you some spring cabbage to go with it.'

'Well, if you're sure.' Fiona turned to Sally. 'We never did steak and kidney pudding at the Epicure. Could you do that, Sall?'

''Course. Nanny often let me make the crust. Let's get the meat on now. We can leave it in the bottom of the Aga while we're out.'

Sally was entranced by Framlingham Castle. She'd never seen a real castle before. When they arrived in the village Fiona announced that as she'd seen it before she'd look round the village shops instead and try to persuade the local butcher to part with some off ration kidney and suet. She left them at the entrance gate, promising to meet them at the pub for lunch in an hour.

Stephen wore civvies this morning; well-cut flannels and a blazer over an open necked shirt. Sally thought that if anything, he looked even handsomer. Together they inspected the medieval well in the castle courtyard and then climbed up to the wooden walkways and made their way round, Stephen pointing out the many things of interest.

Sally looked around her. 'I never knew there were any of these old places still standing,' she said. 'I thought they were just in books at school and on the pictures.'

Stephen took her arm. He found it refreshing to be with a girl who found simple things fascinating. 'Imagine firing arrows from those battlements,' he said, pointing. 'Or tipping boiling oil down on your enemies. War was a whole different bag of tricks in those days. No tanks or aeroplanes — or even guns.'

She turned wide brown eyes on him. 'Oh, but they had hand grenades, didn't they? And bayonets?'

'Well, not exactly. You see . . . ' He saw her lips twitching and shook his head. 'Are you making fun of me, Miss Joy?'

She laughed. 'I did go to school, you know. Not for as long as you, maybe, but we did have the odd history lesson.'

'Sorry. Was I being patronizing?'

She tucked her arm through his. 'I'll forgive you — just this once.'

'Tell me a bit about yourself, Sally. All I know so far is that you're a Londoner.'

'How can you tell?'

'Your accent of course.' He held up his hand. 'You're pulling my leg again!'

'No. I thought I'd lost most of my accent,' she said. 'All those years in Northbridge, living with Fee. I did try, but I suppose old habits die hard. Soon as I went back there I lapsed into it again.'

'You wanted to lose it?'

'Well, in a way, yes.'

'But why? It's such fun.'

'It stamps me though, doesn't it?' she said. 'I know you can never really be what you're not — not that I want to. I'm proud to be a cockney born and bred. It's just that people tend to stick labels on you.'

'What kind of labels?'

'They think you're common and ignorant, just because of the way you speak.'

'Never!'

She looked at him. 'Now you're pulling *my* leg. They do. Your mum, for a start. She makes it pretty clear that she thinks I'm not a good enough friend for her daughter.'

'Ma doesn't mean to give that impression. It's just her way.'

Sally smiled ruefully. 'If she could see that caff where I've been working since the war finished I think she'd have kittens!'

'Really? That bad, was it?'

'Worse!'

'So, tell me about it.'

They sat down on a bench and Sally began to tell him about the *Cosy Café* and Alf Chandler. In spite of her aversion to the café and the memories she was trying so hard to eradicate she managed to make her story sound so funny that Stephen began to chuckle. Responding to his amusement, she warmed to her subject, and by the time she had finished Alf Chandler seemed more like a figure of ridicule than an ogre and she realized for the first time that the bad memories were beginning to fade. When she looked at him he was laughing. She nudged him.

'You wouldn't laugh if you had to work there,' she said.

'I'm sure I wouldn't,' he said 'It's just the way

you tell it. I think you deserve a medal for sticking it as long as you did.'

Sally sighed. 'I don't think the London I remember will ever be the same. I couldn't believe what had happened to it when I first went back. Everywhere — the West End as much as the East. There was a poem we learned at school. One bit of it stuck and I couldn't help remembering it when I looked at all that bomb damage.' She closed her eyes in concentration. '*This is the land of lost content, I see it shining plain. The happy highways where I went, And cannot come again.*'

'A. E. Housman,' Stephen said quietly.

'That's right.' Sally looked at her watch. 'Hey, look at the time. We'd better go. Fee will have finished her shopping by now.'

As they left the ancient building Stephen took her hand. 'Sally, you're a tonic,' he told her. 'I can't remember when I've enjoyed a conversation as much.'

'What are you going to do when you get out of the RAF?' she asked, liking the warmth of his hand holding hers.

'I'm hoping to go to Cambridge University,' he told her. 'I never got the chance to take up my place there when the war started. I want to study law.'

'Brainy, eh?'

He grinned at her. 'Now who's sticking labels on?'

★ ★ ★

Fiona had managed to coax some kidney and suet out of the local butcher and as soon as they had their lunch the three of them set off back to Saltmere. They were gathering ingredients together in the kitchen when Marcia appeared in a state of agitation.

'I've just had the vicar on the phone,' she said. 'He's in a terrible state. The young soprano who was coming over from Colchester to sing at the concert has gone down with tonsillitis and cried off. Poor Mr Newbold has sold out of tickets and he doesn't know what on earth he's going to do.'

Fiona looked at her mother and then at Sally, who was busy grating suet at the table, her back towards her.

'Maybe Sally can help,' she said. 'What do you say, Sall?'

Sally spun round. 'Oh! I don't know.' Her cheeks had reddened and her heart had given a painful lurch.

Marcia looked irritated. 'This is church music, Fiona,' she said with a frown. 'Not amateur night at the local *palais de dance*.'

Sally felt her hackles rise. Who the hell did this toffee-nosed woman think she was? 'Actually I used to sing in the church choir at home in London,' she said. 'Have you got any idea what this girl was going to sing?'

Marcia looked flustered. 'Ave Maria and Panis Angelicus, I think. But the idea of replacing her at such short notice is out of the question surely.'

'Well — is it, Sally?' Fiona interrupted. She stopped stirring her pot of soup and wiped her hands.

65

'Well, I've sung both of those before,' Sally said, determined to show Marcia that she wasn't going to be intimidated into refusing. 'And I'm pretty sure I can remember them.'

'Right. I'll go and phone the vicar now,' Fiona said. 'And then Stephen can run you across to the vicarage and introduce you. I'm sure Mr Newbold will be only too glad of a solution to his problem.'

Half an hour later Sally was standing by the piano in the vicar's study, a sheet of music in her hand and her knees knocking.

'It's so good of you to help us out like this, Miss Joy.' Horace Newbold was a tall, nervous looking man. He seated himself at the piano and looked round at her over the tops of his steel-rimmed spectacles. 'Ready when you are.'

He played the introduction, turning to nod at Sally as her cue came. She took a deep breath and began to sing. It was some years since she'd sung Ave Maria at St Faith's in Bethnal Green, but the words and melody came back to her as though she had sung them yesterday. For a little while she was lost in the beauty of the music and her surroundings seemed to melt away. When she had finished there was complete silence. She looked at the vicar.

'Was — was that all right?' she asked tentatively.

He stared at her for a moment. Then he gave himself a little shake and stood up.

'*All right*, Miss Joy? It was more than all right. It was *exquisite*! Thank you so much!' He grasped both her hands. 'I think God must have sent you here to us today! I'll take you across to the church now and you can see where you'll be performing this evening.'

★ ★ ★

Donald and Stephen were full of praise for the meal the girls had produced and even Marcia was grudgingly appreciative. Fiona's French onion soup was rich and tasty and Sally's suet crust made a light and fluffy topping to the tenderized meat. Finally the apple sponge was a luscious end to the meal.

'I suppose young women feel they are above domestic work now that they've come out of the services,' Marcia remarked. 'The lovely dinner parties we used to give seem doomed to be a thing of the past. All our friends are grumbling about the lack of girls wanting to go into service. It isn't any better in London either. I was talking to Muriel St John-Pickard the other day. The St John-Pickards have moved back to their house in Holland Park and Muriel says there isn't even a *domestic agency* there any more! They haven't been able to entertain friends since they've been back in Town.'

'Maybe some of these ladies should learn to cook for themselves,' Fiona suggested.

Her mother gave her a withering look. 'Don't be facetious, Fiona,' she said.

Stephen gave his sister a sly wink. 'You seemed to consider it good enough for your daughter, Ma,' he challenged.

Marcia sighed. 'It was the last resort. Fiona

67

had neither the talent nor the interest for anything else,' she said scathingly. 'We were at our wits' end.'

Fiona reddened painfully but before she could counter with an angry remark that would trigger a row, Stephen stood up and threw down his napkin. 'Right! You are excused the washing up,' he said, addressing Sally. 'Time I took you over to St Peter's to get ready for your big moment.'

Marcia sighed again. 'Don't remind us of the concert,' she said. 'I only wish we could think of an excuse not to go, but poor Mr Newbold must be tearing his hair out so we must give him our support.' Catching her husband's cautioning look she added quickly, 'I'm sure it's very kind of Sally to volunteer to fill the gap, but you know what I mean.'

Stephen drove Sally across the village to the church. As they drew up outside St Peter's he looked at her.

'Are you all right?'

She turned to him and nodded. 'As all right as I'm going to be, till it's over,' she said.

'You hardly ate a thing at dinner,' he remarked. 'Nervous?'

'A bit. Singing on a full stomach isn't good for the voice anyway. So maybe it's just as well.'

He leaned across and kissed her cheek. 'Well, break a leg anyway. See you later, eh?'

'Yes. See you later.'

★ ★ ★

68

As the strains of Panis Angelicus died away, echoing softly around the beautiful old medieval building there was a brief silence in the church. Then the applause broke out. Startled by its intensity Sally bowed her head in acknowledgement. It was some time since she had sung church music and she could have done with more rehearsal, but the enthusiastic reception assured her that her performance had been more than adequate. The vicar, who had been conducting the choir, stepped forward and held up his hand.

'I'm sure that everyone will agree that we have had a great treat here this evening,' he said. 'Miss Sally Joy is a visitor to the village and she stepped gallantly into the breach for us at very short notice. If it hadn't been for her the concert would have had to be cancelled, but I'm sure you will agree with me when I say that she has delighted us all this evening.' He turned to Sally. 'Thank you for a wonderful performance.' The applause was renewed and Sally bowed again, noticing for the first time that Fiona and Stephen were in the front pew with their parents. She noticed that even Marcia was applauding.

She was putting on her coat in the vestry when Fiona and Stephen rushed in. 'You were *brilliant!*' Fiona said, hugging her. 'Everyone was simply *entranced*. I've never heard you sing that kind of thing before. You were marvellous.'

'Well at least I didn't embarrass you,' Sally muttered, overwhelmed by all the attention.

'Never enjoyed one of the vicar's concerts as much as I did tonight,' Stephen said. 'And I'll let you into a secret,' he whispered close to her ear. 'Even Ma was impressed.'

'Mother's rather tired,' Fiona said. 'Would you let me drive her and Daddy home in your car, Stevie?'

He nodded. 'Of course. You can't do much damage driving it for half a mile, can you?' As he ducked out of the way of the swipe she aimed at him he looked at Sally. 'We'll walk back, shall we? It's a beautiful night.'

There was a clear, starlit sky and a full moon, and as they walked the air was heavy with the honeyed scents of spring. Stephen took her hand.

'You looked like a wicked little angel standing up there in your red dress,' he said. 'And your voice is out of this world.' He looked down at her. 'Sally — I'd like to share a secret with you — something no one knows about yet.'

She looked up at him 'Me? Are you sure?'

'Very sure. Promise it'll be between us — just for now anyway?'

'Of course. I won't say a word. What is it?' Suddenly she was sure that he was about to tell her that he'd met the girl of his dreams and asked her to marry him.

'I've been notified that they're giving me a gong.'

She stopped walking and turned to stare up at him. 'A *gong*? What would you want one of those for?'

He laughed and picked up her hand again. 'I mean a medal. The AFC actually. God knows what I did to deserve it.'

'Oh, *Stephen*!' Sally laughed delightedly. 'Of course you deserve it. They don't hand those things out for nothing.' She was suddenly serious. 'But you should be telling your family, not me.'

'I'll tell them soon. I just wanted to share it with someone first,' he said. 'Telling you has made it feel real. Up till now it's felt a bit like a dream. In the beginning I kept thinking it must be a mistake.'

'I feel honoured,' she whispered. 'Congratulations, Steven. It's wonderful news.'

'Thanks. And you won't say anything?'

'Of course not. It's our secret.'

'Great.' He looked down at her. 'Sally, I'd like very much to see you again. Next time I'm in London perhaps we could meet — have a meal or go to a flick or something. What do you say?'

Sally's heart gave a leap of joy. She longed to say yes, but she couldn't help wondering what Marcia Crowther would think of her darling son, soon to be decorated by the King himself, keeping company with a 'wicked little cockney angel'.

'Well?' He was looking down at her ruefully. 'Does it really take that much thinking about?'

'No. I'd love to see you again, Stephen.' She smiled up at him. 'I'll be staying with Fiona at the hostel till I can find another room. You can find me there any time.'

He smiled and lifted her hand to kiss the fingertips. 'Thanks. I was hoping you'd say that. I'll look forward to it.'

'Me too.' She smiled to herself, remembering

what Fiona had said earlier about changing — being the person you wanted to be. Today she had proved to herself — and maybe to others, that she could put the past behind her. And now Stephen had trusted her with his wonderful secret — and asked to see her again. It was the perfect end to a lovely day.

★ ★ ★

She was just dropping off to sleep when the door opened and Fiona crept in.

'Sally,' she whispered. 'Sall — are you awake?'

Sally turned over. 'I am now. What's up, can't you sleep?'

'No.' Fiona sat down heavily on the edge of the bed. 'Sall, I've had this brilliant idea and I couldn't wait till morning to tell you about it — hear what you think.'

Sally sat up and switched on the bedside lamp and peered at the clock. It was half past one. 'OK, tell me. And it had better be good.'

'We — you and I that is, could do a catering service.'

Sally frowned. 'How do you mean?'

'You heard what Mother was complaining about this evening at dinner; the lack of domestic staff. We could go to people's houses and cook dinner for them. Just like we did here tonight.'

'Could we?' Sally blinked. 'Sounds barmy to me. I mean — what people?'

Fiona shook her head impatiently. 'People like Mother who want to start socializing again — giving dinner and cocktail parties again. We'd advertise — go to their houses and do the food for them.' She reached out and shook Sally gently by the shoulder. 'Well, say something for heaven's sake. What do you think?'

Sally slowly absorbed the idea and began to smile. 'Hey! It might just work. It needs a lot more thinking through, mind.'

'Of course it does, but what about the idea? Does it appeal?'

Sally grinned. 'Yes — yes, I reckon it does!'

★   ★   ★

The following morning at the breakfast table the atmosphere was electric. Fiona was fizzing over with her new idea and had already talked to her father about it. Marcia was taking breakfast in her room as usual, but Donald greeted Sally warmly as she joined them at the table.

'Fiona tells me that you and she are planning an interesting venture together,' he said. 'But I've warned her, with a voice like yours you might want to sing professionally.'

'No fear of that,' Sally assured him 'I love singing but if I had to do it for a living I think all the fun would go out of it. Fee knows that.'

'I've told Daddy about the offer you had. I've also been telling him about my idea,' Fiona beamed across the table at her. 'And guess what he's suggested. He's going to let us move into the family house in Gower Street and work from there! Isn't it exciting?'

'Your London house!' Sally's eyes widened as

she looked at her host. 'That's very kind. Are you really sure?'

'Of course. And it's not as altruistic as it might seem,' Donald said as he buttered a piece of toast. 'There's method in my madness. You see the builders will be working on the house for several weeks and with the place being empty I'd have to pay someone to be around to make sure everything was secure. I know Fiona will keep a weather eye on things, and it will make a useful base for your proposed business at the same time, so — killing two birds with one stone, so to speak.'

'It sounds wonderful,' Sally said, returning the encouraging smile that Stephen gave her.

'Don't worry, the house isn't a wreck,' he assured her. 'The problem is mainly with the roof and the top floor.'

'Absolutely,' Donald put in. 'It really needn't interfere with your life much at all. The first two floors are perfectly habitable.'

'I'm going to raid the kitchen in a minute for some of the things we'll need,' Fiona said. 'Large saucepans for instance. And I seem to remember there's a fish kettle somewhere and a big steamer.'

When she'd excused herself and gone off to the kitchen Donald smiled at Sally. 'Fiona is a very lovely young woman,' he said. 'She might be a little stubborn — gets that from me, I'm afraid, but she has a very sweet and loyal nature. I'm always telling Marcia, the academic life isn't for everyone.' He smiled at Stephen. 'One genius in the family should be enough for any mother.'

'Ma has this habit of making her feel she's a disappointment,' Stephen said. 'I wish she wouldn't do it, especially in front of visitors.'

Donald sighed. 'I'm sure she doesn't mean anything,' he said. 'She's as proud of Fiona as I am — in her own way.' He rolled up his napkin and pushed his chair back from the table. 'I'd better go and see that she doesn't plunder the kitchen too thoroughly. Mrs Hobbs will be giving in her notice if she finds half the utensils missing and we can't have that. I know she isn't exactly a cordon bleu cook but she's all we've got.'

When the door had closed behind him Stephen looked at Sally. 'You must think we're a strange family,' he said. 'Ma would have overlooked Fee's individuality if she'd agreed to toe the line socially, but I'm sure you know how she feels about that.'

Sally laughed. 'I have heard her voice the odd opinion on the subject, yes.'

Stephen laughed. 'You'll get used to us. At least, I hope you will.' He smiled. 'And now that you're going to be living at the family house in Gower Street I'll know exactly where to find you, so there's no escape.'

5

It was a strange feeling for Fiona, stepping in through the front door of number twenty-eight Gower Street. She had not visited the house since before the war when visits to London occurred twice a year for the Crowther children: in summer, when the main purpose was to buy new items of school uniform from Harrods. If they were good there would be a treat as well, a visit to the zoo or the Natural History Museum and Nanny would let them buy ice cream afterwards from the forbidden stop-me-and-buy-one barrow by the park gates. The other visit would be at Christmas to see the pantomime at Drury Lane. It was rare for their parents to come too. As Fiona recalled, it was more often only Nanny Joan who accompanied them. These were the times Fiona loved to remember. In winter the three of them would toast muffins in front of the nursery fire and listen together to the children's hour on the wireless.

Now, as she turned her new key in the lock and stepped over the threshold the echo of the house's familiar scents brought back nostalgic memories. She took a deep breath and turned to Sally. 'Well, here we are. Welcome to Gower Street.'

Sally stepped into the hallway and looked around her at the elegant Georgian features; the ceiling cornice, sculptured with flowers and leaves, the high, moulded skirting boards and the curving staircase with its delicately scrolled banister rail. 'Oh, Fee,' she breathed. 'Are we really going to be allowed to live here?'

'For now,' Fiona said, dropping her suitcase at the foot of the stairs. 'Once we're on our feet we'll find our own place. Come on. Leave your things here and I'll show you round before we unpack.'

On the ground floor there were two large rooms to the front of the house and a smaller one at the back, looking out on to a small garden. All the furniture was shrouded in dust sheets, but the long windows were curtained with floor-length velvet curtains.

'This used to be the dining room,' Fiona told her, opening a door. 'And the one across the hall was the morning room. The little room at the back was used by the housekeeper as an office. Before the war Mother and Daddy used to spend a lot of time in London. They did all their entertaining here, so the housekeeper had plenty to do.' Turning back into the hall she pointed to a baize-covered door at the rear of the staircase. 'The kitchen's downstairs.' She looked at Sally who was still speechless with the splendour of it all. 'Shall we go and have a look? It's likely we'll be spending a lot of our time there.'

Below stairs the kitchen seemed enormous to Sally. There was a cream enamelled Aga sitting in an alcove and the biggest dresser Sally had ever seen and a large Frigidaire refrigerator.

'The Aga will be useful,' Fiona said. 'It was put in just before the war to replace the massive cast iron range that used to be here. And the fridge too of course. We'll have to check that they're both still in good working order. Most of the utensils were taken to Saltmere St Peter when the war began, which is why I raided the kitchen there.'

In the centre of the room was a large deal table with ten chairs. 'There used to be quite a large staff here,' Fiona explained. 'A house-keeper, a cook and a kitchen maid. Then there was a parlour maid and a daily woman for the rough work. When my parents came they used to bring Carter.'

'Carter?'

'He was the butler.'

'A *butler*? You're kidding,' said Sally, wide-eyed.

'No. He was called up at the beginning of the war and killed at Dunkirk.'

'I knew you then. You never said.'

Fiona smiled ruefully. 'What would you have thought back in those days if I'd told you my parents had a butler?'

'See what you mean,' Sally's face said it all and they laughed together.

'There'll never be another Carter,' Fiona said. 'He was a lovely man who had worked up from the lowest domestic job to the highest. He was so proud of his station in life as a butler.' She shook her head. 'The days when people take pride in working as servants are gone. I don't think it's quite sunk in yet for Mother that life will never return to the way it was before the war. Men and women who risked their lives for their country are going to want more than merely to serve those whose only claim to superiority is financial. It's going to be hard for her to realize, but the sooner she does, the better.'

Sally said nothing. It wasn't the first time she had sensed the bitterness that existed between Fiona and her mother. She couldn't understand why someone who had had such a privileged childhood should be resentful when she herself was quite satisfied with her own humble beginnings.

A window and a door to the front of the basement, looked out on to a paved area with steps that rose up to the street above. 'We used to spend a lot of time down here, Stevie and I,' Fiona said. 'Cook used to let us roll out bits of pastry and sometimes, in the afternoons, Patsy, the kitchen maid used to play snap with us.' She smiled and shook her head. 'Looking back, I realize that she couldn't have been all that much older than we were. I think she joined the ATS when the war started.' She looked at Sally. 'Shall we go and look at the bedrooms?'

On the first floor there was a large drawing room, four bedrooms and a bathroom. Sally smiled when Fiona opened the door.

'Oh! It's got a fireplace!'

'Yes. Nanny used to bath us in here, with towels warming on a towel horse in front of the fire. It was lovely and cosy in the winter.' Fiona closed the door. 'You can choose which bedroom you'd like.'

'But which is yours?'

'Stevie and I used to sleep on the top floor,'

Fiona explained. 'We had a day nursery and a night nursery up there and there was a little room for Nanny. I'll show you in a minute. I suggest we both choose rooms at the back, away from the traffic noise.'

It was the top floor that had suffered most from the effects of the bombing. Some of the ceilings were down and daylight could be seen through the holes in the roof. Buckets stood around to catch the rain that dripped through. The furniture had been moved to the driest places and covered with dustsheets but the toys were stacked against one dry wall in the nursery. Sally looked at them in awe — the kind of toys she had only ever seen in books: a rocking horse almost as big as a real one; a train set that ran on real steam, a flounced dolls' cradle and a massive dolls' house full of miniature furniture. Not for the first time, she wondered if she would ever fully comprehend what it must have been like to have such an advantaged upbringing.

As though reading her thoughts Fiona said, 'I doubt whether anyone will live like this again. The war will have made people think differently.'

'Why do you say that?' Sally asked. 'You had a happy childhood, didn't you? You must have been happy with all this.'

But Fiona was shaking her head. 'We spent very little time here, or at home either for that matter once we started school. I hated St Hilary's. I missed Nanny and Stevie. It always felt like a punishment.'

'But it must have been nice in the holidays,' Sally said.

Fiona sighed. 'As far back as I can remember I had the strangest feeling that I didn't belong,' she said. 'Then when I was older I found out about the poverty that existed, right on our very doorstep. Just a few streets away from here, Patsy, the little kitchen maid I told you about, lost her baby brother. There were ten children and when the baby got ill they couldn't afford a doctor and he died.'

'That happened a lot where I used to live,' Sally said. 'It was part of everyday life. Things like diphtheria, bronchitis and pneumonia. They're killers for little kids.'

'But that child only had tonsillitis,' Fiona said. 'A doctor could have cured him easily. He'd probably even have recovered without help if he hadn't been so malnourished. Once I knew that I felt ashamed that families like mine wasted more food in a month than Patsy's family saw in a year.'

'It's the way things are, Fee,' Sally said. 'I think it always will be. You can't go around beating yourself over the head over things you can't change. There'll always be rich and poor, same as there'll always be folks with no jobs — brainy kids and dunces. It's just — just *life*. It's the way things are and there's nothing we can do about it.'

'I know.' Fiona shrugged. 'Oh, come on, we're getting too serious. Let's unpack and start settling in. Then tomorrow we can start making plans.'

★　★　★

They had been at Gower Street for a week, seven busy days during which, as far as was possible with the builders still working on the roof, the house had been made comfortable. Both girls had worked hard. Fiona had found a chimney sweep and had all the chimneys swept. All the dustsheets had been removed and the dull bloom polished from the furniture. The beds were aired, the cobwebs banished and the carpets vacuumed.

To their relief the Aga was found to be in working order and now, with the fire lit, the basement curtains drawn and the remains of their meal cleared away the girls sat at the kitchen table, ready to start making their plan. Fiona had a large notepad in front of her and a freshly sharpened pencil.

'I think we should start by making a few menus,' she said, writing *Menus* in large letters at the top of the page. 'Things like meat, sugar and fats will have to be supplied by the customer while we're still rationed, and we'll have to start scouting round for a good fishmonger and greengrocer.'

'We could always get our vegetables from Nanny Joan,' Sally suggested. 'She might let us have other things too, like eggs and the occasional boiling fowl. Then, in summer there'd be plenty of fruit.'

Fiona's eyes lit up. 'Sally! You're a genius!' The smile left her face abruptly. 'Oh, but how would we transport it up here from Fairfield?'

'That's a point,' Sally agreed. 'Maybe later we could afford to buy a van. We're going to have to get one anyway. How else can we take all the stuff we'll need along to the customers' homes?'

'Taxis, I suppose.'

'We'd lose most of our profit if we had to do that.'

'OK, we'll try and get some kind of vehicle, which means we'll have to get a loan from the bank.' Fiona rubbed out *Menus* and wrote, *See Bank Manager.*

Sally watched her apprehensively. 'Do you think he'll give us one, just like that?' she asked. 'Why should he believe us when we say we can make a go of it? And suppose we fail — how would we pay the loan back?'

'We're not *going* to fail!' After a moment's thought Fiona rubbed out the heading, *See Bank Manager.* 'We won't get a loan without customers,' she said. 'And we can't start working without funds.' She chewed the end of her pencil. 'So where do we start?'

'Do you think Stephen would help?' Sally asked.

'In what way? What does he know about starting a catering business?' Fiona said.

'What do *we* know about it if it comes to that? Three heads are better than two. He might have some ideas.' Sally leaned forward. 'Tell you what, why don't we ask him for dinner? He enjoyed the meal we made at your mum and dad's that weekend. We could ask him to bring a friend if you like. It'd be good practice. Then, if it's successful we could even put on a meal for the bank manager later, just to show him what we can do.'

Fiona looked up. 'Sall, I think you might well have the beginnings of an idea there.'

As the telephone had still to be reconnected Fiona slipped out to the post office and sent Stephen a telegram. It read: *Come for dinner Friday. Bring Ian. Love Fee and Sally.*

The reply came back immediately: *Love to. Stephen and Ian.*

It threw them into a flurry of activity. What to cook? How to obtain the ingredients? They decided on a masculine menu, which they knew would be popular. Vegetable soup, roast beef (if they could find a decent joint) with Yorkshire pudding and horseradish sauce. Treacle pudding and custard for dessert, ending with biscuits and cheese (if they could find anything better than the usual processed mousetrap).

★　★　★

Williamson and Threlfall's, the high-class grocer's shop where Mrs Biggins, the long-departed housekeeper from Gower Street, had always dealt, was still open for business and, to Fiona's delight, the pre-war manager was back in charge. As they handed over their ration books John Martin told Fiona that his job had been kept for him whilst he was away fighting with the Eighth Army in the desert. He was pleased to see her and interested in the new venture the girls were starting. To their delight he found them a piece of Stilton cheese, a jar of extra strong horseradish sauce and a large tin of Golden Syrup — which took most of their points coupons — and a bottle each of port and sherry. They carried their treasure home as though it were gold bullion. A visit to the butcher later resulted in a joint of silverside of beef, which Fiona said would be tender with careful cooking.

On Friday afternoon they lit a fire and laid the table in the dining room. Fiona had found the damask tablecloths, carefully packed away in tissue paper by Mrs Biggins. She had also unearthed the EPNS cutlery once used by the staff. It had been left behind in London as Marcia had considered it valueless. Sally had found a forgotten candelabra with a slight dent in its base at the back of a dusty cupboard. She even found some candles for it too.

By the time the boys were due the dining room fire was burning brightly, the flames glinting on the silver and glasses and the room perfumed by the flower arrangement Fiona had made for the table centre. But best of all was the aroma of the roasting beef drifting mouth-wateringly up the basement stairs.

When the front doorbell rang Sally felt her heart flip. She was looking forward to seeing Stephen again far more than she wanted to admit. She'd thought about him ever since her visit to Saltmere St Peter at Easter, wondering if he would remember his promise to get in touch again. Although she refused to acknowledge the fact, her suggestion that they invite him and his friend to dinner was motivated by more personal reasons than for picking his brains for ideas.

As the bell pealed, rattling the board at the bottom of the basement stairs, she made to dash to answer it then checked, glancing over her shoulder at Fiona who laughed.

'Go on, I know you're dying to see him,' she teased.

Sally made herself walk slowly up the stairs. She took a deep breath, glancing in the hall mirror as she passed and giving her hair a pat before opening the door. She was wearing the only dressy frock she possessed, the red one she'd worn when she'd sung at the Easter concert.

Wearing a smart grey suit, Stephen looked as handsome as she remembered him. He smiled as Sally opened the door and handed her a bunch of tulips.

'Hello there, Sally. Good to see you.' He bent and kissed her cheek. 'I don't think you've met my friend, Ian Jerome. Ian, this is Fee's friend, Sally Joy.'

Ian Jerome was taller than Stephen. He had thick, dark hair, brushed smoothly back and the bluest eyes that Sally had ever seen. She held out her hand.

'Pleased to meet you,' she said shyly.

He smiled. 'How do you do.'

Stephen laughed. 'Oh dear! Formal, aren't we? Where's that sister of mine?' He sniffed the air appreciatively. 'Smells as though the two of you have been busy. We can't wait, can we, Ian? We haven't eaten all day. There's something to be said for being guinea pigs!'

'I heard that!' Fiona put her head round the baize door. 'Guinea pigs! Damned cheek! We've put on our best effort for you two. Come and have a sherry down in the kitchen while we dish up. I refuse to stand on ceremony for my horrid older brother.'

'Not so much of the *older!*' Stephen said as they followed her down the basement stairs. At the bottom he looked around him in surprise. 'Hey! You've made it cosy down here.'

'We live down here most of the time,' Fiona explained. 'It's our dining room, drawing room and office all rolled into one. Can't afford to light fires upstairs every day with the coal shortage, so this is the warmest place in the house. Thank goodness it's April. With a bit of luck it should start warming up soon.' She handed them a glass of sherry each and fetched a vase for the tulips.

'Cheers! Here's to your new business,' Stephen said. 'By the way, what are you going to call yourselves?

The girls looked at each other. 'We haven't thought about a name yet.'

'Well, you'd better start. You can't start advertising till you've got a title.'

'Maybe you can think of one for us,' Sally suggested.

'Mmm, I'll have to think about that.' He drained his glass. 'Now, come on. Don't keep us hanging around talking small talk any longer. We're as hungry as a couple of hunters and besides, I want to hear all your news.'

The meal sent up to the dining room via the dumbwaiter by Fiona and served by Sally, was a success and as the last crumb of Stilton cheese disappeared both young men sat back with sighs of satisfaction.

'That was delicious,' Ian said. 'If you can produce meals like that for your customers I'm sure you'll make a fortune in no time.'

'Shall we go downstairs for coffee?' Fiona suggested. 'The fire's burning low and there's no more coal.'

'Is the piano still OK?' Stephen asked.

Fiona shrugged. 'I've no idea. You know I was never any good at music. All we've done is dust it and replace the dustsheet. We don't use the drawing room.'

'Let's go and see.' He was already on his feet and heading for the stairs.

'In the drawing room he pulled the dustsheet from the baby grand piano and sat down, opening the lid and flexing his fingers. He ran his hands over the keys and winced slightly. 'It could do with a good tuning, but it's better than the old upright in the mess I suppose.' He smiled up at Sally. 'Come on, Sally. I'll never be able to see you in that dress without wanting to hear you sing.'

She backed away. 'Oh no. I can't.'

'Yes you can.' He played a snatch of 'Long Ago and Far Away'. 'Come on. I bet you know this one.'

Sally let him play the first few bars then began to sing the words. When the last chorus came to an end Fiona and Ian clapped enthusiastically.

'That was super!' Ian said. 'Steve told me about the concert where you stepped in at short notice. Now I see what he meant.'

Stephen closed the lid of the piano and pulled the dustsheet back. 'Why don't we go back downstairs for a nice cup of coffee?' he suggested.

The four of them clattered down the basement stairs and Sally filled the kettle and put it on the Aga hotplate.

Fiona sat down and took a deep breath. 'The thing is, Stevie, we've been trying to work out some kind of plan and, to be absolutely honest, neither of us has a clue where to start.'

'Ah, now we get to the ulterior motive,' Stephen said, leaning back on his chair. 'I thought all that grub would have to have a price.'

'Well what are brothers for if it isn't to give advice?'

'Flattery will get you nowhere. Still, it was a good dinner, so fire away.'

'You see, we need cash to start and we can't ask for a bank loan without showing we've got some customers. Then again we can't get the customers without the funds,' Fiona went on. 'We need some transport too, a van or — or something.' She glared at Stephen's amused expression and reached out to slap his hand. 'Don't *laugh*! I'd like to see you do better. We have the know-how as far as the catering goes, we just need to know how to put a business in motion, that's all.'

'Oh — is *that* all?' Stephen said.

Ian leaned forward. 'I might be able to help with the transport,' he offered. 'I'm planning to go into the used car business and I've already managed to buy one or two second-hand vehicles with my gratuity. I could lend you one if you like.' He looked at Fiona. 'I take it you can drive.'

'Yes. But we couldn't possibly accept — it would be too great a responsibility, borrowing a car.'

'Well, I'm not all that busy at the moment,' Ian said. 'I could even come and drive you myself. I'll be entitled to a commercial petrol allowance. After all, I take it that it would be in the evenings?'

'Well, yes.'

He smiled. 'No problem then.'

'As long as you agree to let us buy one from you as soon as we can afford it,' she added.

'Not going to argue with that!' he smiled. 'I'll keep my eye open for a bargain for you.'

'Had you thought of asking Dad, Fee?' Stephen asked. 'For a loan, I mean.'

She shook her head. 'I'd only do that as a very last resort.'

'I don't see why. After all, he'll be paying my expenses at Cambridge. Look, I can lend you some cash if you like. There's all my gratuity money just sitting there in the bank. You might as well use it. A bank loan will cost you a fortune in interest.'

'I can't take your money,' Fiona said.

'We could always pay Stephen back with interest,' Sally suggested. 'Maybe less than the bank would charge us, but he'd still be into pocket.'

'Good girl! I'm all for that,' Stephen said.

'You'd be independent and I'd benefit too. So is it settled then?'

'Well, maybe we could borrow a bit from you,' Fiona conceded. 'Just till we get on our feet.'

'Right. So you've got cash and transport sorted out,' Stephen said. 'What's next — supplies?'

'We've found a good grocer and a butcher,' Fiona told him. 'And Sally had the brilliant idea of buying our fruit and vegetables from Nanny Joan.'

'Great idea,' Stephen said. 'But you'd need to make trips down to Fairfield at least once a week for that.'

'That's OK. I can take you,' Ian said. 'I'll be free on Sundays.'

'Right. So what's next? Have you thought about advertising?' Stephen asked. 'Everyone says it pays to invest in that. You should place advertisements in all those magazines that Ma likes, like *The Lady* and *The Tatler* . . . '

'We can't go out into the country,' Fiona reminded him.

'No, but people will be opening up their London houses now and most of the entertaining is done up in Town anyway.'

'That just leaves the name,' Ian said. 'What are you going to call yourselves?'

For the ten minutes that followed suggestions were tossed back and forth across the table, some facetious, some hilarious and some of Stephen's suggestion downright mischievous.

'Girls for Hire.'

'Stevie, *really*!'

'OK then, Ladies In Waiting,' he offered with a grin.

'Very funny.'

'Chefs in Frocks.'

'*No!*'

'The Food Factory.'

'*Stephen!*'

'Grub Galore?'

'Will you please be serious!'

'How about Dinner At Eight?' Ian said quietly.

The laughter abated as the other three digested this idea then Sally said, 'I really like that. It sounds classy. What about you, Fee?'

'Yes, I like it too. It's simple and it says everything. Thanks, Ian.' Fiona stood up. 'I think this calls for a celebration.' She fetched the precious bottle of port from a cupboard and poured four generous glasses. Stephen raised his.

'Here's to Dinner at Eight,' he said. 'And may God help all who eat it!' He cleared his throat. 'Seriously though, there's just one thing I'd like you to do for me. Could you please keep October 27 free when you're booking; because I have an invitation of my own for you.'

Fiona looked at him. 'What's this, Stevie?'

'Well, it's just that His Majesty has a spare AFC going and it seems he wants me to go to the palace on that day and pick it up. I'd like all of you to be there for the occasion.'

Fiona's eyes filled with tears. '*Oh, Stevie!*' She threw her arms around his neck. 'Why didn't you say anything before? I'm so proud of you. Of course we'll be there, won't we, Sally?'

Sally nodded diffidently, unsure of whether

Stephen meant to include her and whether she had any right to be present at such an auspicious occasion along with all his family.

They were standing at the front door later that evening when Ian said, 'After such a sumptuous dinner I think it's our turn to entertain you. Can we book somewhere for next week — for the four of us?'

'Great idea!' Stephen looked at Sally. 'You will come, won't you?'

'I'd love to,' Sally said. 'You too, eh, Fee?' She glanced at Fiona.

'Well — we are going to be busy,' she said hesitantly.

'Rubbish!' Stephen kissed his sister's cheek. 'An evening off will do you both good and Sally wants to come, don't you, Sally?'

'I think it would be very nice,' she said.

He took her hand. 'Good, that's settled then. See you both next week. We'll let you know when.' He pulled Sally gently towards him and kissed the corner of her mouth, lingering slightly and smiling into her eyes. 'It was great to see you,' he said softly. 'And to hear you sing again,' he said softly. 'Specially that song. Here's to next week, eh?'

When they had waved Stephen's little car off and closed the door Fiona turned to Sally. 'Why did you have to let us in for dinner next week?'

Sally looked at her in surprise. 'What's wrong with having dinner with your brother?'

'It's not just Stevie though, is it?'

'I thought you liked Ian. I think he's smashing and he really likes you. Anyone can tell that by the way he looks at you.'

'Nonsense.' Fiona coloured and turned away. 'I'm wondering if it was wise, agreeing to accept his help. After all, we hardly know him.'

'We asked them here to advise us.'

'Yes, well, it's done now. We've made a business arrangement with him and it doesn't do to mix business with pleasure.'

Sally grinned. 'Oh, so you do admit it'll be a pleasure then?' She followed Fiona down the stairs to where the washing up awaited them. At the bottom Fiona turned to her.

'Let's get one thing straight, Sally,' she said. 'I lost the only man I could ever love in the war. You know how I felt about Mark. He was my soul mate and there'll never be anyone else for me. I don't appreciate people trying to organize dates for me.'

'It's not a date — only a *meal*,' Sally protested. 'For four of us, not just you and him. Are you planning never to speak to any man ever again? 'Cause if you are you might as well become a nun and be done with it.'

They washed up in silence. It was the only time Sally could ever remember Fiona being annoyed with her and it made her unhappy. As she hung the tea towels to dry above the Aga she turned to her.

'Don't let's fall out over it, Fee,' she said. 'You don't have to go if you don't want to. You could always have a headache or something. I just thought that if they wanted to return the compliment and ask us out it was only polite to say yes.'

94

Fiona sighed. 'I know. And of course you're right. Ian is a nice man and he's been very kind. It would be churlish not to accept his invitation. It's just that we're likely to be seeing quite a lot of him anyway and . . . '

'Even if you enjoyed Ian's company you wouldn't be disloyal to Mark's memory, if that's what you think,' Sally argued. 'I never met him but I'm sure he wouldn't want you to live the rest of your life alone and grieving for him.'

Fiona put her arms around Sally and hugged her. 'You're a dear good friend, Sall,' she said. 'And I know you mean well. But in future will you let me decide for myself, please?'

'Of course.' Sally hugged her friend back, relieved that their disagreement was over. But deep inside she had her own thoughts about why Fiona wanted to keep Ian at arms' length. They had exchanged only a few sentences during the evening but the spark of attraction between them had been all too obvious. She guessed that it had been disturbing for Fiona but secretly she hoped that the spark might turn into something brighter and more romantic, given time and encouragement.

6

As soon as the telephone had been reconnected the girls placed advertisements for *Dinner At Eight* in several magazines and had business cards printed. A telephone call to Nanny Joan had secured a promise of fresh vegetables and fruit in season, also whatever else she had available. Everything seemed to be in place and they sat back and waited with bated breath for their first booking.

A week passed and nothing happened. Their hopes began to flag.

'What we need is some personal recommendations,' Fiona said. 'There's really nothing like word of mouth.'

To take their minds off the nerve-racking waiting they composed menus, sitting at the table in the basement and glaring from time to time at the maddeningly silent telephone as though they could will it to ring.

They were still eating breakfast at half past eight one Thursday morning almost two weeks after the advertisements had appeared when the instrument finally made its presence felt. They both jumped to their feet in eagerness to answer it but Sally got there first.

'Good morning. *Dinner At Eight*, at your service.'

'Oh, thank goodness — I mean — good morning.' The female voice at the other end sounded slightly panic stricken. 'Look, my name is Sarah Strickland and I'm in a bit of a muddle. Actually I'm throwing myself on your mercy. I just hope you can help me.'

'I'm sure we'll do our best.' Sally made a face at Fiona who was listening.

'You see it's like this: I've recently got engaged and my fiancé wants me to cook dinner for his parents. I think they want to be reassured that their poor darling boy won't starve if he marries me.'

'I see.' Sally put her hand over the receiver and mouthed, '*I think it's a booking.*'

'The thing is, I've been a bit naughty,' the caller went on. 'I've let him — Nigel — my fiancé — think I'm a super cook and the terrible truth is I can barely boil an egg!'

'Oh dear.'

'I mean — I was going to take some lessons before the wedding, naturally.'

'Naturally.'

'But now he's just telephoned me to say they're coming *tomorrow evening!*' The caller's voice rose to a desperate squeak. 'Do you think you could *possibly* help me out? Oh *do* say you're not booked.'

'I think we're free tomorrow,' Sally said, noisily rustling the pages of Fiona's notebook. 'But if we come and cook dinner for you won't that give the game away?'

'Well — I thought — I wondered if you could sort of — bring something along that I could sort of — warm up myself — er — later.'

By this time Fiona who had her ear pressed to

97

the other side of the receiver took it from Sally. 'Hello. I'm the chef,' she said, winking at Sally. 'First of all, do I take it you are in London?'

'Yes. Holland Park.'

'Can you tell me where you saw our advertisement?'

'Oh, I don't know — some magazine or other.'

'Right. You'd like to order dinner for four people?'

'Yes please.'

'Can you give me any idea what you have in mind. Any special requirements — vegetarian for instance.'

'No — no! I'm sure they'll eat *anything*.'

'And you want us to bring along something you can re-heat?'

'Yes.'

'And be gone before your guests arrive?'

'If you could manage it.'

'In other words you want them to believe you've cooked it yourself.'

'Er — well, yes.'

'So it had better be something fairly simple.'

'Well — not *too* simple. I was hoping to sort of impress them a bit.'

'Would you require the full service?'

'What's that?'

'Laying the table — setting the ambiance, so to speak?'

'Ambiance — oh — yes, please.'

'We can supply tableware: napkins, glasses, cutlery, candles and so on, or do you wish us to use your own?'

'Oh! I hadn't thought of all that. Perhaps

you'd better bring yours?'

'Certainly. So that's dinner for four with the full service at . . . ?'

'Oh — er about seven,' the caller said vaguely.

'Give me your telephone number and I'll ring you back with a suggested menu and a price.'

'Thank you *so* much.'

'I'll get back to you as soon as I can,' Fiona said. She put the receiver down. 'Stupid woman!'

Sally laughed. 'Lesson one. The customer is always right — and never stupid. Just as long as we get paid.'

'We're hardly going to get any word-of-mouth recommendations from her though, are we?'

Sally laughed. 'Not unless she's got lots of crafty mates.'

Half an hour later Fiona rang back with her suggestions.

'How does this sound, Miss Strickland? French onion soup to begin with. Boeuf bourguignon with dauphinoise potatoes for the main course. And torte aux pommes and crème cuite for desert.'

'Are you sure that's the kind of thing they'll believe I made myself.'

'Oh yes. It's all quite basic really,' Fiona assured her. 'And very easy to heat and serve. You would serve the desert cold anyway. I'm afraid it's too short notice for us to provide wines.'

'Oh that's all right. Nigel will do that.'

'And you can manage the coffee?'

'Oh yes. I'm quite good at coffee.'

'Good. I'm afraid we shall have to charge extra

99

for short notice like this,' she said.

'Of course. I quite understand that.'

'We'll have to ask you to pay for a taxi too. You see we can't organize our usual transport at short notice either.'

'That's fine. So — what will all this cost me?'

Fiona mentioned a figure that caused Sally's eyebrows to shoot up. She held her breath but to her surprise the caller seemed quite happy with it.

'We'll be with you at approximately half past five tomorrow afternoon then, Miss Strickland.'

When Fiona had put the phone down Sally shook her head. 'What's Boof something, doe-fin-wise potatoes, tart thingummy and cremm whatsit? You said we'd do beef casserole with cheese and onion spuds, apple tart and custard.'

'And that's what we are doing,' Fiona laughed. 'I just gave the dishes their French names. It sounds more professional.'

'Oh right! I shall have to learn all those,' Sally said. 'You'll have to write them down for me. But why say we need a taxi? You know Ian would have taken us.'

Fiona's face assumed the closed expression Sally was becoming used to at the mention of Ian's name. 'I don't want to impose on him,' she said. 'Not at short notice like this.'

'You mean you don't want to be beholden to him.'

'If you like. It's the same thing.'

'Not quite.' Sally muttered under her breath. She said no more, thinking of the evening when

100

she and Stephen, Fiona and Ian had gone out to dinner together. They'd had a lovely evening and Ian was quite clearly attracted to Fiona. But the more notice he took of her, the more she backed away from him. Sally could see that he was hurt and puzzled by her reaction and later when the four of them were walking back to Gower Street she had a word with Stephen about it.

'Maybe you should explain to Ian that Fee is still upset about Mark,' she said. 'I'm sure she likes him. It's just that she feels disloyal. It'll take time.'

'I know. Poor Fee,' Stephen said. 'I've already told him about Mark, but I don't know how long you can expect the poor bloke to compete with a ghost. He's not made of wood after all.' He pulled her hand through his arm and smiled down at her. 'You're not carrying a torch for anyone, are you?'

'No.'

'That's good. By the way, do you know why I chose that particular song the other night?'

' "Long Ago and Far Away"? No.'

'The words. I took a chance that you knew them all the way through.'

'And I did. It's a lovely song. But what about the words?'

'I think they're so appropriate. They fit *us*, Sally — you and me. Come here.' He drew her into a doorway and pulled her close, his lips meeting hers in a tender, lingering kiss.

For a moment she felt dizzy. Behind her closed eyelids stars exploded and her knees turned to water. No kiss had ever made her feel like that

101

before, but then no kiss had ever meant so much to her. As they drew apart the last line of the song was echoing through her head. *Just one kiss and then I knew that all I longed for long ago was you.* Could he really have meant that?

'Sally!' Fiona nudged her. 'Wake up! No time for daydreaming now! We have work to do.' She was putting on her coat. 'This is our first real engagement. Come on. We'll get round to the butcher's and the grocer's right away. No time to go to down to Fairfield so we'd better get up to the fruit and flower market in Covent Garden first thing in the morning for apples and vegetables.' There were two bright spot of colour in her cheeks and her eyes were dancing. Sally hadn't seen her so excited for a long time.

'Right, I'm coming.'

Next morning they were up at the crack of dawn, walking up to Covent Garden to buy the freshest produce they could find. Fiona even bought spring flowers to make a table decoration. At the butcher's the previous day Fiona had used all her powers of persuasion to charm him into parting with some braising steak. Not as much as she would have liked, but as she told Sally, she would make it up with lots of vegetables and a rich red wine sauce.

Once they got home the kitchen became a hive of activity. Sally was kept busy peeling potatoes and vegetables for Fiona to prepare, gently browning them with the meat and putting them into a casserole with the red wine sauce. Once it was in the oven she set about making the French apple tart. Sally watched as Fiona lined the pastry case with layers of sliced apples and sugar set out in a spiral pattern.

'You can make the dauphinoise potatoes,' she said to Sally, showing her how to layer the potatoes with chopped onion and seasoning, cover with milk and top with grated cheese. Once it had joined the casserole in the Aga Sally looked at the time and saw that it was still only half past ten. She smiled at Fiona.

'I reckon we deserve a coffee,' she said. 'You sit down. I'll make it.'

At four o'clock that afternoon the girls sat in the hall, waiting for the taxi. Everything was packed in boxes insulated with layers of newspaper and tea towels and when the taxi arrived they carefully loaded the boxes and Fiona gave the driver the customer's address. As the cab drew away from the kerb they looked at each other.

'Well, this is it,' Sally said. '*Dinner At Eight* starts here.'

★ ★ ★

Sarah Strickland's flat was on the first floor of a rather grand Edwardian villa in Mayfield Crescent. When she answered their ring at the bell she looked flustered.

'I'm just off to the hairdresser's,' she explained, pulling on her coat. 'But do come up and make a start. I'll be back in an hour.'

She was a tall woman of about thirty with lank fair hair and glasses. Her large front teeth prevented her mouth from closing properly so that she appeared to be perpetually smiling. She took them up a graceful curving staircase to the flat and showed them the dining room and kitchen. The whole place was redolent of affluence, from the gleaming Georgian dining table and elegant chairs to the pristine kitchen, which looked as though no food had ever been prepared in it.

'I'll need to give you some instructions about the food,' Fiona said, somewhat alarmed that her customer was about to leave. 'How to heat and serve it and so on.'

'I can't stop now but I won't be long.' Sarah looked at her watch and gave a little squeak. '*Ooh!* I'm late already. Marcel gets so annoyed when I'm late. It's only round the corner so I won't be long.' She whisked out of the flat, leaving Sally and Fiona staring at each other.

'Well! Talk about leaving things till the last minute!' Fiona exploded. 'Couldn't she have had her hair done this morning — or even yesterday afternoon?'

Sally shrugged, opening the pantry door and taking a sneaky look at the contents. 'She obviously hasn't a clue. Look, there's nothing in here but baked beans and a few tins of soup.'

They carried the box of tableware into the dining room and began to set the table, finishing it with the small floral arrangement that Fiona had made. It looked very nice in the centre of the elegant dining room.

'I've looked in the fridge,' Sally said, standing in the doorway. 'There's nothing in there either, certainly no wine. I wonder when what's his name — Nigel is due.'

Fiona was busy laying the various dishes out on the kitchen table: soup and custard in their respective thermos flasks, the casserole and potatoes and the apple tart. 'I hope she won't be long,' she said. 'I need to tell her how long the potatoes need to brown the cheese. It would be a disaster if she burned them. The bread rolls should really be crisped up too.'

'Well, that's her problem if she must go swanning off to the hairdressers,' Sally said. 'She wants jam on it if you ask me.'

They heard the door slam downstairs and looked at each other in alarm. 'That can't be her back already,' Fiona said.

'One of the other tenants perhaps.' Sally bit her lip. 'At least, I hope so.'

A moment later the door opened and a bald, heavily built man walked in. His surprise matched theirs. 'Oh! Hello there.' He looked from one to the other. 'Sarah about, is she?'

'She's at the hairdresser's,' Sally said.

'Oh, right.' He put the bag he was carrying on the table and began to take out several bottles of wine. 'I'd better put the white in the fridge,' he said. 'And uncork the red. I think it's beef we're having, isn't it?'

'That's right.' Sally and Fiona looked at each other. 'If you want to take the red wine through to the dining room it's all ready,' Fiona told him.

He looked up and smiled. 'Good-o. I take it you two are the caterers.'

'Well, yes.' They exchanged another look.

'Right. Well, I won't keep you. Need anything, do you?'

'Just our cheque,' Sally said boldly, handing him the bill she had carefully made out before they left Gower Street.

He waved it away. 'Ah — 'fraid you'll have to see Sarah about that.'

Downstairs the door slammed again and they heard running footsteps on the stairs. Sarah appeared in the doorway looking flushed and breathless and not at all newly coiffeured. 'Oh — hello,' she said. 'If you've finished you can go now — if you — er — like.'

They followed her into the hallway and Sally said quietly, 'Perhaps you'd like to settle up now, Miss Strickland.'

Sarah turned on her toothy smile. 'Oh, I really can't stop now,' she said. 'Our guests are due any minute.'

'But you said seven,' Fiona reminded her. 'And I need to tell you about reheating the food and the . . . '

'I'll *manage* — honestly. I'm really very grateful. Perhaps you could come back tomorrow. I'll telephone to let you know when it's convenient.' In a state of near panic, Sarah was already edging them towards the door.

'We'll need to collect our equipment,' Fiona said.

'Yes, yes . . . ' Downstairs the bell rang making Sarah almost jump out of her skin. She gave a little scream and clapped her hand over her mouth.

'*Eeek!* They're here. Yes, yes, I'll ring. I'll have

106

your things and your cheque all ready. Goodbye.' She bundled them unceremoniously down the stairs. Opening the front door she assumed her widest and horsiest smile for the smart couple waiting outside.

'Mr and Mrs Haversham. How *lovely* to see you. Do go up. Nigel is already there. I'm just seeing off these two friends who happened to drop in.'

The couple stepped inside, smiling politely at Sally and Fiona. 'I do hope we're not chasing you away,' the woman said.

'No, no, they have to be somewhere, don't you?' Sarah pushed them out through the door and closed it smartly behind them.

Standing on the steps they looked at each other.

'How bizarre,' Fiona said.

'I hope we're going to get paid,' Sally said. 'I didn't like the look of that set-up at all. Nigel knew we were the caterers, yet she said she hadn't told him she couldn't cook.'

'Perhaps she confessed after all.'

'And that couple — they didn't look old enough to be Nigel's mum and dad. He was forty-five if he was a day and they weren't much older than that themselves.'

Fiona shrugged. 'Maybe they married young.' They'd reached the main road and she began scanning the road for a cruising taxi. Sally took her arm.

'Come on, there's an Underground station over there. I think we'd better take the tube. I've got a really bad feeling about this one.'

* ★ ★

All next day they waited for Sarah Strickland's telephone call. In the end Sally decided to make a call herself. She wasn't surprised when there was no reply. 'I think we'd better get over there double quick, Fee,' she said. 'I can smell a rat — several, in fact.'

Their ring at the bell of flat two, twelve Mayfield Crescent brought no reply and they were just turning away when a woman laden with shopping bags came up the steps.

'Can I help you?' she asked.

'We're looking for Miss Strickland, flat two,' Fiona said.

The woman looked puzzled. 'The Grangers live in flat two,' she said. 'And they've gone abroad for six months. The only other person who has access to it is Mr Wilmot, the estate agent. It's up for sale, you see and they left a key with him. They did warn me that he might be along to show prospective buyers round.'

Sally's heart sank. 'So you don't know Miss Strickland at all?'

'No. There is a cleaning lady who comes and goes. Perhaps that's her.'

Sally began to open her mouth but Fiona had noticed something. She nudged Sally into silence. 'Thank you,' she said. 'There's obviously some mistake. We must have the wrong address.'

By the time the woman had disappeared through the door of the ground floor flat Sally was fizzing with impatience.

'We've been conned,' she said. 'It's obviously

108

some kind of swindle. We should call the police.'

Fiona shook her head and pointed to a box half hidden in the corner. 'That looks like our equipment,' she said. 'There might be a cheque inside. We don't really want to be involved in something like this when we're just starting out, do we?'

'A cheque inside? You must be joking,' Sally grumbled. 'I reckon we'll be lucky if all our stuff is there!'

They waited until they were in a taxi before they checked the contents of the box. As Sally had predicted, there was no cheque.

'Look at the state of this tablecloth!' Fiona wailed holding up the stained and crumpled damask. There's even a cigarette burn on it. There's a crack in the casserole dish too.' She sat back on the seat, her eyes filling with tears. 'What a way to start our business! I'm sorry, Sally.'

'Not your fault.' Sally grinned. 'Anyway, don't worry. I already had my suspicions when we were hustled out like that so I slipped one of our cards into that woman's pocket as I passed her on the way out. I stuck our bill in with it. I bet she was surprised when she found it.'

Stephen dropped in at Gower Street later that day. He had taken to dropping in two or three times a week ever since their evening out. As they sat round the table in the basement Fiona regaled him with their disastrous first booking.

'Rotten luck.' He said. 'I think in future you're going to have to ask for your money before you leave.'

'We did try,' Sally told him. 'But they couldn't get rid of us fast enough. It's my guess that Sarah knew her in-laws would arrive before seven and it would give her a good excuse to rush us off the premises.' She went on to tell him how she had slipped a card and their bill into Mrs Haversham's pocket. He laughed.

'Trust you! Well, at least it should make her see her future daughter-in-law in a new light.'

'If Sarah *is* her son's fiancé,' Sally said. 'I doubt it somehow.'

★ ★ ★

It was one morning the following week when the girls were busy with the housework that there was a ring at the front door bell. Sally went to answer it and to her surprise found an elegantly dressed woman standing on the steps. Her face was familiar.

'I'm looking for the two young ladies who run *Dinner At Eight*,' the woman said. Then, looking closer she added, 'Ah yes, we've met before, haven't we? At Mayfield Crescent last Friday evening. I'm Julia Haversham.' She held out her hand.

Sally smiled and shook it. 'Of course. Please come in, Mrs Haversham.'

The woman stepped inside and smiled at Fiona who had joined them in the hall. 'I'm so glad I've found you. I'm afraid we were all badly misled the other evening. I hope you'll allow me to settle this,' She held out the bill that Sally had thrust into her pocket. Sally blushed.

'Oh no, really! I shouldn't have done that. I'm sorry.'

'Please don't be. If it hadn't been for this and your business card my husband and I would have been swindled out of quite a large sum of money. Perhaps you'll allow me to explain?'

Fiona opened the door of the dining room. 'Please come in and have a seat, Mrs Haversham. Can I get you anything — coffee perhaps?'

'No thank you my dear.' The woman sat down at the table and took a cheque out of her handbag. It was already made out to *Dinner At Eight*. 'I think this should make up for your inconvenience,' she said. 'My husband insisted on adding a little bonus by way of our grateful thanks.' She passed the cheque to Fiona and smiled at the two pairs of puzzled eyes facing her across the table.

'Let me explain: my husband and I had been looking for a flat to rent on a short lease and we'd been along to Elliot Wilmot's to see what he had on offer. At the time he had no property for letting on his books. However he did have a very nice flat for sale in Mayfield Crescent. Mr Wilmot told us that the owners were away on an extended trip abroad and he showed us round the flat himself. We liked the place but told him we were only interested in renting. Later that evening a woman rang us at our hotel. She said she was the owner of the flat and that she was back in the country on a flying visit. To our delight she said that she was willing to rent the flat to us on a six-months' lease. She even invited us to join her and her fiancé for dinner last Friday evening so that we could look round again.'

'So who was she?' Sally asked.

'It transpires that Miss Strickland works as a clerk at Elliot Wilmot's office. Apparently she and her accomplice had seen a way to make some quick money out of us. She had a copy made of the key and telephoned us with the bogus invitation.' She smiled ruefully. 'I think you can work the rest out for yourselves.'

'But what stopped you from going ahead with the deal?' Fiona asked.

'We were doubtful when they demanded the whole six months' rent in advance,' Mrs Haversham told them. 'Then I went to get a handkerchief from my coat and found your card and the bill in the pocket. I guessed that you were trying to tell me something.'

'What did you do?' Sally asked.

'I said we needed time to think about it, but once my husband and I were alone I showed him your card and bill and we both agreed there was something fishy about the deal. Why wasn't this offer made to us through the estate agent for instance? Why did they want all the rent in advance? We telephoned Mr Wilmot the following morning and told him everything. He recognized the description of Miss Strickland and informed the police at once and she and her accomplice are now in custody.'

There was a stunned silence as the girls took in the story. 'That was our very first booking,'

Fiona said at last. 'Not what you'd call an auspicious start.'

'Maybe it was our first and last,' Sally added.

'Not at all,' Mrs Haversham said with a smile. 'The meal was the only good thing about the evening. I shall certainly recommend you to my friends. Mr Wilmot has since found us a very nice flat not very far from here. Maybe you could come and cook a dinner for our flat-warming party once we're settled in.'

As Fiona closed the front door she turned to Sally and waved the cheque delightedly.

'You're a genius, Sally! If you hadn't put that card in Mrs Haversham's pocket we might never have got *Dinner At Eight* off the ground.'

Sally laughed. 'You always said that word-of-mouth was the best advertisement, didn't you?'

7

At last bookings for *Dinner At Eight* had started to come in, several of them recommendations from Mrs Haversham. At first they had only the occasional dinner party, but as spring turned to summer the girls found that they were doing at least two dinners a week and some buffets and cocktail parties as well. Ian had continued to transport them and the arrangement worked well, but Fiona insisted on paying him. Sally thought this was faintly insulting.

'He wants to do it as a favour — until he finds us a second-hand van.'

Fiona disagreed. 'We're keeping proper books so whatever form of transport we use, it has to be paid for and noted,' she argued. 'After all, if we had our own vehicle it wouldn't run on water, would it?'

Sally couldn't dispute the basic logic of this but she guessed rightly that Ian longed to do something that would make Fiona warm towards him. At the moment he seemed to be fighting a losing battle.

Sally and Stephen had been out several times on their own; to the cinema or sometimes just for a walk in the park, now green and fragrant with burgeoning summer. While he waited to go to Cambridge he was working with Ian, helping him to get his used car business up and running.

Sally thought Stephen was the loveliest man

she had ever met and her feelings towards him were deepening week by week. It was clear that he was fond of her too. They enjoyed each other's company, laughed a lot and shared many of the same interests. Everything should have been perfect, but the misgivings she had had from the beginning refused to go away. He clearly had no idea of the width of the social gulf between them or the difference in their backgrounds and upbringing, not to mention their education. If they continued to see each other she was worried that she might eventually let him down in front of his friends. He thought she was funny now, with her East London accent and the quick cockney wit that he seemed to bring out in her, but there might come a time when he would see her in a different light. And as for his parents . . . Sally closed her mind to the image of his mother's shock and horror should things become serious between Stephen and her.

It was in early June when she had an invitation to Jenny's birthday party. It was to take place on a Saturday evening, the most likely time for a dinner party booking but Fiona insisted that Sally should accept.

'You've worked so hard and we don't have any bookings for next weekend,' she said.

'But we still might get one for Saturday.'

'Then we'll turn it down for once. I think you should go,' Fiona said firmly. 'You haven't had a break since your illness and I don't want you cracking up on me.'

Sally laughed. 'Thanks! You know damned

well I'm as fit as a butcher's dog now.'

Fiona smiled. 'OK; as a matter of fact I thought of going to Fairfield next Saturday anyway to see Nanny Joan. All the new season's fruit and vegetables will be ready soon and I want to make sure the arrangements are in place and talk prices with her. I don't want her out of pocket and I know what she's like.'

'I see, so you want to get away without me,' Sally joked. 'How are you going to get there, by train?'

Fiona turned away but not before Sally had seen the faint blush that coloured her cheeks. 'As a matter of fact Ian is taking me,' she said.

Sally knew better than to tease her friend. 'Oh. That's nice,' she said, smiling delightedly to herself. Perhaps things were looking up between those two at last.

When Stephen asked her out for the following Saturday and she told him she had been invited to Jenny's party he looked crestfallen.

'Oh — right.'

'Why don't you come with me?' she asked on impulse. 'You've never been to a good old East End knees-up, have you?'

If she thought he was going to be put off she was wrong.

His face lit up. 'Would you really like me to come too?'

' 'Course I would.'

'OK then I'd love to.'

'Good! I'll drop Jenny a note and let her know.'

The moment he eagerly snapped up her

invitation Sally developed misgivings. She was sure that it would be the kiss of death to their relationship. When Stephen saw her in her own environment he would see that they were poles apart. But then that had been her intention, hadn't it? She lay awake that night, agonizing over losing the only man she had ever felt deeply for. (She carefully avoided the word love, even in her own mind.) Before the war they would never even have met. People lived their whole lives within their own class and environment and rarely married anyone outside it. She turned over and punched her pillow. What was she thinking about? Who was she kidding? Stephen had never given the impression that he was serious about her, had he? And this time next week it would all be over between them so where was the point in worrying about it?

* * *

The extended Gifford family lived in a tall Victorian house in Florence Street. Along with many other buildings in the area it had suffered its share of bomb damage, but the Gifford family had never contemplated moving out, even during repairs. Why would they when most of them had been born in the house?

Jenny, her parents and three brothers lived and ate in the basement, where there was a large kitchen, a scullery and a living room. Mrs Gifford's elderly parents, affectionately known as Gramps and Granma, occupied the two ground floor rooms. The family slept in the four bedrooms above and the three top floor rooms had been made into a flat for Jenny's married sister, Greta, her recently demobbed husband and their baby son.

There had always been a happy and relaxed atmosphere in the house that Sally loved. Everyone was welcome and somehow, even with rationing and shortages, there was always somehow enough food to go round.

They drove out to the East End in Stephen's little car, which he parked outside the house. The front door was never locked and as they let themselves in Stephen almost fell over a pram and two bicycles propped against the wall in the hallway.

'There's nowhere else to leave things like that,' Sally explained. 'At least, not where they wouldn't get 'alf-inched.'

Stephen looked at her. 'Half-inched?'

She laughed. 'Pinched. It's rhyming slang; you'll probably be hearing a lot of that before the night is through.'

He laughed and slipped an arm round her. 'You're full of surprises, Sally Joy!'

The door leading to the basement opened and Jenny popped her head round it. 'Oh, Sall, it's you. I'm dead chuffed you could come. And you've brought Stephen.' She held out her hand. 'Pleased to meet you, Steve. Come on down both of you. Almost everyone's here and Mum's put on the best spread you've ever seen.' She tucked her arm through Sally's. 'I can't wait for you to meet Gerry, Sall.'

As they reached the bottom of the stairs.

Jenny's mother, Kate, was coming out of the scullery carrying two large plates of sandwiches. She was a plump, motherly woman with a ready smile and when she saw Sally she beamed with pleasure.

'Well, well, little Sally Joy! Long time no see, gel!' She put down the plates on a table and enveloped Sally in a warm hug, smiling at Stephen over her shoulder. 'We used to call her our little bundle of joy,' she laughed. 'Not so little now though.' She held Sally at arms' length and studied her. 'I had a card from your Gran the other day love. She seems to be lovin' it down there.' She shook her head as she looked Sally up and down. 'Just look at you! Turned out a real little smasher an' no mistake gel. Breakin' all the boys' hearts now, I bet.' She winked at Stephen. 'Now then — who's this 'andsome feller?'

'This is Stephen, Auntie Kate. Stephen Crowther. He's my friend Fiona's brother.'

'Lovely to meet you, Steve,' Kate said, taking Stephen's hand between both of hers. 'Come on in and meet my mob.'

In the basement living room the chairs and the upright piano had been moved back against the walls and the table, as Jenny had predicted, was groaning with the buffet supper her mother had prepared. There were introductions all round. Sally had never met Gerry Browning, Jenny's fiancé or her sister's husband Patrick, not to mention the latest member of the Gifford clan, chubby little Sam, who sat on his proud grandfather's knee.

119

From time to time Sally glanced at Stephen, wondering if he was finding it all a little overwhelming, but he seemed to be enjoying himself, chatting to Jenny's brother Johnny who had also been in the RAF.

They ate, talked and laughed, catching up with all the news and the happenings of the intervening war years. Everyone did justice to the food and the abundance of beer that the boys had contributed to the party and soon everyone was in a mellow mood. Eventually, the plates cleared and the table leaves folded down, it was time for the entertainment. They played charades and Stephen delighted Sally by entering into the spirit of the game with an acting skill that surprised her. Then someone asked Jenny what she would like next.

'I want Sally to give us a song,' she said.

Sally shook her head. 'No. You don't want to hear me.'

'Yes, I do. It's my birthday so you have to do as I say!' Jenny insisted. There was a roar of agreement from the others in which Stephen joined.

'Come on, Sally,' he said. 'They want to hear you and so do I. I'll accompany you if that's all right.' He moved over to the piano. ''A Nightingale Sang in Berkeley Square'. Let's have that.'

Everyone settled down to listen as Sally sang the popular romantic song but if she thought she was going to get away with just the one she was wrong. As the last note died away there was a cry of 'More!' She shook her head in protest but

Stephen looked up at her and said quietly,

'Shall we have 'Long Ago and Far Away'?'

He played the introduction and Sally sang the song with feeling, remembering what Stephen had said about the words. As she came to the last line he glanced up at her with the special tender look that told her he remembered too. Before her voice could falter she stopped singing and said,

'Oh, come on you lot! I'm not going to do all the work. Everyone join in!' And the building reverberated with their combined voices as they all joined in with a hearty reprise.

Later, when she was up in Jenny's bedroom, putting on her coat to leave, Jenny told her that she and Gerry had set their wedding date.

'It's August 10 at St Faith's,' she said. 'Gerry's got the job he wanted as a theatre technician now so there's nothing to wait for. We've even got our name down for one of the hospital flats. It'll be so handy — no queuing up for buses.'

'That's wonderful, Jenny. You'll have to let Fee and me do your reception buffet.'

'Don't know that we'll be able to run to that,' Jenny said. 'Anyway, I want you to be bridesmaid.' She looked at Sally thoughtfully. 'What about you and Steve?'

'What do you mean — what about us?'

'You really like him, don't you?'

Sally shrugged. 'He's OK.'

Jenny laughed. 'Oh come off it, Sally Joy! You don't fool me, I know you too well. You're potty about him. I saw it in your face when you sang that song.'

Sally turned away to pick up her handbag.

'We're chalk and cheese, Jenny. It'd never work.'

'Why not? He's smashing. I know he talks a bit posh but that don't matter. Anyway so do you now.'

'No I don't!' Sally protested. Unable to work out whether this was a compliment or not, she added, 'I don't really — do I?'

'You do a bit. I expect you've got it off your friend Fiona. Anyway, as I said, it don't matter. He really likes you. Anyone can see that.'

Sally sighed and sat down on the edge of the bed. 'You should see the place where he grew up, Jenny. It's like something off the pictures. And he's off to Cambridge University in a couple of months' time — going to be a lawyer. I don't suppose I'll be seeing him again after that. Anyway, he's not our sort. I'd never fit in.'

'But he obviously enjoyed himself tonight, with all of us,' Jenny pointed out. 'And you and him — you look so good together.'

'In wartime things were different,' Sally argued. 'All sorts of people mixed together and Stephen got used to that like we all did. But it's peacetime now. Things will get back to normal soon. Once Stephen gets among his own sort at university he'll realize that I'm not for him.'

'So what about you and Fiona then? Are you saying that isn't working either?'

Sally shook her head. 'Fee's different. She hates all that snobby stuff.'

'And Steve likes it?' She laughed. 'I don't think so. Not if tonight was anything to go by. He was just like one of us.'

Sally forced a smile. 'Well, it's fun for now,'

she said. 'Fine for as long as it lasts. Just let's leave it at that.'

★　★　★

Fiona and Ian spent a pleasant day with Nanny Joan. The smallholding was flourishing. There were early strawberries and new potatoes, peas and the first tomatoes and lettuce from the heated greenhouse.

'If only there were some way to preserve all this,' Nanny complained. 'The trouble is, it all comes at once. Not that I'm complaining. The market stall is doing good business.'

'I read where they're bringing out frozen fruit and vegetables soon,' Ian said. 'After that I daresay it'll only be a matter of time before everyone has their own deep freezing cabinet in the kitchen.'

Fiona laughed. 'What an idea! That'll be the day! It would be wonderful though.'

Joan had cooked a special lunch, which they all enjoyed. After a walk round the smallholding and a discussion about the future of *Dinner At Eight* Ian had gone to the local garage to buy petrol leaving Joan and Fiona to pack up the box of supplies. From time to time Joan glanced at Fiona and at last she said, 'I approve.'

Fiona looked up in surprise. 'Approve? Of what?'

'Not of what — of whom! Of that young man, of course.'

Fiona sighed and dropped her gaze to the box

123

again. 'I thought you were talking about our business.'

'Stuff and nonsense!' Joan said in her forthright way. 'If you don't snap him up then you're not the young woman I thought you were.'

Fiona shook her head. 'Nanny! I haven't the vaguest idea what you're talking about.'

'I think you have. It's not like you to beat about the bush, Fiona. But I'll say no more,' Joan closed down the lid of the box. 'Except this — when you're young you think there's plenty of time — plenty more fish in the sea, as they say. Well, you can take it from me that there isn't, and it's a hard lesson to learn when it's too late.'

Fiona hugged her. 'Darling Nanny. You and your platitudes! Don't worry about me. I've got more important things to think about at the moment and I'm happy.'

'Well, I won't argue with that,' Joan said hugging her back. 'That's all I've ever wanted for my girl.'

★ ★ ★

Fiona was quiet on the drive back to London. Ian looked at her from time to time, wondering where her thoughts were. At last he gave her a gentle challenge.

'Penny for them.'

She smiled at him. 'Not worth it really. I never see Nanny Joan without feeling a bit nostalgic. She was a big part of my childhood. The best part really, apart from Stevie.'

124

'She is a lovely person,' he agreed. 'A really strong lady. And that place of hers — she must put in hours of work to keep it going. Does she have any help?'

'There's an old chap who comes in and helps her with the really heavy work,' Fiona told him. 'But she does most of it herself.'

He glanced at her guessing at her worrying thoughts. Nanny was over fifty now. What would happen when she was too old to carry on with all that hard physical work?

'What do you say we stop somewhere for a drink and a sandwich?' Ian asked. 'We passed some nice village pubs on the way this morning.'

She nodded. 'Ok.'

They found a pleasant looking pub in a village on the outskirts of Colchester. It had oak beams and an inglenook fireplace. It seemed dim after the bright evening sunshine outside but there was a jug of forsythia on the bar, its bright yellow colour bringing the sunlight indoors. They were the only two customers in the bar and the smiling landlady made them thick cheese and pickle sandwiches accompanied by crisp lettuce and tomato. Ian ordered two pints of the local ale with which to wash it down. And as they both took a drink from the thick glass mugs Ian smiled at her.

'I like a girl who enjoys a pint.'

She laughed. 'I think I proved to you and Stevie that I could keep up with you both when we went on a pub crawl that weekend in Saltmere St Peter.'

He laughed. 'You did indeed. That was a night, wasn't it?'

'Certainly was.' Fiona took a bite of her sandwich. 'One of the happier things the war taught me — how to drink beer and enjoy doorstep sarnies.'

'Steve told me about your fiancé,' Ian said quietly. 'I'm sorry.'

She shook her head. 'Mark wasn't even that really. We never got around to getting officially engaged,' she said. 'In normal times we would probably have been married by now and set up in a home of our own.' Looking up she saw that his face was thoughtful and suddenly, with a flash of intuition she asked, 'Did you lose someone too, Ian?'

His eyes met hers and he said, 'It's not something I talk about much.'

'Oh. I'm sorry. I didn't mean to . . . '

'No *no*! It's all right,' he said quickly. 'I'd really like to tell you — if it wouldn't bore you too much.'

'Of course it wouldn't.'

'Ok. Shall we move?'

They took their plates and mugs to a corner of the bar by the window where the last of the evening sun shone in.

'I've never even told Steve,' Ian said. 'At least, not the details.' He paused to take a drink from his mug. 'You realize of course that I haven't had his education. All I aspired to was the local grammar and I left there after school cert. at seventeen and went on to technical college. I'd never have had the chance to train as a pilot if it

126

hadn't been for the war. I started off as a flight engineer. The lads were dropping like flies and they needed every bod they could get their hands on to train.' He bit into his sandwich and chewed thoughtfully. 'I was so proud of myself when I got my wings. I'd known Maureen since school. You could say we'd grown up together and when I got my commission I asked her to marry me. I managed to get a forty-eight-hour pass and we were married at the register office in Southampton where our folks lived. It was a quiet wedding, but I thought we were the happiest couple alive at the time. After that I was on ops for months. Maureen came up sometimes for a weekend, but other than that we hardly saw each other. When I did get a few hours off I was always so dog-tired I could hardly speak.' He sighed. 'Well, after a while she stopped coming. I couldn't really blame her and to tell the truth we were under so much pressure that I hardly noticed. But as soon as I got leave I went home. Maureen was living with my folks. They'd made the front room into a bed-sit for us. She was still at work when I arrived and Mum and Dad asked me in for a cup of tea. I could see they were worried about something and eventually Mum told me Maureen had been seeing someone else — some American soldier. Mum said she'd even brought him home and she was pretty sure he'd stayed the night.' He shook his head. 'Dad kept butting in. He didn't want her to go on — kept trying to backtrack and say they didn't know for sure — had no proof, but by then I was seeing red. I went and sat in our room and waited for her. It was winter and dark by the time she got home. When I challenged her with it I expected her to deny it, but she didn't. She just stood there and told me what a dead loss I was as a husband and how much better this Yank was. She said our marriage had been a bad mistake and she was going to get a divorce as soon as she could and marry him — go back to the States after the war.'

Fiona could see his hand shaking as he picked up his beer mug. Fearfully she asked, 'What did you do, Ian?'

He drew a long shuddering breath. 'To say that I was hurt and upset would be an understatement. I was so angry that it scared the living daylights out of me. I wouldn't have believed I was capable of such a rage. It was like a fire inside me. She stood there with her hands on her hips, this horrible sneer on her lips and her eyes mocking me. She went into every detail of their relationship — goading me with it. I think she wanted me to hit her and I knew that if I stayed in that room with her for one more minute I'd do something terrible. It might sound cowardly, but I never even spoke. I just turned and walked out. I walked and walked, down by the docks. It was raining and I didn't have my greatcoat but I didn't care. For me the end of the world might as well have come there and then. I'd loved Maureen for as long as I could remember. I thought she loved me too, and now she'd turned into this stranger that I didn't even recognize, less than a year after our wedding. Why? Why?

'I reckoned it had to be my fault she'd turned out like that. Even when the siren went I kept on walking. The planes came and the bombs started to fall, and all I wanted was for one to fall on me so that the agonizing pain would go away. In the end an air raid warden dragged me into a shelter and I spent the rest of the night there, shivering in my soaking wet uniform.'

He was quiet for a moment and Fiona's hand crept along the counter to touch his fingers. He stared at it for a moment then raised his eyes to hers.

'In the morning when we came out of the shelter there was devastation everywhere but I hardly noticed. All I wanted was to get home. I'd had all night to think and I was determined to talk to her — to make her see sense. I couldn't believe she could stop loving me just like that after all these years. I was ready to take all the blame myself — to promise her that things would be different. Then I turned the corner of our road — and I just stood there. There was nothing left. The whole road had been flattened by a direct hit. Everything was gone — my home, my folks, my wife, my marriage — my life. All I could think was that if I hadn't walked — if I'd had the guts to have it out with her, I'd have been dead too, and believe me, that was all I wanted at that moment. It felt like the end of the world.'

'Oh, Ian!' There were tears on her cheeks now. She felt so guilty. Her own loss had been terrible but his was so much worse. At least Mark and she had shared his last leave together. They had never stopped loving each other. There were no bitter memories, no regrets. And she still had so much compared to Ian. His hand turned over suddenly, his fingers closing tightly round hers.

'Thanks for listening, Fiona,' he said. 'I don't often unburden myself like that. Sorry if I've upset you.'

'Perhaps you should talk about it more,' she said, her hand still in his. 'It doesn't do to bottle things up.'

'Do you talk?'

She smiled ruefully. 'Not really. Not enough, I suppose. Mark was Stevie's friend. They were at school together and joined the RAF at the same time. We fell in love and he was killed during the Battle of Britain. We can't go back unfortunately. We can't change anything, can we?' She drained the last of her beer. 'I suppose we should be moving on,' she said. And suddenly she knew that she meant much more than just continuing the drive back to London.

★ ★ ★

'I like your friends,' Stephen was driving them home. Sally turned to look at his profile in the light of the street lamps.

'They've always been like the family I never really had,' she said. 'Auntie Kate always made me welcome. I used to be round at their house every Sunday afternoon.' She laughed. 'They all brought their mates home on a Sunday and when Kate was laying the table for tea I used to secretly count the cups and saucers, hoping I'd be staying too. I always was.'

'They're a very close family,' Stephen said.

'Yes. That why I used to love being with them. I thought it must be wonderful, being part of a big family,' Sally said. 'My mother walked out on me when I was a baby. I only had Gran and Grandpa.'

'At least they were always there when you were growing up,' he said.

She looked at him. 'Your mum adores you,' she said. 'Your dad too I daresay. And you've got Fee.'

'Never saw much of them when I was at boarding school,' he told her. 'I hated it. I was so bloody homesick — blubbing away like a baby after lights out — wanting Nanny.' He glanced at her. 'I was only eight at the time, mind. I soon learned to toughen up. Anyway, when we were at home the parents weren't around much — always off somewhere — skiing holidays or cruises, hunt balls and cocktail parties. Even when they were at home they were entertaining and we had to be kept out of the way. Not the thing to have grubby noisy little brats milling around. That's why we both still cling to Nanny Joan. She was our rock.' He turned to smile at her. 'It wasn't the way you think it was, you know, all privilege and cosseting. I was bullied mercilessly at school until I was big enough to stand up for myself. And not only by older boys. Some of the masters were pretty sadistic too.'

'Did you ever try to run away?'

He smiled. 'Only once. Those POW films have

nothing on what it was like being caught and brought back.'

Sally's eyes widened. 'You're kidding!'

He laughed. 'Well, yes. It was pretty bad though. If you can stick that you can stick anything. I was quite glad to get into the RAF.' He pulled the car off the road into a side street and switched off the engine. 'I hope you realize that I'm trying as hard as I can to get the sympathy vote here,' he said, his eyes laughing into hers. 'You're supposed to be stroking my brow by now.'

She laughed. 'Do you really want me to stroke your brow?'

'I'd rather have you kiss me.'

The kiss lasted for quite a long time till with a sigh she drew away and let her head rest against his shoulder. His arm felt warm and strong around her. 'Everything has been mapped out for you so far, so how do you see your future life, Stevie?' she asked.

He sighed. 'Well, I've got to try and get this legal degree first. After that I suppose it'll be a job with a firm of solicitors to get some experience under my belt and then try for the bar.'

She twisted her head to look up at him. 'The bar?'

He laughed. 'As in barrister — not pulling pints,' he explained. 'You know, gown and wig and all that.'

'Oh.' She sighed. She tried to picture him in the black, bat-like gown and white curled wig that she'd only seen in films. Somehow it didn't go with happy-go-lucky, debonair Stevie. Suddenly in her mind's eye she saw him as a little dot on the horizon, getting further and further away from her. But for now she was here in his arms, his breath warm against her ear, his heart beating close to hers. And she knew that she must make the best of it while she could.

Their goodnight outside 28 Gower Street lasted for quite a while till Sally noticed the time. Stepping out of the car she ran up the steps and stood watching until the little car disappeared round the corner. She let herself in and crept quietly up the stairs, but seeing that there was still a light under Fiona's door she tapped gently.

'Come in.'

Sally slipped inside and sat on the end of Fiona's bed. 'Did you have a good day at Fairfield?'

'Yes. I've brought a boxful of gorgeous goodies back. They're all in the fridge. Oh and someone rang up after we got back and booked a boardroom cocktail party for Marvel Electricals next Wednesday lunchtime. Oh, and guess who the managing director is?'

'Go on, tell me.'

'Mr Haversham, no less! They've been so good to us.'

'We deserve it,' Sally said. 'We do a good job. So how was Nanny Joan?'

'Just as she always is. She sent her love.'

'Ian all right?'

'He was telling me on the way home that he's a bit worried about his business. That garage he's renting in Edgware is part of a bombed-damaged

133

factory. It was all he could afford but it isn't secure enough. He's afraid it's only a matter of time before there's a break-in. You know how valuable good second-hand cars are at the moment and he has a lot of money tied up in them. If he can't find a better place soon he might have to sell up for whatever he can get and give up.'

'That'd be a shame.'

'How was the party?'

'Lovely. Stevie enjoyed it too.'

'I rather think he'd enjoy anything as long as you were with him,' Fiona said. 'He's pretty besotted, Sally.'

'No!' Sally shook her head. 'We enjoy each other's company, that's all. Once he goes Cambridge he'll meet lots of other girls.'

'He's not a two-timer,' Fiona said. 'He laughs and makes flippant jokes but his feelings go quite deep.'

'We're poles apart,' Sally said. 'I'm not kidding myself about that. Stevie has a good career ahead of him. I'd only hold him back.'

'Who told you that?'

'I'm not stupid, Fee. We're happy enough at the moment though and I'm quite prepared for him to move on when the time comes.' Changing the subject she said, 'Jenny and Gerry have set the date for their wedding. It's August 10. I've been wondering what to get for a wedding present and on the way home I thought, why don't I do the wedding breakfast for her?'

'What a good idea. Yes, I'm all for that,' Fiona said. 'We'll do it together.'

Sally looked at her friend properly for the first time. Fee looked different tonight. More relaxed. In spite of the lateness of the hour she didn't seem at all sleepy. In fact there was an elated air about her.

'So you had a nice time then — with Ian, I mean?' She asked hesitantly.

'Yes — fine.'

'You got on OK?'

'Of course. Why wouldn't we?'

'You obviously talked.'

'Well, we'd hardly spend the whole day in silence, would we?'

'You know what I mean.' Sally stood up. Fee obviously wasn't giving anything away. 'Oh well, time we were asleep, I suppose. See you in the morning.' She headed for the door but as she took hold of the door handle Fiona said,

'He's had a terrible time, Sall. But he doesn't talk about it much. If I tell you, you'll keep it to yourself, won't you? He hasn't even told Stevie.'

'Of course I won't say anything.' Sally was back on the edge of the bed instantly. 'What happened, Fee?'

When Fiona had finished telling her Ian's story Sally's eyes were moist too. 'Oh God! Poor Ian. His entire family. How awful.'

'The fact that he'd walked out on his wife after a row must have been hard to come to terms with too.'

'But you say she'd been unfaithful — even wanted to leave him.'

'He was on his way back — convinced he could talk her out of it.'

'Maybe it would never have worked,' Sally said. 'Sometimes these things happen for the best. It was a long time ago now. Is he over it?'

'Do you ever get over something like that?'

'Maybe he needs someone to help him,' Sally ventured. 'He must like you a lot to entrust you with his deepest feelings.'

'Mmm. Can't resist it, can you?' Fiona smiled in spite of herself. 'I think you were right when you said we should be asleep.' She plumped up her pillow and lay down. 'Night-night, Sally.'

'Night-night.' Sally paused in the doorway. 'You can hide your head all you like, Fiona Crowther but you can't hide your feelings — not from me.'

8

'Is that old wind-up gramophone still up in the nursery?' Stephen asked suddenly.

It was Sunday evening and the four of them had been having a meal in the kitchen at Gower Street. It had been Sally's impromptu idea to invite the boys as they had food left over from the previous evening's catering. As they enjoyed their coffee all four of them were in a relaxed mood. Stephen especially was full of fun and as they shared the washing-up together he asked his sister about the old gramophone.

Fiona laughed. 'What on earth do you want that for?'

'I thought we might have a dance,' he said. 'That's if the bombing didn't damage the records.'

'There's a perfectly good piano upstairs,' Fiona pointed out.

'I'd have to play it though, and I want to dance too. Besides we'd have to roll back the carpet. It's easier down here.'

The four of them trooped up to the top floor to search. It was Stephen who found it, tucked away at the bottom of a cupboard along with the dusty collection of old wax records.

'Fee and I learned to dance with the aid of this old friend,' he announced. 'Nanny Joan taught us, do you remember, Fee?'

'I certainly do, and I hope you're better at it

than you used to be. As I remember, your feet spent more time on my toes than on the floor!'

He grinned. 'I've had plenty of practice since those days. I think you'll find that I could give Fred Astaire a run for his money now.'

They carried the machine and records downstairs and Sally got out a duster and began to dust off their find.

'These are old,' she remarked, peering at the record labels. ''Smoke Gets in Your Eyes', 'September in the Rain'. Oh and here's 'The Folks Who Live on the Hill'. I remember hearing them on the wireless when I was a kid.'

'All good for dancing to though. And look, there's even a packet of new needles.' Stephen screwed one into the pick-up head and began to wind the machine up. 'OK, let's have 'Smoke Gets in Your Eyes'.'

Sally put the record on to the turntable and gently lowered the needle on to it. To the surprise of all four of them the music began. It was slightly crackly but quite loud and clear. Ian turned to Fiona and bowed. 'May I have the pleasure?'

Stephen didn't bother to ask. Grabbing Sally by the waist he pulled her close. 'If my memory serves me right this is a slow foxtrot,' he said against her ear. 'But don't worry. I only know two steps so I'll be doing one of those anyway. I always find that as long as the conversation's interesting enough my partners don't seem to mind.'

Sally laughed and did her best to fit her steps to his. 'Pity there isn't anything we can jive to,' she said as the record ended. 'I used to be pretty hot at that at the factory dances.' To her delight at the bottom of the pile she found something suitable. 'Oh look 'Hold Tight'! We could jive to that. Come on all of you.' She put the record on and the cheerful, jumpy tune boomed out. All four began to jive and Sally was delighted to find that Stephen was as adept at the dance as she was. But just as they were all getting into the swing of it the gramophone began to run down. The music slowed and the sound became so distorted that all four of them collapsed with laughter, clinging to each other helplessly.

'*What on earth is going on here?*' Marcia Crowther stood on the stairs glowering down at them while Donald peered over her shoulder. 'We've been standing on the doorstep, ringing the bell for ages. No wonder you couldn't hear with the racket you're making. Then we found that the door wasn't even locked! The whole place could have been cleared while you were down here cavorting!'

'Mother!' Fiona looked shocked. 'And Daddy — what are you doing here?'

'You might well ask.' Marcia came down the rest of the stairs and sank on to a chair. 'Your father had a letter from the builders to say that the work on the roof was finished so we wanted to come and make sure everything was completed satisfactorily. We've had an invitation to the St John-Pickards' dinner party next Thursday too so we thought we'd kill two birds with one stone.' She looked at Stephen. 'I've been waiting for a letter from you,' she

139

admonished. 'It's weeks since you telephoned or wrote.' She looked at Fiona. 'And you — I take it that hare-brained scheme of yours has fizzled out?'

'As a matter of fact it's going extremely well,' Fiona told her. 'We've started to get really busy.'

'And they've got you to thank for it, Ma,' Stephen put in.

'*Me?*' Marcia looked scandalized. 'It had nothing to do with me.'

'Oh, but it was your idea,' Stephen said wickedly. 'And I'm sure Fee and Sally are really grateful to you.'

Marcia shook her shoulders irritably. 'As you're so good at providing food perhaps one of you would be kind enough to make us some tea and sandwiches,' she said. 'Your father and I have had a long drive. 'And Sally — kindly go upstairs and prepare our room please. It's the large one at the back, overlooking the garden. You'll find clean sheets in the airing cupboard. Oh and make sure they're the pure linen ones.'

As Sally began to climb the stairs Marcia called out, 'The bed will need to be aired thoroughly, so you'd better put three hot water bottles in it and light the gas fire.'

When Sally had disappeared Fiona turned to her mother angrily. 'Sally is not a servant, Mother,' she said.

Marcia raised her eyebrows. 'Did I say she was? I don't think it's unreasonable to ask her to do some small tasks for me, seeing that she's had rent-free accommodation in my house for several months.'

'That's hardy fair, dear,' Donald put in. 'We've been grateful to the girls for keeping an eye on things for us here, haven't we?'

'That remains to be seen when we've inspected the work.' Marcia looked round the kitchen disdainfully. 'It seems that both my children have developed a taste for living like domestics. No prizes for guessing whose influence brought that about!'

Ian, who had been looking distinctly uncomfortable, glanced at Stephen. 'I think perhaps I should be going.'

'I'll come with you,' Stephen said. 'But not till I've said goodnight to Sally.'

'That won't be necessary,' Marcia told him. 'I shall pass on your excuses. Goodnight, Stephen. We shall be here until next weekend, so I trust you'll make time to see us again before we leave.' She waved a dismissive hand in Ian's direction. 'Goodnight.'

'Goodnight, Mrs Crowther.'

When the boys reached the hall Stephen turned to his friend. 'You go and start the car. I'm going to find Sally.' He ran up the stairs and found her in the master bedroom, making up the bed. Without a word he grasped her shoulders and turned her towards him, kissing her hard. 'You are not to take any notice of Ma,' he told her. 'They're not staying long, so just bite your tongue and put up with her. She'll never change, I'm afraid, but she'll have to learn eventually that she can't treat people like dirt any more.' He looked into her eyes. 'You won't say anything to muck things up for us, will you darling?'

141

She gave him a rueful smile. 'You know what I'm like. It won't be easy, but I think I know which side my bread is buttered.'

He kissed her again. 'Do I qualify as the butter?'

She rubbed her cheek against his. 'No — you're the *jam*,' she whispered. 'Now go before your mum catches us. I'll see you soon.'

She went out on to the landing with him and watched him run down the stairs. At the bottom he turned and looked up at her. She blew him a kiss, the word *darling* singing inside her head like heavenly music.

Later, after everyone had retired for the night there was a tap on Sally's door and Fiona slipped inside and perched on the end of her bed.

'Sorry about Mother,' she said.

'It's all right. I understand.'

'Poor Ian looked so embarrassed,' Fiona said. 'There's something I should tell you. It could be a problem.'

'About you and Ian?'

Fiona shook her head. 'You've got a one-track mind where Ian is concerned,' she said. 'No, it's the St John-Pickards' party.'

'What about it?'

'We're doing it.'

'I knew that but . . . ' Sally's mouth dropped open. 'Oh! I see what you mean. You think it'll embarrass your mum.'

'That's the understatement of the year!'

'Just tell her it's us, then if she's that bothered she can make some excuse and not go.'

'I can't do that. She's looking forward to it so

142

much. It's the first London party she's been to since before the war.' She sighed. 'I promise you, Sally, she'd be seriously humiliated to think her hostess knew that she was the cook's mother.'

Sally sat up in bed and hugged her knees. 'What we need is a waitress,' she said. 'If we stayed out of the way in the kitchen your mum need never know we did the catering.'

'Yes, but where would we get a reliable waitress at this late stage? The party is on Thursday.'

Sally was thoughtful then suddenly her face lit up. 'I know — Annie!' she said. 'If only we could get her we'd be home and dry. She's had experience as a parlour maid, remember?'

Fiona looked doubtful. 'Do you know where to find her?'

'She gave me her address. She mentioned that she was going to live with a sister in Islington, didn't she?'

'That was ages ago. She might have moved by now.'

'Her sister would know where she was though.'

'She might. We had so many addresses of people we never kept in touch with though. Are you sure you still have it?'

'I wrote it down in my little book,' Sally said. 'Hang on. I'll have a look.' She slipped out of bed and found the address book in her handbag. Leafing through it she said. 'Yes, here it it. Annie Thurston, 14 Tavistock Terrace, Islington. I vote we go and see her tomorrow.'

'I don't know.' Fiona shook her head. 'We

can't really afford to start taking on staff'

'It's only for this once,' Sally argued. 'Anyway, can we afford to cancel a booking? It wouldn't do our reputation much good, would it?'

★ ★ ★

The following morning both girls were looking forward to getting out of the house. Marcia had been up since before seven, stalking round the house, looking into every nook and cranny and pointing out to her husband that the whole place was in need of redecoration.

'It's all so *shabby*, Donald!' she wailed. 'We couldn't possibly do any entertaining here until it's smartened up. While we're here we'd better see about getting an interior designer in.'

Donald looked aghast. 'An interior designer? I was thinking along the lines of a lick of paint here and there.'

Marcia stared at him. 'Donald — *really*! Can you possibly be so out of touch?' Later when, armed with her book of clothing coupons, his wife had gone off to Bond Street to buy a new frock for the dinner party, Donald came down to the kitchen where Fiona made him a fortifying cup of coffee.

'You know what your mother is when she's got the bit between her teeth,' he said. 'I don't think she quite realizes that things like wallpaper and carpets are still in short supply. Still, knowing her, I daresay she'll find someone who knows where to find these things.' He looked at the girls. 'It does mean one thing though. With the house full of workmen we're going to need you as caretakers for quite a few months to come.' He smiled. 'I take it that arrangement will suit you?'

They smiled their agreement. 'Daddy,' Fiona cleared her throat. 'We've got a problem.'

Donald tapped his breast pocket. 'Cash? You're short?'

'No, no! It's this party on Thursday at the St John-Pickards'.'

'What about it?'

'Sally and I are doing the catering.'

'Jolly good!' Donald rubbed his hands together. 'I know I'm in for a good dinner then. No snoek or whale meat!' He chuckled.

'You're missing the point, Dad. Mother will be mortified. It will ruin the evening for her. It'll make things pretty impossible for us too.'

'Oh!' Donald's face fell. 'Yes — I see what you mean.'

'We thought we'd try and find a waitress,' Sally put in. 'I usually do the waiting, you see. We do know of someone . . . '

'If we can find her,' Fiona added.

'And with you on our side . . . '

'Mother doesn't know the name of our firm,' Fiona said. 'So even if Mrs St John-Pickard mentions it, it won't mean anything to her.'

'Well, I'll help in any way I can,' Donald said doubtfully. 'But I don't really see what I can do.'

'Well, to begin with, could you drive us out to Islington?' Fiona asked.

Donald stood up and took out his car keys.

'I'm at your service, ladies. Your chauffeur for the day!'

* * *

They found Tavistock Terrace without much trouble; a little row of Victorian houses which like so many others, had suffered its fair share of bomb damage. Number 14 sported a tie-bar and two stout props. Fiona pulled a face at Sally.

'You knock.'

A woman in a print overall and a hairnet answered the door. She looked at the car standing at the kerb and then the two young women standing at the door.

'If you're from the Council I hope something's gonna be done about this place soon,' she said. 'Before the bleedin' lot falls down round our ears!'

'We're not from the Council,' Sally said. 'We're looking for Annie Thurston. Does she still live here?'

The woman didn't reply, instead she turned her head and bellowed up the stairs, '*Annie! Two young gels 'ere t'see yer.*' She looked from one to the other with a sniff. 'Daresay she'll be down in a minute,' she muttered then wandered back down the hallway to disappear through a door.

Fiona looked at Sally. 'Charming!'

Sally grinned. 'Can't imagine *her* waiting table at the St John-Pickards'!'

They were still chuckling when they heard a door shut and the familiar figure of Annie

146

appeared at the top of the stairs. When she saw them her face lit up in a smile.

'Sall and Fee!' she exclaimed. 'Well, well. Thought I'd seen the last of you two! 'Ow are you, luvs?'

Fiona came straight to the point. 'We're here to ask you a favour, Annie,' she said. 'I know we should have looked you up long ago and this is an imposition really but . . . '

'Come on, spit it out gel!' Annie laughed. 'First of all, is there any money in it? If there is the answer's yes!'

'Oh you'd get paid, yes,' Sally put in. 'Fee and I have started a catering business and we've got a slight problem. How would you feel about waiting table for a dinner party? It's just for the one occasion.'

Annie smiled. 'It'd be smashing to get back into harness,' she said. 'All I've had is the odd cleanin' job. I haven't been able to get a proper job anywhere since we left the factory. I'm fed up being on the dole and living here with Ada and her old man — proper old misery-guts, he is. And as you can see, this house is no palace!'

'Is there anywhere we can go for a coffee?' Sally said. 'Then we can tell you about the job.'

'There's a caff round the corner,' Annie told them. 'It's not very posh but it's clean. Just let me get my coat.'

Fiona asked her father to give them half an hour and the three of them went round the corner to the Beehive Café.

Annie's eyes grew round as they told her

about *Dinner At Eight*. 'That's smashing!' she said. 'Good luck to the pair of you.'

'We just need a waitress for this one party,' Fiona explained. She explained about her mother's unannounced visit and her invitation to the St John-Pickards' party. 'I just want to keep a low profile so as not to embarrass her. It's this Thursday and we'd arrange for you to be picked up and brought home again afterwards. Could you do it?'

'Don't see why not. The going rate per hour, is it?'

Fiona nodded. 'And a little bit more if we get away with it.'

'OK then, you're on. Mum's the word — in more ways than one!'

They all laughed at Annie's unintended wit then suddenly Sally remembered the uniform she wore for waiting table. It was the black dress she'd worn for her job at Lyons before the war with a little lace apron and cap that Fiona had found tucked away at Gower Street. She looked at Annie's ample figure and realised that she would never get into it. 'Er — what will Annie wear?' she asked Fiona. 'I don't think my uniform will . . . '

Annie burst out laughing. 'I should say not, love! I'd never get into your little frock. It'd be bursting at the seams. All the fellers'd be getting' an eyeful before the soup was cold! No, it's all right, I've still got the uniform I had when I was with the Frobishers in Eaton Square. I think it still fits, but I can always let it out a bit if it don't. I'll give it a good sponge and press and I'll get my hair done nice. I won't let you down, don't worry.'

* * *

Before the St John-Pickards' dinner party the girls had the boardroom buffet lunch to cater for. They particularly wanted it to be a success because the Havershams had brought them so much business. They rose early on Wednesday morning and by eight o'clock Sally had cut several plates of tiny sandwiches with assorted fillings. Fiona had made miniature sausage rolls and cheese straws and the kitchen was redolent with delicious smells. Sally was busy cutting some of Nanny Joan's fresh tomatoes into water lily shapes when Marcia appeared on the basement stairs. She wore a pink lace negligee, her long hair, usually worn in a chignon, hung in a braid down her back.

'What on earth are you doing?' she demanded, glowering at Sally who was working at the table. Fiona came out of the larder.

'We're preparing for a boardroom buffet luncheon, Mother,' she said.

'Well I would like some breakfast,' Marcia said. 'I'll have porridge, toast and coffee.'

'That's all right,' Fiona said. 'You can use the toaster, the kettle is on the boil and I'm not using the hob at the moment.'

Marcia drew herself up, wrapping the negligee tightly round her. 'Are you suggesting that I make it myself?'

'Isn't that what you do at home?'

'Certainly not! Mrs Hobbs comes in at eight.'

'Well I'm sorry, Mother, but as you haven't brought Mrs Hobbs with you you'll have to get it yourself,' Fiona told her. 'Sally and I are extremely busy.'

Marcia stared at them, her face a study of indignation, but at that moment Donald's face appeared over her shoulder.

'It's all right, dear, I'll get it,' he said. 'Fiona and Sally really must get on with their work.'

A tight-lipped Marcia turned and flounced back up the stairs.

Fiona looked at her father. 'Sorry, Dad.'

'Don't worry.' Donald winked at them. 'Mrs Hobbs doesn't come in to get our breakfast,' he said quietly. 'I usually get it anyway, so it's nothing out of the ordinary.'

As it was a weekday morning they were obliged to take a cab to Mr Haversham's office, loading the boxes of food, plates and glasses into the luggage compartment. In the boardroom they laid the table with their largest damask cloth and set out the plates of food. In the small adjacent kitchen Fiona put the bottles of wine to chill in the ice bucket she had brought and put out glasses on the silver trays. Then both girls changed into the plain black frocks they had decided to wear for the occasion.

Mr Haversham arrived at half-past twelve and pronounced everything satisfactory.

'It all looks quite delicious,' he said rubbing his hands. 'And I couldn't ask for two more attractive hostesses. This luncheon is in celebration of a merger my company is making with a

150

larger firm. It's something of a coup for us and I especially want it to go with a swing.' He smiled at them. 'You two young ladies are making quite a name for yourselves. My wife has recommended you all over town. We're about to move into our new flat; a very smart one in Knightsbridge, thanks to this merger. I know Julia is going to ask you to cater for our flat-warming party soon.'

'We'd be delighted,' Fiona said.

'And perhaps we should give you a special rate after all the good business you've brought us,' Sally put in.

'Not at all. You're not to think of it.' Mr Haversham looked at his watch. 'I'd better go downstairs and welcome my guests now,' he said. 'And I'll give you this before I forget. Thank you both very much.' He took an envelope out of his inside pocket and handed it to Fiona. 'You'll find a little bonus included, just in case you think there's some mistake.'

It was late afternoon by the time the girls had returned to Gower Street and unpacked all their boxes. Marcia was out visiting friends so Donald lent them a hand. 'You know, what you girls need is a van,' he remarked.

'That's what we're saving up for,' Fiona said.

'There's no need for that. You know I'll lend you the money.'

'No, Dad. We want to stand on our own feet,' she told him.

'It could just be a loan. You could pay me back.'

'I know. But this way we're working for what

we need,' Fiona said. 'We want to do it on our own, don't we, Sall?'

'That's right, Mr Crowther. And we're doing well. We've worked out that by next Christmas we'll be able to ask Ian to look for that bargain for us.'

He smiled. 'Well, I admire you for wanting to be independent. Tell you what, when you do get it let me pay to have your sign painted on the side. Call it my Christmas present to you both. Can't you just see it buzzing around London?' He painted the words with his hands. '*Dinner At Eight*. And your telephone number underneath! How's that?'

* * *

Fiona was nervous about the St John-Pickards' dinner party. They left Gower Street earlier than necessary and arranged for Ian to pick Annie up separately. The menu that Muriel had chosen was simple. Consommé, coq au vin with a selection of vegetables and a fruit syllabub for dessert. The wines were being provided by the St John-Pickards.

Sally and Fiona laid the table together and then took themselves off to the kitchen, hoping not to have to cross paths with Marcia.

At half past seven Ian delivered Annie to the back door. When she took off her coat both girls gasped. She looked the part perfectly in her black dress and starched cap and apron. Her hair was neatly coiled in the nape of her neck and she wore black stockings and

152

sensible black button and bar shoes.

'Annie, you've done us proud,' Sally declared. 'You look wonderful.'

Annie beamed with delight. 'I reckon I've lost a bit of weight since the war ended,' she said. 'I used to eat well at the canteen but with our Ada's cookin' no one don't ask for no seconds!' She raised her eyes to the ceiling expressively and the girls laughed.

The evening went well and Muriel came through to the kitchen to thank them when her guests had repaired to the drawing room for coffee.

'The maid you brought with you was excellent,' she said. 'I only wish I could find one like her. Servants are so hard to find nowadays.'

Annie came through to the kitchen with her laden tray and insisted on staying to help with the washing up.

'D'you know, I've really enjoyed m'self tonight,' she said. 'One o'them ladies in there even asked me for my name and address on the quiet. Keep your fingers crossed. I reckon I might get offered a job.'

Ian collected Annie and took her home then returned for the girls and all their equipment. By the time Marcia and Donald arrived home just after midnight everything had been put away and Stephen and Ian were enjoying a late night coffee with the girls in the kitchen. When Marcia came trotting down the basement stairs on her high-heeled evening shoes she looked flushed and pleased with herself. Stephen stood up and kissed his mother on both cheeks.

'I take it you've had a lovely evening, Ma'.' He said grinning at the others over her shoulder. 'You look positively radiant.'

'I feel it,' Marcia said. 'This evening was delightful. Wonderful to enjoy a sophisticated dinner party again with intelligent conversation that wasn't about war and shortages!' She sank into the chair that Stephen had vacated. 'And such delicious food. Muriel had hired this marvellous maid for the evening. I managed to talk to her later. She told me she was parlour maid for Henry Frobisher before the war.' She looked at Donald. 'He used to be an M.P. didn't he?'

Donald nodded. 'That's right. Represented a constituency in Surrey if my memory serves me right.'

Marcia's smile widened. 'I've almost decided to offer her a room and a retainer to move in here for when we come up to Town.' She pointed to the coffee pot on the table. 'Stephen darling, pour your father and me a cup of coffee, there's a dear.' She took out her cigarette case and inserted a cigarette into its jewelled holder. 'Fiona, you had better get the old day nursery ready for her. It could benefit you too you know. So that she's not idling her time away when we're not here she could lend a hand with your little catering business. Her name is Annie Thurston, by the way. But I think *Anne* sounds much more suitable, don't you?' She accepted the light that Ian offered her and drew reflectively on her cigarette. 'Or do you think *Thurston* sounds better as she's older?'

154

'You'll have to work that out between you dear,' Donald's face a study in nonchalance, but the others were working hard to keep smiles at bay. Once he had escorted his wife upstairs again they let out their collective breath with a sigh.

'*Phew*! I thought I was going to explode!' Stephen said.

'Did you see Dad?' Fiona asked. 'How does he keep a straight face like that?'

'Plenty of practice,' Stephen reminded her. 'He's an expert at getting his own way and making her think it was her idea. I wouldn't mind betting he's at the bottom of this wheeze.'

'So — looks as if you're about to have a housemate!' Ian said.

'And a free helpmate.' Sally added. 'Couldn't be better!'

The four looked at each other and all burst out laughing.

'Good old Ma,' Stephen said. 'Good old Dad too!'

9

'Oh, Sally, that would be *lovely* Are you really sure?'

Jenny and Sally sat opposite each other over coffee in a newly opened coffee bar in Oxford Street. Sally had just proposed that her wedding present to Jenny would be a buffet reception, especially catered for by *Dinner At Eight*.

'Of course we're sure,' she said. 'This means Fiona as well as me, and of course we've got Annie. Stephen and his friend Ian have offered their help too, if that's OK with you.'

'Of course it is,' Jenny agreed. 'Mum's already made my cake but it'll save her such a lot of work. Now she can concentrate on just icing it and making herself look nice.' Her smile faded for a moment. 'Oh — does this mean you can't be my bridesmaid though?'

'No. I'll try and fit that in as well,' Sally promised. 'That's why we need loads of free help from the boys.'

'And I want you to sing too,' Jenny added. 'Oh, do say you will — at the church as well as at the reception. Since my party everyone wants to hear you again.'

'I'll think about it.'

'And do you think your boyfriend, Stephen, will play the piano for you?'

'He's not really my boyfriend, but yes, I'm sure he will.' She laughed. 'I can see you've got it all planned. Looks like I'm going to have my work cut out over the next few weeks!' She took out a pad and pencil. 'Shall we talk about the food first? What kind of buffet would you like?

The wedding date was set for August 10 and during the weeks that followed preparations gathered momentum alarmingly fast. In between their *Dinner At Eight* engagements Sally was measured and fitted for her dress, which was to be made by Jenny's aunt who was also making her wedding dress. Aunty Jessie had owned a draper's shop before the war and had hoarded several bolts of material, which had been carefully wrapped in tissue paper and stored away in her wardrobe throughout the war. Sally was to wear peach coloured taffeta and Jenny's dress was to be of white lace, lined with silk. No recycled parachute nylon for her!

The buffet was to be fairly simple and although the numbers would be greater than *Dinner At Eight* had ever catered for before the girls were confident that they could do it all on the day before the wedding so that everything would be fresh.

Annie was now comfortably ensconced in what had been the day nursery on the top floor. She was quite excited at the prospect of being involved with a wedding and she was more than willing to help in whatever way she could. When Donald and Marcia weren't in residence at Gower Street there wasn't much for her to do in the house except keep an eye on the decorators that Marcia had engaged. The girls were more than grateful for her capable assistance.

A week before Jenny's big day Sally and Fiona invited her and her fiancé, Gerry, to Gower Street for a meal along with Stephen and Ian. The six of them enjoyed a relaxed evening while they talked about the final arrangements for he wedding.

'I want you to sing 'Ave Maria' at the church,' Jenny announced. 'I thought it would be nice if you sang while Gerry and I are signing the register. Is that all right?'

Sally resignedly agreed.

'Then after the speeches at the reception maybe a few nice songs. You know, nice soppy ones.'

'I'll try to think of some,' Sally laughed. 'And Stephen says he'll accompany me.'

'Sure thing!' Stephen said. 'I'm quite looking forward to this. It'll be the first post-war wedding I've been to. Most of my chums who got hitched during the war had a swift pint and a ham roll in the pub afterwards — if they got the time. This sounds as though it's going to be a really slap-up do!'

Gerry, who had been silent most of the evening cleared his throat. 'Er — look, I'm sorry but I've got a bit of bad news,' he said. 'I hate to chuck a spanner in the works but my Uncle Harry who was going to drive Jen to the church can't do it. His car has bust its big end and he says it's a write-off.'

'Oh, Gerry!' Jenny turned to him. 'Why didn't you say something before? I thought we were all set for transport. What am I supposed to do now — queue up for a number eleven bus?'

158

'Taxi?' Gerry suggested.

'I think I can do better than that for you,' Ian put in. 'I know where I can get hold of a vintage Bentley. All polished up with white ribbons it'll look great. And I'll drive you too if you like.'

Jenny's eyes sparkled. 'Oh! What wonderful friends you all are!' She clapped her hands in delight. 'Oh, I can't wait for next week, can you, Gerry?'

Gerry blushed a deep red. 'N-no,' he said. 'No, neither can I.'

★   ★   ★

August 10 was a beautiful summer day and Sally, Fiona and Annie were up early putting the finishing touches to the buffet. Ian arrived at nine o'clock and took them along with all their boxes to the church hall where the wedding reception was to be held. There the three of them set about laying everything out. Kate Gifford arrived soon after with the wedding cake she had made. With an apron over her wedding outfit she unpacked the cake from its box and began assembling the three tiers, finally putting the tiny bride and bridegroom on the top beneath their arch of lily-of-the-valley. The four of them stood back to admire the result.

'It's beautiful, Auntie Kate,' Sally said. 'You've really done Jenny proud.'

'Couldn't do less,' Kate said, misty-eyed. 'I've done the same for all my kids and Jenny's the last to go. I've been saving up the ingredients for this cake for ages. All three tiers are cake you know, not one real and two cardboard like a lot of folks had to do when the war was on.' She sighed and looked at Sally. 'Here! I don't know what you're doin' still here, gel. You've only got half an hour before you're due at the church!'

Sally looked at her watch in panic. 'Blimey! You're right. I'd better get changed.'

The ceremony went off without a hitch. The church was cool and fragrant with the scent of roses and Jenny looked radiant in her white lace dress as she walked down the aisle on her father's arm. Afterwards, while the newly-weds signed the register in the vestry Sally walked up the chancel steps to sing 'Ave Maria'.

It seemed no time at all before they were all at the church hall enjoying the buffet the girls had worked so hard over. After the speeches Sally sang again, this time a medley of popular songs, then at last she was free to mingle with the other guests. She was sitting chatting to Jenny's sister when a man stopped in front of her.

'Well, well. If it isn't little Sally Joy!'

She looked up. 'That's right.'

'Dance?' He nodded towards the floor, which had been cleared for dancing.

'OK, thanks.' There was something vaguely familiar about the dark eyes audaciously eyeing her. His dark hair was smoothed back with hair cream and he wore a well-cut dark suit. Suddenly his name sprang out of her memory.

'You're Maxie Feldman!'

He laughed. 'Well, I was last time I looked in the mirror.'

She and Maxie had been at school together. In

those days he had been a scruffy little kid from the flats, now demolished by the blitz. There was a large family of Feldmans of which Maxie was the eldest. His Dad had been a tailor and they'd been poor just like everyone else, but in spite of his obvious poverty Maxie had always been a smart kid, always ready with a slick answer. Although he was small and skinny he was never bullied. He was clever too, always near the top of the class and brilliant with arithmetic. She wasn't surprised that he'd obviously done well for himself.

His face broke into a grin and for a second she caught a glimpse of a gold filling. 'I like to be called Max now if you don't mind,' he said. 'Let's sit the next one out and you can tell me what you've been up to,' he said. 'It must be — what — seven years?'

'Must be,' Sally smiled. 'Before the war certainly. Last time I saw you, you were working with your old man.' She took in the smart suit and expensive shoes he wore; his sleek hair and carefully manicured hands. 'You look as if you've done all right for yourself. Take to the tailoring, did you?'

He laughed. 'You're joking! No — a couple of my brothers took over Dad's business but I never really had the feel for it. I did all right though.'

'I can see that. I suppose you got called up. Where did you get to in the war?'

'Never moved from here. Army never took me — unfit.'

'Unfit?' Sally raised her eyebrows. 'You look OK to me.'

His smiled faded. 'You don't always see what's underneath. Flat feet.'

'Oh. I'm sorry to hear that.' Sally tried not to smile. 'Flat feet' was usually a euphemism for someone who'd pulled strings to get out of being called up.

'It's OK. I live with it.' The music stopped and he took her arm. 'Come on, let me get you a drink. I reckon you'n' me've got some catching up to do.'

They found a couple of chairs on the far side of the room and Max returned with two glasses of wine. Sally took a sip of hers. 'So — what do you do, Max?'

'Oh, a bit of this and a bit of that,' he said. 'Matter of fact I've got a club not far from here.'

'Club?'

'Yeah — you know — nightclub. You should come over one evening — bring a few mates. It's a nice little place. I call it the *Pink Parrot*. I got a loan, a licence and so on and started it up in '41. We stayed open all through the blitz. A lot of folks used to come down there instead of going to the shelters. It's in the basement, see — underneath Brewsters the grocers.' He beamed with pride. 'I've just bought that too, so the place is all mine now — flat upstairs too.' He looked at her. 'Look, Sally — we have a cabaret at the weekends. I'd like to book you to come and sing for me.'

Sally laughed. 'Go on! I only sing for fun. It's just a hobby.'

'So why not turn pro'? That's a real talent you've got, Sall. Nothing wrong with making it

162

work for you, is there?'

'You've got me all wrong,' she said. 'My friend and I have a catering business, *Dinner At Eight*. We did the buffet for the wedding. It keeps us pretty busy. There isn't time for much else.'

'Very nice too! It sounds like hard work to me though. Wouldn't you find singing more fun? It'd only be at weekends and I'd pay you well.'

'Thanks for the offer, Max, but we're at our busiest at weekends. It wouldn't really work.'

'Oh well, it was just an idea, but if you change your mind the offer stands.' He took a card from his pocket and handed it to her. 'You can reach me at that number most of the time. By the way, who's the geezer with the Bentley?'

'That's Ian Jerome. He was in the RAF with Stephen who played the piano for me earlier. He's trying to get a used car business started.'

Max's eyes lit up with interest. 'Really? Now that *is* interesting. I've got a little garage m'self as it happens. I've only just bought it — on Commercial Road. So, this feller — what's-'is-name, Jerome? Doing OK, is he?'

'Finding it hard to get suitable premises, I think,' Sally told him. 'He's storing his cars on a bomb-site in Edgware at the moment but he's not too happy with the arrangement.

'I just might be able to help,' Max said. 'I've been looking for a bloke with a bit of know-how.'

'He's over there. Come on, I'll introduce you.'

At half past four the bride and groom departed for their honeymoon in Bournemouth. Outside the church hall everyone gathered to see them off to Waterloo Station in the Bentley, driven by Ian. Later when Sally and Fiona were packing up Ian reappeared looking for Fiona.

'I've hardly seen you all day,' he said. 'Any chance we could do something together this evening?'

'We've been invited to stay on for the party,' Fiona said. 'But these people are more Sally's friends than mine. I was thinking of leaving soon. Annie's looking tired too. I daresay she'd appreciate a lift home.'

'I'll take you both. Perhaps we could have a chat later. I've got something rather important to tell you.'

Fiona wouldn't let Sally help load the car. 'You've worked really hard today,' she said. 'Now you deserve to have some fun. Ian and I will take everything home and unpack. You stay on with Stevie and enjoy yourselves.' She watched with a smile as her brother claimed Sally and whisked her off to dance. 'Shall we go?' she asked Ian.

When they were on their way Fiona looked at Ian. 'What was it you wanted to tell me?'

He smiled. 'It could be that I won't have to give up the business after all.'

She smiled. 'Oh, Ian, that's really good news. How come?'

'A chap Sally introduced me to has just bought a garage on Commercial Road. He doesn't know much about cars and he's looking for a partner who'll do the buying and selling and run the mechanical side of things.'

'Have you agreed?'

'We're meeting next week at the place he's bought to discuss the pros and cons. I get the impression that he's prepared to offer me a partnership.'

'In return for an investment, I take it?'

'Well, of course. He's a businessman. Anyway, nothing's settled yet. We'll have to see how things turn out.'

★ ★ ★

'Who's the character with the draped suit?' Stephen looked down at Sally as they circled the dance floor. 'He looks a bit of a wide-boy to me.'

Sally laughed. 'His name's Max Feldman. We went to the same school. It seems he's quite a smart businessman these days. He was always bright at school and now he owns a nightclub, a grocer's shop *and* a garage.'

Stephen's expression was sceptical. 'Mmm. I take it he avoided the call-up. It takes more than two years to make that kind of progress.'

'He's got a problem with his feet apparently.'

Stephen laughed. 'You don't say!'

'Don't look like that. Max had a rough childhood. He deserves to do well.' She glanced up at him. 'Actually he offered me a job.'

He stopped dancing to look down at her. 'A job? What kind of job?'

'Singing at his club. It's all right. I turned it down.'

'I should hope so.'

Sally bridled. 'Only because Fee and I are busy most weekends,' she said. 'I'd probably have taken it otherwise.'

'Then you've got less sense than I credited you with.'

'He just wanted to do me a favour.'

'Do himself one, you mean!'

'Max is OK. Do you really think I'd have anything to do with him if he was into anything dodgy?'

He grinned good-naturedly. 'OK, you win. I'm judging him without knowing him.' He pulled her close again. 'Can't you tell when I'm being madly jealous?' he whispered. 'Seeing you sitting there, deep in conversation with him made me want to come over and punch his head for him.'

She laughed. 'I don't believe a word of it. You're far too civilized for that.'

'Don't you know that you bring out all my primitive instincts?' he whispered.

She laughed. 'Sorry, can't see you as the he-man type somehow.'

He assumed a mortally wounded expression. 'Now that *really* hurts!'

She laughed. 'You might change your mind when you hear that he's offered Ian a partnership in his garage.'

'Has he now? What does Ian say?'

'I think they've arranged to meet and talk about it. We'll have to wait and see. You might have to eat your words about Max yet.'

★ ★ ★

At Gower Street Ian helped Fiona and Annie to unpack all the boxes from the Bentley. When everything was put away the older woman gave a sigh.

'If you don't mind I think I'll turn in love,' she said. 'It's been a smashing day but I'm more'n ready for my bed.'

'Of course. You go on up, Annie,' Fiona said. 'And thanks again for all your help. We couldn't have managed without you.'

When Annie had gone Fiona looked at Ian. 'Coffee?'

'Thanks. I'm gasping.' He sat down gratefully at the kitchen table while Fiona filled the kettle.

'What's this important thing you wanted to talk about?' she asked.

'If I do go in with this Feldman chap I won't be handling any commercial vehicles,' he told her. 'Feldman has already made it clear that he's only interested in cars for private use — the upper end of the market.'

'I see.' Fiona sat down opposite him. 'So, will that make a difference?'

'It means that I'll have to sell off a couple of vans I bought recently and it occurred to me that one of them in particular would suit you.'

Fiona's eyes lit up. 'Oh, Ian!'

'It's in good condition, registered just before the war and a very low mileage on the clock. It's a plain colour so you could have the name and phone number on the side. It'd be a free advertisement as you drove around in it.'

Fiona sighed, remembering her father's offer. 'It's very tempting, Ian, but we haven't got that kind of cash yet. Sally and I worked it out that it would be at least next Christmas before we're ready to make that kind of outlay.'

'I'd let you have it for what I paid,' he told her. 'And I wouldn't expect you to pay all the money at once. You could spread it over.' He bit his lip. 'I only wish I could afford to give it to you, but . . .'

'*Ian*! You know perfectly well that we wouldn't let you do any such thing! Dad offered to lend us the money to buy a van but I wouldn't accept the offer.' She smiled gently at his crestfallen expression. 'We really mustn't overreach ourselves and neither must you. Anyway, you'll be needing all the money you can scrape together to buy into the business, won't you?'

'Well, yes, but if you'd like the van we could surely come to some arrangement.'

'Better not,' Fiona said reluctantly. 'Ian, I know Sally would agree with me. It has to be a business deal or nothing.'

He looked at her. 'Business aside, Fee, I think you know that I'd do anything for you.' Reaching across the table he covered her hand with his and the look in his eyes made her heart contract.

'Why are you so good to me, Ian?'

'I'm sure you know the answer to that.' He stood up, drew her to her feet and pulled her gently towards him. She didn't pull away but closed her eyes, relaxing in his arms as he gently kissed her.

'It's all right, I know how you feel,' he said. 'I know that Mark still occupies your heart and you still grieve for him, but you're much too young and far too lovely to lock up your heart forever. You have to let go some time and when you do

168

I'd like to think it might be me you turn to.'

'I know.' She hid her face against his shoulder. 'And I want you to know that if anyone could fill the emptiness it would be you.'

His arms tightened around her. 'That's all I need to know. I can wait, Fee. You'd be surprised how patient I can be.'

★ ★ ★

It was well after midnight when the wedding party finally broke up. Stephen and Sally went back to the Giffords' house where Sally changed out of her bridesmaid's dress into her own clothes before they set off to drive back to the West End. Sally sank into the passenger seat of the little two-seater with a sigh.

'It's good to sit down. I feel as though I've been on my feet since dawn.'

'Don't worry, soon have you home.' Stephen pressed the starter, but nothing happened. He pressed again. This time the engine gave an asthmatic cough. He turned to look at her. 'Have to use the handle,' he said. He got out of the car and went round to get the starting handle from the boot. Inserting it at the front he swung — nothing. Two more tries brought no result. He looked up. 'Could you pull out the choke for me next time, Sally?' She did as he asked and he tried one more time — another cough and a dying groan. He straightened up with a sigh.

'Looks as if the battery's flat. I'm afraid we're going to have to leave her here tonight and hike it home.' He opened the passenger door and held out a hand to help her out. 'I love this old buggy most of the time, but letting us down tonight of all nights is the last straw.' He aimed a kick at one of the car's front tyres. 'Hear that? I hate your guts, you little swine.' He slipped an arm round Sally's shoulders. 'Poor darling. Never mind, if we step it out it shouldn't take too long, and with a bit of luck we might see a stray cabby on his way home.'

Sally was glad of the comfort of his arm around her as they walked. 'A great wedding, wasn't it?' she said.

'Super.' He paused and looked down at her. 'Look, Sall, I've met your friends and been to a party and a wedding with all of them, so how about you coming to the Palace to see me get my gong? Only a matter of weeks to go now.'

Sally shook her head. 'I don't know. That's a whole different cup of tea, Stephen.'

'I don't see why. Surely I'm entitled to invite my girlfriend. It's only fair that you come. Besides, Dad tells me he's booked a table for lunch afterwards at the Savoy.'

'It's for you and your family,' she protested. 'It's a formal occasion.' She looked up at him. 'And you know as well as I do that your mother wouldn't like it. I'd feel I was spoiling her day.'

'What about *my* day?' He frowned. 'It's my show, not hers. I'm entitled to have whoever I like there and I want you, Sally.'

'It would make an atmosphere — me being there. You know it would. Anyway, Stephen, the *Savoy*! I mean — it isn't exactly *me*, is it?' She grinned up at him. 'Go on, admit it. I'd be like a sparrow in a crowd of peacocks.'

'What rubbish! I think the Savoy is exactly the right setting for you. Anyway, if anyone were to make an atmosphere it'd be Ma, not you.'

She gave him a wry smile. 'So you admit that she'd disapprove?'

He sighed. 'She's going to have to get used to having you around, Sall, so we might as well start as we mean to go on.'

Sally smiled wistfully to herself. 'That's as may be,' she said softly. 'Once you get to Cambridge things will be different.'

'In what way?'

'Oh, I don't know. New people to meet — new places to go — so much to learn. Life will change for you, Stevie.'

'But not the way I feel about you,' he told her. 'Nothing's ever going to change that.'

She slipped her arm around his waist and hugged him. 'I'll be there at the Palace, Stevie, don't you worry. I wouldn't miss it for the world. I'll be right there in the front of the crowd to see you come out in your uniform with your medal pinned to your chest and I'll be the proudest girl in all that crowd. I just won't be with your party, that's all. That's for you and your mum and dad and Fee. Don't push it any more, love. I mean it. It would only spoil the day for everyone.'

He stopped walking and drew her into a nearby shop doorway where he crushed her close and kissed her till she was breathless. 'I love you, Sally Joy,' he whispered against her hair. 'You're maddeningly stubborn and irritatingly bolshie, but you're the warmest — the loveliest girl I've

171

ever known and I'll always want you in my life — always.'

'And I hope I'll always be there.' She rubbed her cheek against his, loving the roughness of his early morning stubble against her skin. 'I love you too, Stevie,' she whispered. 'And that's why I want your special day to be perfect. So can we not talk about it any more, please?'

The sound of an engine and the swing of headlights coming round the corner galvanized Stephen into action. 'Quick!' He grabbed her hand. 'It's a cab.'

The good-natured cab driver was indeed on his way home but he responded to their frantic waving and stopped.

'Where d'you wanna go, mate?'

'Gower Street.'

'OK, hop in. It ain't much outa me way.'

As they sank gratefully into the back seat Stephen drew her to him. 'I can't face going all the way back to Edgware tonight. I think I'll doss down on the sofa in the kitchen tonight,' he said. 'Is that all right with you?'

'Lovely.' Sally said happily, knowing as well as he did that he wouldn't be going anywhere near the sofa.

10

Sally wakened early next morning to find Stephen already dressed and about to leave. She looked up at him sleepily.

'Where are you going?'

'I'm off to Edgware to get Ian to give me a lift over to Hackney to pick up the car. He'll have to tow me back to the garage so that I can put the battery on charge.'

'What's the time?'

He looked at his watch. 'Just after six.'

'It's still the middle of the night. Don't go yet. Ian won't be up for hours yet and anyway you haven't had any breakfast.'

'Shh.' He bent down to put a finger against her lips. 'To tell you the truth I don't want to set my little sister a bad example.'

Sally laughed and reached up to wind her arms around his neck. 'It's a bit late for that, isn't it?'

'Well then, I don't want her to think I'm taking advantage of you. Does that sound more like it?'

'Not much. Fee knows me better than to imagine anyone could ever do that.' She pulled him down and kissed him. 'At least wait while I get up and take me with you.'

'And how will you explain your absence?'

'I'll leave a note.' She looked into his eyes. 'You really are bothered, aren't you — about what Fee will think of you staying the night?'

He detached her arms from around his neck and stood up. 'Unhand me, woman. Enough of your evil temptations.' He smiled down at her apologetically. 'Car repairs are chaps' stuff. You'd be bored rigid. Anyway, you must have forgotten that Ian is driving us all down to Fairford later this morning, so it's vital to get the car sorted out before we go.' He bent over her. 'Say goodbye like a good girl.' He kissed her lingeringly, then whispered, 'And thank you sweetheart.'

'What for?'

'What do you think? For last night.'

Sally coloured. 'I don't need thanking!'

He sat on the edge of the bed and looked into her eyes. 'It was the first time for you, wasn't it? Did you think I wouldn't realize what that meant to you?'

She avoided his eyes. 'Well, I . . . '

'I'm so proud and honoured that it was me,' he interrupted softly. A finger under her chin he raised her face to make her look at him. 'You're lovely, Sally, really special. I'd never do anything to hurt you and I meant what I said last night. I love you.' He kissed her once more and stood up. 'And now I'm off before you weaken my resolve. See you later.'

'OK, you win. See you later.' She watched him walk out of the room and close the door softly behind him, then lay down again, her body weak with yearning and her heart aching with melancholy. She knew now that she was irreversibly, head over heels in love with Stephen.

She hadn't meant to let things go so far but last night she had found him totally irresistible.

Closing her eyes she relived the earlier hours of this morning when they had tumbled into bed together to make love. Stephen had been so sweet, so tender and gentle, yet he had aroused her to a passion she had never experienced before with his softly caressing hands and his ardent kisses. She knew all the time that she should not be allowing it to happen, that she was hurtling headlong towards the point of no return. She knew now that ahead lay only heartache. They were such poles apart, she and Stephen. It would inevitably end, and when it did she would suffer only tears and heartbreak.

She rolled on to her back and gazed at the early morning sunlight making patterns on the ceiling. Well, so be it, she told herself resignedly. All her bridges were well and truly burned now, but at least there would be last night to remember and cherish. No one could ever rob her of that.

★ ★ ★

'I've taken Annie's breakfast up on a tray,' Fiona said. 'Poor old love worked so hard yesterday. I thought she deserved a treat.' She poured Sally a cup of tea, her favourite breakfast beverage and looked up at her enquiringly. 'So — what time did you and Stevie leave the party?'

'It was after midnight,' Sally told her. 'And then the car wouldn't start so we started to walk home.'

175

'*Walk?* All that way! You must have been exhausted by the time you got home.'

'Well, no. We were lucky enough to catch a cruising taxi before we'd walked too far.'

'That was a bit of luck, especially at that hour.' Fiona peered at her friend. 'Are you all right? You look a bit preoccupied.'

Sally took a deep breath. 'Fee, there's something I think you should know.'

'You mean about Stevie staying the night?'

Sally gasped. 'You know!'

'Yes. Look, I'm sorry but I woke up about four and peeped in to reassure myself that you'd go home safely.'

'Oh Lord!'

'It's OK.'

'No! It's unforgivable — it's your house and . . . '

Fiona was smiling. 'You looked so sweet, the pair of you, fast asleep in each other's arms like the babes in the wood.' She reached across the table to pat Sally's hand. 'Don't look so mortified, darling. I'm delighted for you both. It's been clear to me for weeks that Stevie was besotted with you. And now I know that you love him too. Believe me, there's no one I'd rather have as a prospective sister-in-law.'

'Wait a minute!' Sally held up her hand. 'Look, Fee, I know I should have put a stop to things before this. I never meant it to go so far. Stephen and I are not right for each other. You must know that. That word you used, it says it all — *besotted.*'

Fiona shook her head. 'It's only a word.'

'Yes, one you've used before and it means it can't last. Once he gets to Cambridge he'll realize the truth of it. Anyway, can you imagine your mother's face if she knew?'

Fiona shook her head. 'Stevie's not a starry-eyed kid. He's fought in a war and won a medal. He's his own man, Sally. As I see it, Mother doesn't come into the equation.'

'I bet *she* doesn't see it that way! And I don't blame her. She wants the best for him like any mother would. Look, Fee, I'm not some silly schoolgirl. I realize that when Stephen goes off to university he'll be caught up in all the new things in his life. He'll meet people — girls, with more in common with him than I have and . . . '

'Stevie's not like that,' Fiona protested. 'He's not fickle. When he feels things he feels them deeply. I know him. You'll see.'

'Well, I'm not banking on anything,' Sally said. 'I'm making the most of him while I've got him and trying not to look too far ahead.' She reached for a piece of toast and buttered it. 'How long did Ian stay last night?'

Fiona laughed. 'That's a loaded question if ever I heard one! Not as long at Stevie, shall we say.'

'Oh, I wasn't prying,' Sally said quickly. She looked up at her friend. 'You do like him though, don't you?'

'Yes, very much. It rather looks as though his business venture has taken an upturn, thanks to that old school friend of yours. It looks as though he might be going into partnership with him if things work out. He says that if he does he'll

177

have to get rid of any commercial vehicles he has, and as a result he's offered us a van he happens to have at cost price.'

'Can we afford it?'

'Well, no, but I have been thinking about it,' Fiona said. 'When Dad was here he offered to lend us the money to buy a van. Naturally I refused. Ian did offer to let us pay it off in instalments but I know he needs the cash, so I was thinking — as this is such a good opportunity I wondered if we could borrow the money from Dad after all.'

Sally looked doubtful. 'It would mean we'd have to wait a lot longer to be in profit.'

'True, but that's what business is all about. And we really do need a van, Sall. If Ian takes this partnership offer he'll probably have to put in extra hours which means he may not be so free to ferry us about.'

'Did he say that?'

'No, but it wouldn't be fair to expect it really, would it? It was only meant to be a temporary measure anyway.'

'Are you sure this isn't just you not wanting to be indebted to him?'

'Not at all!' Fiona shrugged. 'OK, I suppose it was a daft idea. Trying to run before we can walk.'

But Sally was biting her lip thoughtfully. 'On the other hand — if we had to start taking cabs every time . . . ' She looked up. 'Fee, how would you feel about me taking an extra job?'

Fiona looked startled. 'What kind of job?'

'Ian wasn't the only one who had an offer

from Max Feldman last night,' she said. 'Did you know that he owns a club?'

'No. A garage *and* a club?'

'Yes. It's called the *Pink Parrot* and it's above a grocer's shop in Hackney.' Sally smiled. 'Actually he owns the shop too now — and the flat above it!'

'Your Max Feldman sounds like quite an enterprising chap!'

'Yes, I always knew he would be one day.'

'So what's this job he offered you?'

'He asked me if I'd sing at the club — only at weekends. I turned him down because the weekend is our busiest time. But he'd pay me well and if Annie wouldn't mind doing the odd spot of waiting I could still help you with the cooking and preparation. It'd help pay for the van without dipping into our working float.'

'It's an awful lot of extra work for you, Sall.'

'Singing isn't work. And anyway, the minute we'd paid the van off I'd stop.' She looked up expectantly. 'What do you say?'

'We'd have to ask Annie.'

'Of course, but it would only be Fridays and Saturdays.'

'And if Mother and Dad were up here to stay she obviously wouldn't be free to do it. In fact it might be better all round if Mother didn't know about the arrangement.'

'OK. On those occasions I'd tell Max I couldn't work. I'll make him understand all our conditions before I agree.'

Fiona's eyes lit up. 'It might just work. Maybe we could do it.'

'You bet we could! Shall I go and give Max a ring?'

'Yes, go on. Then tonight I'll ring Dad and tell him I'll accept his loan.' She looked at her watch. 'Heavens! Look at the time. We'd better get dressed before the boys are back to take us down to Nanny Joan's. I want the Havershams' housewarming party next Wednesday to be really special.'

★ ★ ★

It was midday before they arrived at Moon Cottage. Nanny Joan had a delicious Sunday roast waiting for them, complete with a succulent Yorkshire pudding and Stephen's favourite apple pie to follow.

'You've done us proud, Nanny,' he said as he pushed his chair back with a satisfied sigh. 'How on earth do you do it?'

'I don't eat much meat so I've been saving up my ration,' she told them as she cleared away the plates. 'All the rest is home grown as you know.' She looked round the table. 'Now don't you get thinking you're taking it easy this afternoon. I know you all had a late night last night, but there's plenty to do if you're to get stocked up.' She laid a hand on Sally's shoulder. 'You can help me with the washing up, dear, and the lads can help Fiona with the picking and packing.'

'Wouldn't it be lovely if we could deep freeze all that lovely produce?' Fiona said with a sigh.

'Never you mind your newfangled deep freezers,' Nanny said. 'Folks've been preserving fruit and vegetables for centuries. If you look in my larder you'll see jars of jam and bottled fruit, apple puree and salted beans still there from last year's crop. I daresay that was one thing they *didn't* teach you at that cordon bleu cookery school.'

'You're right, Nanny, they didn't,' Fiona agreed with a smile.

'Well, any week now I'll be starting my preserving, so if you girls want to come and stay for a few days you could learn how to do it and go back to London with enough fruit to last you through the winter. How about it?'

Fiona looked at Sally who smiled her approval. 'How could we refuse an offer like that?' she said. 'A few days in the country *and* a cookery lesson! We'll keep some mid-week days free, say the week after next?' She looked at Nanny. 'Would that be all right?'

'Suits me fine. I'll look forward to it.' Nanny began to load a tray with dishes.

'Annie will still be at home to take any enquiries we might get,' Sally said.

'What they haven't told you is that they're soon going to be mobile,' Stephen said. 'Ian has found them a van and Dad's going to have the name painted on the side for them.'

'Well, that's good news I'm sure,' Nanny said. 'But just you mind you don't go driving too fast and having an accident.'

'Now then Nanny, you know what a good driver I am,' Fiona reminded her. 'That time when you sprained your wrist I drove you to town and back, remember? And I was only seventeen at the time.'

'I remember it very well. And I have to admit I had no complaints.' Nanny looked round the table. 'Well, that's enough chatting. Off you go now and we'll all have a nice cup of tea when you've finished.'

Stephen groaned. 'Slave driver! She feeds us till we can hardly walk and then starts cracking the whip to make us jump about!'

Ian stood up. 'Mrs Harvey is right though. If we don't make a move we'll never get the car loaded up.'

The three of them went off, Fiona and Stephen grumbling loudly. Sally laughed.

'They go back to being kids when they're with you, Nanny,' she said as she carried the tray out to the scullery.

Nanny Joan was smiling. 'I know, bless them, and I wouldn't have it any other way.' She poured hot water from the kettle into the sink. 'The happiest time of my life that was, when those two were little.'

Sally glanced at her. 'Ian called you *Mrs*. Are you a widow?'

Nanny shook her head. 'No, love. Most nannies, like cooks are addressed as Mrs. It's sort of traditional. I never had a husband.'

'That's a shame.' Sally dried a plate. 'You'd have made a lovely wife and mum.'

'I'm not saying I've never been in love mind,' Nanny said quietly. 'Nor had my heart broken. But those two were all the babies I ever wanted.'

'They're lucky to have you,' Sally said wistfully. 'I never knew my mum.'

Nanny looked at her. 'Did you never ask your grandmother about her?'

Sally shrugged. 'Yes, a lot at one time, especially when I first started school. But Gran never seemed to want to talk about her. All she told me was that her name was Ethel and that she took off soon after I was born and hasn't been heard of since. For all I know she's probably dead by now, what with the blitz and everything.'

'So you don't know anything about your father either?'

'No.'

Nanny dried her hands on the roller towel that hung behind the door. 'You could find out, you know. Everyone is entitled to know who they are and where they come from. It'd surely be on your birth certificate.'

'I don't know where that is. It's sure to have been lost when Gran and Grandpa's place got bombed.'

'You can get a copy, you know — from Somerset House,' Nanny told her. 'You should have one anyway as the original is lost. Never know when you might need it.'

Sally nodded. 'Maybe I'll look into that sometime. If I tell the truth I'm just a little bit scared of what I might find out.'

'Ignorance is bliss in some cases, I grant you, but it's usually better to know — unless . . .'

'Unless what?'

Nanny shrugged her shoulders. 'Circumstances. Maybe your gran made a promise.'

'What kind of promise?'

'Oh, I don't know. People have their reasons for keeping things quiet. Sometimes the truth can hurt. I daresay your gran knew what was best for you back then. But you're a grown woman now and I'd advise you to get a copy of that certificate.'

'OK, I'll think about it.'

★ ★ ★

The four of them drove back to Gower Street that evening tired but happy. The boot of the Bentley was packed with fresh produce and as Ian drove Sally began to hum a popular song. The others soon joined in. One song followed another and they sang every song they could think of until finally the songs dried up and they fell silent.

Sitting in the back with her head on Stephen's shoulder Sally looked up at him. 'I've got something to tell you,' she whispered.

He drew her closer. 'I know, you're going to tell me how wonderful I am — as if I didn't already know.'

She laughed. 'Big head! No such thing. Fee and I talked this morning and we decided that if we're going to buy Ian's van I should accept the job that Max offered me.'

He looked at her. 'You're joking!'

'No. It makes sense, Stevie. I rang Max this morning and I'm going over to talk to him about it tomorrow morning.'

He shook his head. 'Well, you know what I think about it.'

'Yes, but it's for the sake of the business. You want us to succeed, don't you?'

His mouth tightened. 'It has nothing to do with me. I don't even know why you're bothering to tell me if you've already made your mind up.' He withdrew his arm from around her and moved away stiffly.

Sally's heart sank. 'Oh, Stevie, don't be stuffy about it. It'll only be a couple of nights a week and as soon as we've paid for the van I'll stop.'

'As I said, it's really none of my business.' He turned his head to stare out of the window and didn't speak again until Ian pulled up outside number 28 Gower Street and they all got out to unpack the boxes of produce.

When everything was put away Sally put the kettle on for coffee and the four of them sat round the kitchen table to drink it. Sally kept glancing at Stephen but he avoided her eyes. The tension did not escape Fiona's notice and at last she felt obliged to speak.

'Have you two fallen out or something?'

Stephen looked at his sister. 'I'm shocked and surprised at you, letting Sally sing in some seedy little East End night club,' he said. 'I can't see *you* risking your reputation for the sake of your precious business!'

Fiona's eyes darkened. '*Reputation?* What on earth are you talking about? Sally wants to do it. I'm neither making or letting her. We discussed it as business partners.'

'Dad offered to lend you the money to buy a van. I even offered you my gratuity money, so why couldn't you just accept it? Why do you have to be so bloody independent?'

'You know perfectly well that you're going to need every penny you can lay your hands on at Cambridge. And as a matter of fact we *are* accepting Dad's offer,' Fiona told him.

'This is just a way of paying him back quicker,' Sally put in.

'Yes, and if Max Feldman is good enough for Ian to go into business with then what's wrong with Sally working for him?' Fiona asked.

'Come off it. I think we all know what's expected of girls who work in that kind of place,' Stephen said.

There was a stunned silence for a moment, then Sally turned to him angrily. 'That's a rotten thing to suggest! Max and I have known each other since we were kids. He'd never expose me to anything like that. Anyway, how do you know so much about it?'

Ian, who had been looking uncomfortable, cleared his throat. 'Look, I feel that all this is my fault,' he said. 'If I hadn't offered you the van none of this would have happened.'

Fiona reached out her hand to touch his arm. 'Don't you dare apologize,' she said stoutly. 'We're very grateful for your kind offer. I know you could have got a better price for it if you'd advertised. Stevie's just being bloody-minded. Sally's happy to take the singing job for a few months and I'm happy to manage with Annie's help. And that's all about it.'

'It's none of my business, you mean! Right, nothing more to be said then, is there?' Stephen got up from the table and walked up the basement stairs. The other three looked help-lessly at each other, then Sally jumped up and ran after him. She caught up with him in the hall just as he had reached the front door.

'*Stevie!* Don't leave like this — please!'

As he turned to her she saw the hurt in his eyes. 'I don't want my girl working in that kind of place.'

'What kind of place? You've never even been there!'

'I've been in places like it.'

'Why are you being so snobbish about it?' she asked. 'Are you afraid some of your friends might get to know? Would it make you ashamed of me?'

'That has nothing to do with it. You don't have to do this,' he said stubbornly.

'*And I don't have to do as you tell me either!*'

For a long moment they stared at each other, Sally's heart thudding against her ribs. Then Stephen said, 'I thought you loved me, Sally. I thought that last night meant something special to you.'

'I *do*. And of course it did.' As she looked at him standing there, his eyes glinting and his mouth set in an obstinate line he seemed to her suddenly as vulnerable as a small boy. She stepped up to him and put her arms around him. 'Oh, Stevie, I'd never do anything to hurt you. You know I wouldn't. I'm not about to make a career out of singing in nightclubs. It's just for a little while to help us buy the van.' She looked up at him. 'You're not going to blame Fee or poor Ian for it, or let it come between us, are you? I couldn't bear that.'

His arms remained at his sides and his body felt rigid and unyielding in her arms. 'You must have a pretty low opinion of me if you think I'd do that,' he said stubbornly.

'She dropped her arms and looked up at him. 'We're going to have to agree to differ on this one, Stevie.'

'Yes — well, as you've just said, you don't have to do anything just to please me.'

'That's not what I said. Look, Stevie, I've been trying to tell you that I'm not right for you — that what we have can't last,' she said gently. 'Don't you see — by being like this you're just proving me right.'

'All right, as you think we're so horribly incompatible, maybe we should stop seeing one another as from now to avoid any more hurt.'

A lump filled her throat and she felt the tears welling up in her eyes. 'Is — is that really what you want?'

'You say it won't last, so maybe it's for the best.' He pulled the door open. 'Tell Ian I'll be waiting in the car.'

As she appeared at the top of the basement stairs Fiona and Ian looked up at her. 'Is everything all right?' Fiona asked anxiously.

'No, not really.' Sally slowly descended the stairs. 'It looks as though we're finished.' She looked at Ian. 'He asked me to tell you he's waiting in the car.'

'Right.' Ian got up and smiled apologetically at Fiona. 'Better go, I suppose.' As she began to get up he held up his hand, looking at Sally's bowed

188

head. 'It's OK. I'll see myself out.'

'Thanks for taking us to Fairfield. And see if you can knock some sense into my idiot brother. 'Night, Ian.'

When he had gone Sally laid her head down on her arms and burst into tears.

Fiona stroked her shoulder. 'Oh darling don't. He'll come round. It's just his ridiculous male pride,' she said. 'I wouldn't mind betting that even as we speak he's regretting what he said to you.'

'I bet he isn't!'

'I think I've worked out what's biting him,' Fiona said. 'Dad will be paying his expenses at Cambridge. He feels he's taken a step backwards in depending on Dad again. It can't be easy after what he did all through the war. He probably envies our independence — even resents it a little.'

Sally looked up with swimming eyes. 'And he's happy to dump me just for that?' she asked. 'Has he always been this bolshie?'

'I'm afraid so. It's a male pride thing.'

Sally sighed. 'It's beginning to look as if I was right about us being completely wrong for each other, isn't it?'

* * *

It was with a heavy heart that Sally took the Underground to Hackney the following morning for her meeting with Max. They had arranged to meet at the club and Sally had been looking forward to seeing the inside of the place after

189

what she'd heard about it from Max. Since last night however, she was having difficulty keeping her mind on the coming meeting as she came out of the Underground station into the sunlight.

She had lain awake into the early hours, worrying about her row with Stephen and smarting at some of the things they'd said to each other. She had been angry — had almost lost her temper with him, but he had remained so cold and controlled — so sure that he was in the right. She could scarcely believe that he could have such an attitude in this day and age when the war had brought women so much closer to equality. One moment she was convinced that she was better off without him, the next her heart was aching to turn back the clock and have him back again.

Next to Brewster's grocer's shop there was a door with a painted sign above it. *The Pink Parrot* was printed in bright pink letters and below it a strange looking bird that looked to Sally more like an eagle than a parrot. She pushed open the door and descended a dusty staircase at the bottom of which was a small hallway with a reception desk — unmanned at the moment. At the end of the hall was a multicoloured bead curtain. Sally held it back and stepped through.

What had once been a cellar had been transformed. The vaulted ceiling had been painted dark blue and was sprinkled with silver stars. Two cleaning women were busy vacuuming the dark blue carpet that covered the floor, all

190

except for the miniscule dance floor in the centre around which tables were clustered, chairs upturned on top of them. There was a dais at the far end on which stood an upright piano, some music stands and a couple of spotlights, extinguished at the moment. On the other side of the room was a bar where Max was seated on a stool. He wore a black polo-neck sweater and slacks, his jacket slung over a nearby chair. He held up his hand in greeting.

'Hi, Sally!' She noticed that he wore an expensive looking gold watch on his extended wrist. 'Come and have a drink.' He nodded to the barman who was busy polishing glasses and re-stocking the shelves behind the bar. 'Pour the lady a gin and tonic, Bert. Better make it a double, she looks like she's had a rough night.'

'Thanks, Max.' Sally hitched herself up on to a stool beside him. 'Always knew how to flatter a girl, didn't you?' She waved the drink away. 'No thanks. It's a bit early for me.'

Max took out a silver cigarette case and flipped it open. 'OK. Fag then?'

'No, but I wouldn't mind a coffee if there's one going.'

Max nodded at the barman who put down his cloth and disappeared through a door at the back. Max smiled at her over the flame of his lighter as he lit his cigarette. 'So — what d'you think of the place?'

'Very nice.'

'Just had it all done up,' he told her. 'Carpet cost me an arm and a leg — export reject — know a bloke.' He tapped the side of his nose.

'Paint's not easy to come by either, but now that the fellers are filtering back from the services it's easier to get labour.'

'It looks very smart.'

'Hope so. Plannin' to go up-market.' He took a drag on his cigarette and smiled at her. 'You've changed your mind about the job then? Still susceptible to the old Feldman charm, eh?'

'Don't know about that, but I'll come and sing for you two nights a week if you still want me. I will have to make some conditions though.' She named them and he smiled.

'That's OK. I'll pay you by the night. Come when you can, as long as you let me know in advance. I'm expecting you to be a big draw.'

'Well, I hope you won't be disappointed.' Bert returned and placed a steaming cup of coffee on the bar in front of her. She lifted the cup took a grateful drink. 'Mmm — I needed that.'

'Thought so.' Max looked at her, one eyebrow raised. 'What's up darlin'?' he asked. 'Hung over, or had a bust up with your feller?'

'He doesn't approve of me singing in an East End night club if you must know.'

'But you're going ahead anyway. Good for you! He looked a bit of a toffee-nosed geezer to me anyway. I'm meeting his mate at lunchtime. I hope he isn't the same.' He looked at Sally appreciatively. 'I can't say I really blame him though,' he said. 'You've grown up a real little cracker, Sall. You're gonna have the fellers fallin' over themselves.'

'Well they needn't bother. I'm not interested.'

'Off blokes eh?'

'You could say that.'

'Right.' He stubbed out his cigarette. 'Let's get down to business then.' He named the figure he intended to pay Sally per night and she tried not to look impressed.

'Sounds OK to me,' she said nonchalantly.

'Of course there'll be a bonus if the business picks up like I'm expecting it to.'

'Sounds good.'

'Have you got any nice photos?' he asked. 'I thought we could have one blown up and stick it up outside to draw in the punters.'

Sally grinned. 'Like that sign with the parrot, you mean?'

He shrugged. 'Oh that. I'll be getting a neon sign now that the restrictions are off. Might have the entrance widened too — make it more eye-catching. Which reminds me. I take it you've got a few nice gownless evening straps?' He winked. 'You know the kind of thing — slinky, sexy little numbers.'

'I haven't really,' she told him. 'I haven't got any photos either. I haven't had any call for that kind of thing lately.'

He reached for his jacket and drew out his wallet. 'Better get yourself a couple then — for starters anyway. We can arrange for some photos later.' He withdrew some notes. 'Here, take this and get yourself kitted out.'

She stared at the notes he held out to her. 'I can't take all that, Max. And anyway, what about coupons?'

He pushed the notes into her hand. ''Course you can take it. It'll all go down as expenses. And don't worry about coupons. I know a very high class second-hand place.' He scribbled down an address on a scrap of paper and passed it to her. 'Go to this shop. It's only a couple of streets from here. The owner's name is Saskia Marks. Just tell her Max sent you. She'll fix you up OK.'

She looked at the scribbled name on the paper. The shop was called *After Dark*. 'Don't tell me you own that too!'

'No. Sass owes me a couple of favours. I want you to knock 'em dead darlin'. Oh, and if you're worried about getting back up West at closing time, don't be. I'll see that you get home safe and sound.'

'That's very good of you.'

'Not at all.' He grinned at her. 'Got to protect my investment, eh? Start this coming Saturday?'

'Right.'

'Turn up about ten. I'll sort out a dressing room for you. Sing two or three numbers at half ten and then another show at midnight, OK?'

'What about music? I'll need to rehearse with a pianist.'

He shook his head. 'No need. Dave plays by ear anyway. He'll follow you OK, he's brilliant.'

* * *

Sally found *After Dark* without much trouble. For a moment she stood outside surveying the contents of the window. It didn't look the kind of place that would have the type of gown Max had suggested. What was on display looked well worn

194

and slightly scruffy. But this was the place all right, so after a moment's hesitation she pushed open the door and went inside.

Saskia Mills was a heavily built, middle aged woman with dark hair piled high on her head. She wore a black dress and a lot of heavy gold jewellery. Her beady eyes swept over Sally from head to foot as she stepped forward.

'Yes? What can I do for you?'

'Max Feldman sent me,' Sally said. 'I'm going to sing for him at the club and he thought you might have a couple of suitable evening dresses that would fit me.'

Saskia's features relaxed and she suddenly became friendly and helpful. 'Max? Of course. Come this way dear.' She led the way through a door at the back of the shop and pulled back a curtain to reveal clothes of a very different kind from the ones Sally had seen in the window. The woman looked at her. 'Let's see — you're very small. Maybe this.' She drew out an elegant long black velvet dress. It was backless with shoe-string straps and scattered with silver sequins. 'I think this would suit you. Like to try it on? Just through there dear. There's a mirror.'

The dress fitted perfectly and Sally felt a little thrill of excitement. She had never owned such a sophisticated garment in her life. Saskia tapped on the door and looked in.

'I've just found this,' she said. 'It's be lovely with your colouring.' The dress that hung from the hanger she handed in was a creation in bias-cut scarlet silk. Sally took off the black dress

195

and slipped it on. It clung to her body like a second skin.

'You'd have to go without a bra in that,' Saskia said. 'But then you don't need one with a figure like yours.' She stood back smiling admiringly at Sally's reflection in the mirror. 'You look every inch a star if you don't mind me saying so dear,' she remarked. 'I haven't heard you sing, but Max usually knows when he's on to a good thing and I reckon he's found himself a winner this time.'

She found a pair of silver evening sandals to go with the dresses and after Sally had paid her she found that she still had some money over.

'Max won't want the change, so why don't you get your hair done?' Saskia suggested. 'My sister has a hairdressing salon two doors down. Her name's Rachel. Tell her I sent you and she'll do you proud. I guarantee it.'

★   ★   ★

When Fiona saw the dresses she was sceptical. 'All without coupons? Are you sure this Max is on the level?' she asked.

Sally smiled. 'Saskia's is supposed to be a second-hand shop, but as far as the things in the back room are concerned I get the distinct impression that it's a case of 'ask no questions'.'

'Well, those dresses don't look second-hand to me,' Fiona said.

'Maybe they've only been worn once,' Sally suggested. 'Or even bought and never worn. It happens.'

Fiona looked doubtful. 'Mmm — well, I hope you're right.'

'I'm sure Max knows a few dodges but he wouldn't get into anything illegal,' Sally assured her. 'He's too clever for that.'

'Well, I hope you're right because Ian has just rung me,' Fiona said. 'He's thrilled to bits. He met Max at lunchtime at the new premises and he's going into business with him next week. He's starting to drive all his cars over there right away.'

'He didn't happen to say whether Stephen had changed his mind about me, did he?' Sally asked, her eyes hopeful.

'I'm afraid not. Sorry love. But the good news is that he's bringing the van round for us on Friday.' Fiona smiled. 'Just think, Sall. This time next week we'll be mobile!'

11

The following Tuesday was the day the Havershams had chosen for their house-warming party. The girls were up bright and early to prepare the food. Mrs Haversham had chosen a buffet and Sally prepared the salads, tomato with olive oil and basil, cucumber in vinaigrette, lettuce, walnut and baby spinach and all the others she had been taught by Fiona. She had become a dab hand at making dressings, even experimenting and adding a few concoctions of her own.

The chickens they had brought from Nanny Joan's had been cooked the day before, very slowly, as the birds had not been in the first flush of youth. Fiona had thinly sliced the breast meat for the buffet and made the less tender parts into a mousse, which she decorated with rosettes of radish and mint leaves. With a choice of Fiona's delicious desserts and crisp French bread from their local bakery, the girls were packed and ready to go by six o'clock.

It was just before their cab was due to arrive that the telephone rang. Fiona answered it. 'Good evening, *Dinner At Eight* at your service.'

The voice at the other end sounded tetchy. 'Oh, *really* darling, I do wish you'd make the effort to find out who's calling before you make that silly announcement. It could be anyone.'

Fiona put her hand over the mouthpiece and

mouthed at Sally, '*Mother*.' 'Sorry,' she said into the telephone. 'What can I do for you?'

'I just wanted to tell you that your father and I will be coming up to Town at the end of the week for a few days,' Marcia said. 'I'm anxious to inspect the new decor and do some shopping. So will you please ask Annie to see that our room is ready? We'll arrive on Friday evening around six, but we shan't require dinner as we're dining out before the theatre. Stephen managed to get us seats for the ballet.'

'Right. Look forward to seeing you both,' Fiona said. 'Have to go now, Mother. We have a party to cater for this evening and our transport will be here any minute.'

'Fiona — *Fiona*! Wait a minute,' her mother said. 'Please remember what I said. I don't want my friends to think we're reduced to running a business from our London address. When you answer the telephone just give the number. That should suffice.'

'Yes, Mother.' As Fiona replaced the receiver she pulled a face at Sally. 'Honestly! My mother is such a snob. And she still behaves as though this place is fully staffed — *shan't require dinner* indeed! Who does she think is going to prepare it?'

'I suppose she thinks we would,' Sally said as she began to carry the boxes up the basement stairs. 'After all, what's the good of having a daughter who runs a catering service if she can't cook dinner for you?'

'That's all very well when it suits her,' Fiona complained. 'She hates the thought of any of her friends knowing that her daughter is working for a living — especially at *cooking*. On the other hand she doesn't mind taking advantage of the situation!'

'Just as well we'll be down in Fairfield for part of next week,' Sally reminded her.

Fiona nodded. 'As you say, *just as well*!'

★　★　★

The Havershams' flat in Knightsbridge was on the fourth floor of an elegant Edwardian block and it took three trips in the small lift to get all the boxes up to it. The flat was impressive. It had a large square entrance hall with pale oak panelled walls and a black and white tiled floor. The dining room had a glass enclosed balcony, which looked down on to a paved courtyard with potted shrubs and flowering plants. As it was a warm evening the doors were open to the gentle evening breeze. Mrs Haversham was delighted with the food and when everything was laid out the girls changed into their black dresses and prepared to circulate with drinks and be on hand to help the guests. The Havershams had invited about twenty guests, enough to fill the flat without overcrowding, and everyone seemed to be enjoying themselves. Once the buffet had been served the girls were free to begin clearing up. In the kitchen as they washed up Mrs Haversham thanked them. 'Several people have already asked for your name,' she told them. '*Dinner At Eight* is really becoming popular. The salads were so wonderfully fresh. I don't know

200

how you do it. The so-called fresh produce I buy in London is always so limp.'

'We have a special supplier in the country,' Fiona told her.

'Well it was absolutely delicious, so you'd better be prepared for lots more bookings,' Mrs Haversham said as she handed them their cheque. 'Thank you both so very much. Now, when you're ready can I get someone to help you down with the boxes?'

'Would you mind if we left them here until tomorrow?' Fiona asked. 'We came tonight in a cab but we're taking delivery of our very own van tomorrow, so we could collect in style.'

'Your own van. How exciting! Can I get someone to run you home?'

Sally laughed. 'There's no hurry so we'll catch the tube, thanks. We're used to it.'

As the train rumbled homewards they talked about the success of the evening's work.

'I love that flat,' Sally said dreamily. 'One of these days I'm going to have one just like it.'

Fiona laughed. 'When we're an international company, you mean?'

A sudden thought struck Sally and she looked at Fiona in alarm. 'I've just thought — your folks are coming up on Friday and Saturday's my first gig at the club! If we get a booking Annie won't be able to help you.'

'I'll just say we can't do it, don't worry.'

'That's no good,' Sally protested. 'We want all the business we can get. It's no use me doing extra work to pay for the van if *Dinner At Eight* can't function because of it.'

Fiona shook her head. 'You let me worry about it,' she said calmly. 'There's no booking for Saturday at the moment. If one comes then I'll cope somehow.'

Sally was silent for a moment, then she said, 'I've been thinking about what your mum said tonight. Maybe we should find somewhere of our own.'

'Why should we?' Fiona protested. 'Mother was glad enough for us to caretake when all the building and decorating was being done. She can't have it all her own way, can she?'

'It *is* her house,' Sally pointed out.

'It's my home too.'

Sally said nothing. It was all very well for Fiona, but she still felt beholden to the Crowthers and she knew that Marcia resented her. She longed for *Dinner At Eight* to be fully independent. Working from an address of their own would be so much better in her view.

Annie was waiting up for them when they arrived home. 'I took a telephone call for you,' she said. 'I wrote it down.' She consulted the notepad by the telephone in the kitchen. 'A Mrs Bennett from Mill Hill. She wants to know if you do cocktail parties. I said you'd ring her back.'

'When was it for?' Fiona asked.

Annie squinted at what she'd written on the pad. 'Saturday,' she said. 'Saturday evening. Your ma and pa are coming this weekend, aren't they?'

'Yes.' Sally groaned.

Fiona looked unconcerned. 'It's only a cocktail party,' she said. 'You can help me with the preparations, Sall and I'm sure I can manage the party by myself.' She picked up the pad. 'I'll ring them back now before they contact someone else.'

They were having a late breakfast the following morning when a hooting in the street sent both of them rushing up the stairs. Ian sat outside in the little white van smiling. Sally gasped.

'Oh my God — *look*!'

On the side of the van, painted in eye-catching purple letters were the words:

FIONA AND SALLY INVITE YOU TO — DINNER AT EIGHT
DINNER PARTIES AND OTHER OCCASIONS CATERED FOR

Beneath, was the telephone number in equally large print.

Fiona gazed at it with tears in her eyes. 'Oh! It's amazing! Thank you so much, Ian.'

'Don't thank me. Your father telephoned me and asked me to have it done as a surprise,' he explained. 'I'm glad you like it.' He looked at them enquiringly. 'Who's going to have first go then?'

Sally shrugged. 'I can't drive, so it has to be Fee.' She nudged her friend. 'Go on, take her round the block and I'll have some coffee ready for when you get back.' By the time they arrived back Sally had a pot of coffee brewing on the Aga. She looked up as they clattered excitedly down the stairs. 'Well — does she go all right?'

'She's absolutely fantastic!' Fiona flopped down in a chair. 'I was a bit nervous to start with. It's so long since I drove that I wasn't sure I could still do it.'

'She was fine,' Ian said. 'Negotiated the traffic better than any taxi driver. You'll have to take lessons now, Sally.'

'I suppose I will.' As they drank their coffee Sally ached to ask after Stephen, but she didn't know how to bring up the subject. Several times she opened her mouth to frame the question, but somehow she couldn't find the right words.

'Isn't it this weekend you're starting your cabaret spot at Max's club,' Ian asked suddenly, almost as though reading her thoughts.

'Yes.' She looked at Fiona. 'And I'm a bit worried because Fee has taken a booking for Saturday evening.'

Fiona shook her head. 'I keep telling you, it's only a cocktail party. We'll do most of the work together beforehand and they're providing their own wines and other drinks so that's not a problem. I'm sure I'll manage the party on my own, especially now that we've got the van.'

'I'm not doing anything on Saturday evening,' Ian said. 'May I offer my best waitering service?'

Both girls stared at him. '*You?*' they chorused.

'Well! No need to look so horrified. I've got black trousers and a clean white shirt and I'm sure handing round a few drinks and canapés won't tax either of my brain cells too severely.'

Fiona laughed. 'It's not that. We'd be really grateful and I'm sure you'd do it with great aplomb, but do you really want to?'

The look on his face clearly said, *As long as I'm with you of course I want to.* But he said, 'I've offered my services. Take me or leave me.'

'She'll take you,' Sally put in. 'And it'll be a great relief to me, I can tell you.'

* * *

Donald and Marcia Crowther arrived in a taxi soon after six on Friday evening, Marcia complaining loudly about the state of the train.

'It's really too bad. The car *would* have to break down just when we needed it,' she said. 'You should have seen the state of that railway carriage. First class too! I don't know what the LMS is coming to. It would never have been allowed before the war.'

'A lot of things wouldn't have been allowed before the war,' Donald told her with a sigh. 'Anyway, we're here now. And we don't really need the car in Town dear, do we?'

Marcia sighed. 'Well, I just hope there's plenty of hot water. I need a good long soak and a lie down before we go out.' As she began to climb the stairs Donald winked at the girls.

'You mustn't mind your mother,' he said to Fiona. 'She'll soon cheer up when she sees Stephen and settles into her seat at the theatre. A good evening out will do her the world of good.'

As he followed his wife up the stairs Fiona looked at Sally. 'Hear that? *As soon as she sees Stephen.* I'm just the also-ran.'

'I'm sure he didn't mean it like that,' Sally said.

Fiona waved a hand. 'Oh, it doesn't matter. I'm used to it.'

All next morning the girls were busy making canapés for the cocktail party. Marcia put in an appearance halfway through the morning and began picking at the ingredients.

'I must say these look very appetizing darling.'

'Well I'm glad you approve,' Fiona said. 'But could you stop eating them, please, Mother. We'll be here all day at this rate.' She looked up. 'Did you enjoy the ballet by the way?'

'It was pleasant enough,' Marcia said. 'But I couldn't help worrying a little about poor Stephen. He's looking so peaky and I'm sure he's lost weight.' She helped herself to another canapé. 'I'm convinced he doesn't eat properly. He just picked at his dinner last night. I would have thought that you could invite him over for the occasional meal, Fiona. After all, he is your only brother.' She sighed. 'Young people nowadays are so selfish.'

Fiona glanced at Sally out of the corner of her eye and saw that her colour had deepened. 'So — did you see anyone you knew at the theatre?' she asked.

'As a matter of fact we did,' Marcia said. 'Jonathan and Gilly Knowles. You remember, we spent one or two skiing holidays with them before the war. They've been vegetating down in Cornwall and they've only just moved back up to Town. They've invited us to have dinner with them at a new place they've discovered in Chelsea and then on to some nightspot.' She pursed her lips. 'I hope it's all right. Jonathan has rather strange taste sometimes. Still, I suppose it'll be better than mouldering in the country. I get so sick of having nothing to do but listen to the radio or go to Women's Institute meetings.'

Everyone had left that evening before Sally was ready to set out for Hackney. Annie had volunteered to press the dresses for her. She packed them both carefully in tissue paper so that they wouldn't crease and Sally added the sandals, her make-up bag and a dressing gown to the small suitcase. As the hands of the clock moved round to nine-thirty Sally's heart was beginning to beat faster and butterflies were doing a jig in her stomach. Why had she thought she could do this? she asked herself. Singing at parties or even in the church at Saltmere St Peter was one thing, but standing up in front of a crowd of people in a nightclub was something else. If only she could have had a run-through. She hadn't even met the pianist who was to accompany her! Suppose they didn't like her? Suppose they talked all through her cabaret and didn't even listen? Suppose her voice gave out and she ended up squeaking? The dreadful things that could happen were too frightening to think about.

Finally she said goodbye to Annie and set off to take the Underground to Hackney. Too late to back out now. Maybe this would be her first and last gig at the *Pink Parrot*. She almost hoped it would be.

The dressing room that Max had set aside for her was little more than a cupboard, but it had a card table a chair and a mirror at which to do her make-up and hair. He had also found her a rail on which to hang up her clothes. In one corner was a shelf on which stood a jug of water and a basin.

Sally looked round at the brown-painted brick walls in despair. The little room had a cold, clammy, subterranean feel to it. It was hardly star treatment, but it would have to do. She unpacked her case and hung up the two evening dresses then she undressed and put on the dressing gown she had brought. Her hands shook as she made up her face at the spotted mirror and combed her unruly curls, adding a diamante clip that Fiona had lent her. Slipping out of the dressing gown she climbed into the black gown and fastened the zip.

A sudden loud knock on the door startled her. 'Can I come in darlin'?' Without waiting for permission Max walked in, looking sleek and immaculate his dinner jacket. His eyes widened when he saw her.

'Blimey gel, you're a sight for sore eyes an' no mistake.' Grasping her shoulders he kissed her soundly. 'I see Sass done you proud. Love the clobber! All right, are you? Ready an' all that?'

'I suppose so — as I'll ever be.'

'The band are on their supper break so I've brought Dave to meet you,' he said, beckoning to someone standing outside the door. 'He's your pianist. Come in and meet Sally, Dave.'

Dave Grant was a middle-aged man with grey hair swept back from his brow. He had kind blue eyes and a friendly smile. 'Hello, Sally,' he said, holding out his hand. 'I've heard a lot about you.

What numbers are you doing?'

Sally shook his hand and named the three songs she had chosen. He nodded reassuringly.

'Nothing there I don't know and I'm used to accompanying singers. Just give me the first couple of bars now, will you love? So's I can get the key.'

She cleared her throat and sang the first line of 'You'll Never Know'. Dave nodded.

'That's fine. OK then, I'll just give you a couple of introductory bars and when you start I'll follow you. Don't worry about a thing.'

Max looked at her. 'OK then, love?'

She swallowed hard. 'I suppose so.'

Holding both her hands Max stood back and looked her over from head to foot. 'Lookin' like that you could knock 'em dead without even openin' your north an' south!' He looked at his watch. 'OK, it's about time. Follow me.'

At the end of the corridor he paused outside a door. 'Give the fellers a moment to get to their places then I'll go on and announce you. Don't worry, I'll come and take you on.'

She nodded, her mouth dry. Standing there in the corridor she heard the mumble of voices as the musicians returned to their places. Then a roll on the drums as Max stood up to make his announcement.

'This evening, ladies and gentlemen, Miss Sally Joy is our cabaret artist. A young local singer whose popularity is rising fast. Mark my words, she going to be a big hit and when she is you'll be able to say you saw her first at the *Pink Parrot*! So please will you give a big hand to

Miss *Sally Joy*!' The door opened and Max took her hand and led her to the front of the stand. The spotlights and all eyes were trained on her expectantly. She glanced at Dave who gave her an encouraging wink and played the opening bars.

Sally took a deep breath and began to sing her first number, 'You'll Never Know'. The moment the first notes left her throat she relaxed. Her nerves calmed and she began to enjoy herself. The crowd was silent, even the people clustered round the bar stopped talking to listen. Dave followed her pace and tempo perfectly. At the end the applause was enthusiastic. At a seat to one side Max beamed up at her throughout the song and as it came to an end and she took a bow he gave her a surreptitious wink and thumbs-up sign.

She was halfway through her second song when a movement at the back of the room caught her eyes and her heart almost stopped. More customers had just arrived and were making their way towards a table at the edge of the dance floor. Elegant in evening dress, Marcia and Donald Crowther and two other people sat down. Sally's heart gave a lurch but she managed to continue. It was only when she spotted one other person joining them that her throat almost closed up.

As Stephen took his seat their eyes met and held as the song came to an end. She took her bow then turned to Dave and bent to whisper something in his ear. He nodded and began to play the first few bars of the title she'd mentioned. Her eyes fixed on Stephen, Sally began to sing 'Long Ago And Far Away'.

Her voice was low and husky and by the time she came to the last line of the final chorus it throbbed with emotion: '*All I longed for long ago was you*'.

There was a moment's silence before the applause began, louder and even more enthusiastic than before. Sally took her bow and left the stand. Outside in the corridor Max joined her.

'That was terrific, gel! Want to go on again? Go on, do an encore. They love you.' Then he caught sight of her tear-filled eyes. 'You all right, love?'

She shook her head. 'Not really. I need a minute.'

'Hey! You're all of a tremble!' He patted her shoulder. 'OK, don't worry about it. Leave 'em wantin' more, I always say. You'll be all right for the second spot?'

She nodded. 'Yes. I'll be fine. Thanks, Max.'

'I'll get someone to bring you a coffee and something to eat,' he said. 'Go and have a nice sit down.'

In the dressing room, still trembling, she took off the dress and pulled on her dressing gown. Who would have thought that Stephen and his parents would turn up at the *Pink Parrot*? Of all the places in London they could go it would have to be here — and tonight of all nights!

There was a soft tap on the door. Max's promised refreshments. She wasn't sure that she'd be able to swallow food but she called out, 'Come in.'

211

The door opened. She looked up and her heart almost stopped at the reflection she saw in the mirror. She sprang to her feet. '*Stevie!*'

He came in and closed the door, then she was in his arms and he was kissing her eyes — her throat, finally her lips. She closed her eyes and clung to him, drowning in his kiss.

'Oh, Stevie, I thought you'd gone for ever.'

'I'm sorry I was such an idiot,' he whispered against her hair. 'I've been through seven kinds of agony every day since.' He held her away and looked down at her. 'I thought you'd never want to see me again after the things I said. You were so lovely tonight, darling. I was so proud of you. And you sang our special song. Was it for me?'

'Of course it was. Couldn't you tell?'

'I love you, Sally,' he said, holding her close. 'I love you so much. Please don't ever let's quarrel again.'

'Never! I love you too, Stevie.'

Outside the door the waitress with the tray paused, her hand raised to knock. Then she turned and tiptoed quietly away.

★   ★   ★

Fiona and Ian were in high spirits as they drove back to Gower Street. The cocktail party had been a big success and Ian had proved the perfect waiter. The hostess had congratulated Fiona as she handed her cheque over.

'You're very lucky to have found such a personable young man to do your waiting,' she

212

said. 'I'm sure he's an asset to your catering firm.'

Fiona passed on the message to Ian as they drove away. 'Maybe it's something you should take up as a second career,' she joked.

'I may hold you to that.' Ian glanced at his watch. 'It's half past eleven.' He looked at her.

'I know.' She smiled. 'Are you thinking what I'm thinking?'

'I thought we might catch Sally's second spot at the *Pink Parrot*.'

'Me too.' He turned the van round. 'Right! Hackney, here we come!'

When they arrived at the club it was packed. They managed to find two spare stools at the bar just as Sally appeared for her second cabaret spot of the evening. She wore the red dress and looked quite stunning. Ian ordered two gin and tonics and they settled down to watch.

'There's something different about her tonight,' he remarked. 'An air of — I don't know what to call it — starry-eyedness.'

Fiona nodded. 'Yes and I think I've just spotted the reason for it.' She pointed to where Stephen sat on the fringe of the dance floor, his eyes firmly fixed on Sally.

'If I'm not very much mistaken those two have made up,' she said.

Ian grinned. 'Not before time! He's been like a bear with a sore head ever since their row. Perhaps he'll be a bit easier to live with now.'

After the cabaret Sally came out to join Stephen and the two of them joined the others on the tiny dance floor. Ian looked at Fiona.

'Well, those two only have eyes for each other. Like to dance?'

They stepped on to the floor and began to circle the crowded floor. 'I envy them,' Ian said. Fiona looked up at him.

'Do you — why?'

'Just look at them. The rest of the world might as well have fallen to bits for all they know or care. It's an enviable state to be in.'

'We both remember it, don't we?'

He looked down at her, his eyes dark. 'Is that all you're prepared to settle for, Fiona? For the rest of your life — remembering what it was like to be in love? With every year that passes it gets further and further away.'

'I've learned to be — realistic,' she said, avoiding his eyes.

'And does being realistic mean that you can't see what's in front of your nose? Or is it just that you don't *want* to see it?' His tone was almost angry and she looked up at him sharply.

'No, of course it's not that. It's just that it's easy to — to imagine things — to let oneself be — persuaded into false emotions.'

'False emotions?'

She shrugged. 'Oh, I don't know. I'm putting it badly. I just can't take anything for granted any more.'

'The war's over now, Fee.'

'I know it is. I just . . . ' She shook her head. 'Shall we sit down?'

Their stools at the bar had been taken and they were now reduced to standing. Ian caught

214

the barman's eye and ordered two more drinks. He turned to her.

'Look, Fee, there's something I have to say. After tonight — now that you've got the van and there's nothing you need me for any more, I shan't be seeing you again.'

Her heart gave a lurch. 'Ian! *Why?*'

'Do I really have to tell you that? It's too painful. I've been hoping that something might develop between us. I didn't want to rush you so I waited. Sometimes you even seem to be warming towards me. And then next time we meet you're as distant as ever. I can't do it any more, Fee.'

She reached out to touch his arm. 'Ian — Look, please — I . . . '

'*Hello!* What are you two doing here?' Fiona turned to see Stephen and Sally standing behind her. 'We're off now. Are you staying on or are you coming too?'

Fiona made herself smile. 'I think we're ready to go too, aren't we, Ian?'

He nodded. 'We only dropped in to catch your spot, Sally. You were terrific.'

'Yes, terrific,' Fiona echoed.

Sally looked at her friend. 'Are you all right? Party go off OK?'

'Oh, absolutely fine. Ian was a definite hit.'

But Sally had seen the look in Fiona's eyes and she knew there was something wrong. 'That's OK then,' she said, deciding to wait till they were alone to quiz her friend. She linked her arm through Fiona's. 'See you at home then.'

Stephen and Sally took a long time to say

goodnight. The street was deserted apart from Stephen's little car, its top open to the balmy night air. He sighed, his arm around Sally as they snuggled close.

'I could stay like this all night. If the folks weren't in residence I could . . . '

'I know. But they are.'

'Shall I see you tomorrow?'

'Have you forgotten? Fee and I are going to Fairfield tomorrow till Thursday.'

'Drat! Tell you what, shall I drive down and bring you home?'

'If you like, I know Nanny Joan will be pleased to see you.'

'And what about you? Will you be pleased to see me?'

'What do you think?' She stared up at the sky and sighed. 'I can see the moon and count the stars from here.'

'Which one would you like?' he asked. 'Just name it and I'll get it for you.'

She laughed. 'You're crazy. How many drinks did you have while you were waiting for me?'

He shook his head. 'I don't need alcohol when I've got you. You're more intoxicating than a whole lake full of booze.'

★   ★   ★

With the whole house slumbering Sally took off her shoes and crept up the stairs, acutely aware of every creak of the floorboards. Outside Fiona's door she paused then tapped softly. Hearing Fiona call 'Come in,' she slipped inside,

216

closing the door carefully behind her. Fiona had drawn back the curtains and moonlight flooded the room. Sally sat down on the bed.

'OK, what happened?'

Fiona burst into tears. 'It's Ian. He doesn't want to see me any more.'

'Oh, Fee! But why?'

'He says I blow hot and cold and he can't take it any more.'

'He said that?'

'Not in so many words but that's what it amounted to.'

Sally reached for her friend's hand. 'Oh.'

'Is that all you've got to say — *Oh*?'

'Well, you haven't exactly encouraged him, have you? I mean, it's been clear to me for ages that he adores you — yet you . . . '

'I *what*?'

'Well, nothing really. That's just it — nothing.'

'But I do like him, Sally.'

'Maybe just *liking* isn't what he wants.'

'I'm fond of him then.'

'Fee — are you afraid of the word *love*?'

'No!' She fumbled under the pillow for a handkerchief. 'Not the *word*.'

'Of the feeling then — the emotion? Are you afraid to let yourself feel too much in case you get hurt again?'

Fiona sighed and blew her nose. 'I suppose that's it.'

'We all have to risk losing,' Sally said softly. 'I know all too well that I'm risking losing Stevie. I thought I had lost him and I know how much it hurt. Tonight we made up again and now I risk it all over again. But I have to keep telling myself that the happiness I'm feeling right now is worth the risk.' She put her arms round Fiona and hugged her. 'If you can't do the same, Fee you'll go through your life without living at all.'

12

Sally was halfway down the stairs on Monday morning when she heard the post clatter through the letterbox. Taking Nanny Joan's advice she had applied for a replacement birth certificate and ever since she had eagerly awaited its arrival. Hurrying down the stairs she scooped up the bundle of letter from the mat and looked quickly through them. On the last one the words *Somerset House* were printed in the corner of the long envelope and her heart gave a little skip of excitement mixed with apprehension.

She had just started down the basement stairs, hoping to share the contents with Fiona who was making breakfast when the sound of voices halted her. The louder of the two was Marcia's, complaining bitterly.

'I've never felt so embarrassed in my life, Fiona. It was bad enough being dragged along to that sleazy little East End club by Jonathan, but when the cabaret began and Stephen announced to all and sundry that the singer was his — his *girlfriend*! I could have dropped through the floor with shame! Honestly! There she stood, half naked like some cheap little floozie in front of all those *frightful* people.'

'I'm sure she wasn't half naked, Mother. I saw the dress and it was perfectly respectable. And Sally took the job to help us pay Dad back for the van Ian found for us.'

'It's no use making excuses. I know what I saw with my own eyes,' Marcia insisted. 'I don't know what's become of you, Fiona. Since you went off to work in that awful factory place you seem to have lost all sense of class and breeding. What is worse, you've got poor Stephen embroiled in this mess too.'

'You seem to forget, Mother, that Stephen is a grown man,' Fiona put in. 'He's not in the least influenced by me and never has been.'

But Marcia wasn't listening. 'And to add insult to injury,' she went on, 'I find that this *Ian* person you seem to have got yourself caught up with is a *used car salesman*. Not only that but he's actually implicated with the horrid little man who owns that dreadful *Pink Parrot* place!'

'In partnership, Mother. Not *implicated*.' Fiona corrected. 'And you seem to forget that Ian was Stephen's friend first.'

'That was during the war when they were both in uniform,' Marcia said with a dismissive wave of her hand. 'Anyway, whatever his association with that Feldman man might be, it has to be highly questionable. You weren't brought up to mix with such people. I really can't think *why* we bothered to spend money on an expensive private education when all you wanted was to mix with the lowest of the low! But then I suppose I shouldn't really be surprised.'

'What does that mean exactly?' Fiona asked.

But Marcia had no intention of elucidating. She turned on her heel and began to march up the stairs. When she noticed Sally, still standing at the top, she paused only to give her a look of

220

sheer contempt before brushing past her into the hall.

Sally came down to the kitchen and found Fiona sitting white-faced at the table. 'I'm sorry,' she said. 'I couldn't help overhearing.'

'I know. I saw you standing at the top of the stairs but I couldn't shut her up.'

Sally smiled wryly. 'Don't worry. I wasn't under any misapprehensions about her feelings for me.'

'A good thing we're getting out of here for a few days,' Fiona said. 'I suggest we have a quick breakfast and get on our way. I'm beginning to think you were right; we should look for a place of our own.' She got up and went to the Aga to fetch the teapot. 'She didn't even give me the chance to tell her she needn't worry about Ian any more.'

'You are going to get in touch with him before we go, aren't you?' Sally asked. 'Poor Ian. He's probably feeling really miserable this morning.'

'What's the point?' Fiona said without turning round. 'He'll be better off without me in the end. He deserves someone who can return his feelings.'

'And you can't? Are you sure, Fee? Do you really want to throw away the chance of happiness?'

Fiona turned and began to pour the tea. 'There's some fresh toast keeping warm in the oven,' she said, tight-lipped. 'Or did you want some bacon?'

'Did you hear what I said?'

'If you don't mind I really don't want to talk

221

about it any more, Sally.' Fiona reached out for the post. 'Anything there for me?'

Sally suddenly remembered her letter and sat down at the table. 'I think the others are bills but there's one for me. It's from Somerset House. I think it's my birth certificate.'

'Are you going to open it then?'

Sally took a deep breath and slid her thumb under the envelope's flap. Drawing out the certificate she unfolded it and steeled herself to look. 'I'm registered as Sarah Jane Joy, but it says Ethel Mays under *Mother's Name*.' She looked up at Fiona. '*Mays* — not Joy.'

'That means she must have been married,' Fiona said, looking over Sally's shoulder. 'What does it say under *Father's Name*?'

Sally unfolded the rest of the document and her heart plummeted. 'It says *unknown*.' She sighed. 'Well, I always knew I was illegitimate so that's no surprise, but I did hope I'd at least get a name.' She folded the certificate and put it back into the envelope. 'I bet your mother would love to get a look at that,' she said as she stuffed it into her pocket. 'It would prove that everything she said about me was true.'

'That's rubbish!' Fiona said. 'You had no control over what happened before you were born. If she ever bothered to get to know people before passing judgement . . . Oh, anyway, it's none of her business.' She sat down opposite. 'I do think there are some questions you need to ask though, Sally.'

'I know,' Sally looked thoughtful. 'I think I'll drop a line to Gran. I'll write her a quick letter and post it on the way.' She glanced up at the clock. 'Come on, we'd better make a start.'

★ ★ ★

At Moon Cottage Nanny Joan had baskets of fruit and vegetables ready picked and waiting to be bottled, puréed, jammed and salted ready for use during the winter. She kept the girls busy for the two days that followed, demonstrating the bottling process of filling the Kilner jars and heating them in the oven to the correct temperature; boiling fruit and sugar for jam until the gelling point was reached, and layering runner beans with salt. They worked hard, pausing only for meals and by Wednesday Nanny's larder shelves were groaning under the weight of jars of bottled plums and gooseberries, strawberry and raspberry jams, apple purée and salted runner beans. It had been enjoyable work, but when the girls retired to the room they were sharing that night Fiona confided to Sally her concern about Nanny's health.

'Have you seen the way she keeps holding her back?' she asked.

Sally nodded. 'Well, yes, but we've worked very hard over the last three days. My back's been aching at the end of the day too and I'm a lot younger than Nanny.'

'It's not just that,' Fiona said. 'She looks drawn and heavy-eyed. I know her so well and I definitely feel there's something wrong.'

'Why don't you ask her?'

Fiona gave a wry smile. 'Knowing Nanny I can

imagine what she'll say. She'd rather die than admit she was anything but fighting fit.'

'Would you like to stay on for a couple of days?'

Fiona sighed. 'I would really. We have no bookings till next week.' She looked at Sally. 'But Stevie's coming to fetch you tomorrow, isn't he?'

'I'll stay on with you if you want me to. Stevie will understand.' Sally looked at her friend. 'But I thought maybe you and she would enjoy having some time together — just the two of you.'

'That might be nice, and maybe I'd get her to confide in me if there is something wrong. Would you mind, Sally?'

''Course not.'

*　*　*

Stephen arrived the following morning and after coffee and a walk round the garden Nanny and Fiona waved them off.

'Fee's decided to stay on then,' Stephen said as they reached the end of the lane.

'Yes. She's a bit worried that Nanny's not herself,' Sally told him. 'There's nothing to hurry back for so I suggested she stay till the end of the week.'

'The folks have gone by the way,' Stephen looked at her. 'In case you were wondering.'

Sally pulled a face. 'Fee and your mum had a row on Sunday morning.'

'I know. I didn't get off scot-free either.'

'It was about me, wasn't it? Your mum hates me.'

224

'She doesn't even know you properly so how can she hate you?'

'She hates everything I stand for,' Sally said. 'My background and education; the fact that I'm from the East End. And seeing me at the club on Saturday night was the last straw. I actually heard her describe me as 'the lowest of the low'.'

'Just ignore her!'

'I can't, Stephen. She loathes the idea of you and me being together and she's not much keener on Ian. And poor Fee gets the blame for all of it.'

Stephen sighed. 'Ma's a bit of a dinosaur. She's got to come to terms with the fact that the world has changed.'

'I don't think she ever will.'

'Well, no need to worry about her for the moment. She and Dad have gone home — and they've taken Annie with them.'

'Taken Annie — but why?'

'Ma's got some kind of soirée planned for next weekend and she needs her to help. They're putting her on the train back on Monday. Ma isn't satisfied with the way her bedroom has been papered and she's got the decorator coming back again, so she needs Annie back in Town next week to supervise.'

Sally groaned. 'More workmen!'

'Yes, but don't you see what it means for us my darling? For the next three days we have the house all to ourselves.'

'Oh!' Sally's heart gave a lurch. 'I don't know, Stevie. Suppose your parents find out?'

'So what if they do?' Stephen drew the car on

to the forecourt of a tiny thatched pub, switched off the engine and turned to her. 'Listen darling. There's something I haven't told you. I'm off to Cambridge at the end of next week and I've no idea when I'll be able to get back again apart from a flying visit at the end of October for my little trip to the palace. This is a heaven-sent opportunity to spend some time together, just the two of us.' He looked into her troubled face and pulled her into his arms. 'Oh, Sally darling, don't look like that. I shan't be gone forever and we'll write to each other, won't we? I'll come up to Town as often as I can. And you can even come and visit me in Cambridge if you like.'

'Why do you have to go so soon?' she asked. 'I thought the term didn't begin till October.'

'It doesn't, but I've been offered the chance to share a set with a couple of other chaps.'

'A set of what?'

'Rooms — lodgings. It'll be cheaper, sharing, but I need to meet them to see if we hit it off and make arrangements for moving in.'

'I see.'

'Look, I vote we get some lunch here. You'll like this place.' He looked at her. 'You are hungry, aren't you?'

She shook her head. 'Not very.'

'You will be when you see the menu,' he told her. 'They do a wonderful game pie here — pastry that melts in the mouth and locally shot birds.'

Sally shuddered slightly. All that country stuff! It only pointed up for her the ever-widening gulf between them.

Back at Gower Street there was a postcard for Sally from her grandmother.

Dear Sally, My old friend Ada Briggs is going into hospital with her leg next month so I'll be coming up to see her. I'll be staying at Bethnal Green with Ada's daughter Mary. I'll ring you at the number you gave me in your letter and we'll meet up. Hoping this finds you as it leaves me. Love from Gran.

Sally put the card into her handbag. Maybe Gran could answer some of the questions that were buzzing round in her head. Meantime she was too preoccupied with the thought of Stephen's imminent departure to think about it.

The three days and nights that followed were blissful. Stephen took her to all the places she'd never visited, Kew Gardens, The Tower and Hampton Court. They went to the cinema and saw *The Wicked Lady*, a thrilling tale about a female highwayman, and *Brief Encounter*, a sad film about an impossible romance that made Sally cry. It reminded her too painfully of the brief encounter that she and Stephen had enjoyed for she was convinced that it was destined to be brief. By sharing these last days with him she knew she was making the future even harder for herself, but it would have been impossible to resist this opportunity to have him all to herself for three precious days. Every night when he held her in his arms after their rapturous lovemaking she stored the memory deep inside her heart, knowing that she must make the best of what she had of him now, cherishing each and every kiss and caress, every loving look and tender word.

★ ★ ★

At Moon Cottage Fiona managed to persuade Nanny Joan to take things easy after their busy days preserving produce. She rose early herself to feed the hens and collect the eggs. Now that the season was coming to an end there was less to do in the market garden and to her surprise Nanny agreed to stay in bed later in the mornings, though she drew the line at the suggestion of breakfast in bed. On the day they went to market it was clear to Fiona that Nanny was feeling ill. At the end of the day she looked utterly exhausted and willingly agreed to let Fiona drive the pick-up home and make supper while she rested. But even then, when Fiona asked her if she was feeling all right her answer was the same.

'Bless you child, of course I am. Just not getting any younger, that's all.'

'Then maybe it's time you had more help around the place,' Fiona suggested. 'Or even retired.'

Nanny's eyes opened wide. '*Retire?* My dear girl, I'm not ready for that yet. No, I hope to carry this place on for many a year yet. If I need help there's always old Jerry Makepeace, at the end of the lane. He's always glad to earn himself a few extra shillings.'

'Well, if you say so. But you'll have to take more care of yourself. Slow down a little,' Fiona said. To her mind Nanny was looking alarmingly pale and drawn and still surreptitiously rubbing her back when she thought no one was looking. But she knew better than to press the subject further.

She had planned to drive back to London on Monday morning, the van packed with jars of the produce they had conserved for their store cupboard at home. As usual she was up early to feed the hens and vacuum round the kitchen and living room. She was a little surprised when she came in from the garden to find that Nanny wasn't up so, on impulse made breakfast and carried a tray upstairs to her.

There was no response to her tap on the door and when she pushed it open the sight that met her eyes filled her with horror. Nanny Joan lay on top of the bedclothes half dressed, her body twisted and her face ashen and contorted with agony. Fiona put the tray down and hurried across the room.

'*Nanny!* What is it — what's wrong?'

Between clenched teeth the older woman ground out the words, 'Pain. It's terrible.'

'Where, Nanny? Where does it hurt?'

'My back.'

'Maybe you've strained something. I'm going downstairs to ring for the doctor.' For once Nanny didn't argue and Fiona ran down the stairs and dialled the number with shaking fingers.

Half an hour later as the doctor came down the stairs Fiona was waiting at the bottom, her face anxious. 'What is it, Doctor? Has she pulled a muscle?'

He shook his head. 'I'm afraid it's more serious than that. I suspect a kidney stone,' he told her. 'May I use your telephone to ring for an ambulance? She needs an immediate X-ray and if I'm right, an operation.'

Fiona rode in the ambulance to the hospital with Nanny, holding her hand and reassuring her all the way that she would look after everything at Moon Cottage. 'Just you concentrate on getting well, she said, patting her hand. 'I'll get Jerry Makepeace in to help and I'll stay on just as long as you're laid up.'

She saw Nanny settled at the hospital. An X-ray had confirmed the doctor's diagnosis and she was to have an operation that afternoon. Before she left to catch the bus back to Fairfield the ward sister gave her a list of the things Nanny would need once she was back on the ward and told her to ring around four o'clock that afternoon for news.

Getting off the bus at the end of the lane Fiona decided to call in at Jerry Makepeace's cottage to tell him about Nanny. Jerry was a tiny man of indeterminate age. His back was bent but there was strength in the sinewy arms and hands. His kindly face was as wrinkled and brown as an over-ripe apple and his bright blue eyes were full of compassion as he listened to Fiona's news.

'Dear me, I'm right sorry to hear that, miss,' he said. 'A lovely woman, Mrs Harvey is. Strong as an ox an' all. She's been right good to me, she has. But truth to tell I've thought for a week or two now that there were somethin' up. Right poorly she bin lookin'. But don't you worry miss. I'll see everything's kept in order, never you fear. I'll be up there first thing in the mornin'.'

Back at Moon Cottage Fiona rang Sally. 'I was right. Nanny's ill,' she said. 'It's a kidney stone. They've taken her into hospital and she has to have an operation so I'll have to stay on here for a while. You'd better cancel all our bookings till further notice, until we see how Nanny gets on. Oh, and could you let Stephen know please?'

'Of course I will. Oh, Fee, I'm so sorry. Give her my love when you see her and don't worry about things here.'

Fiona busied herself around the house and garden for the rest of the day, trying to take her mind off Nanny and her operation. She could not shake off the memory of her white face that morning, contorted with pain. The mere idea of anything awful happening to her was unthinkable. Nanny had always been there for her and Stephen. Just the thought of her not being around any more was enough to bring tears to her eyes. She hardly knew how to wait for the hands of the clock to move round to four o'clock.

At half past three she made herself a cup of tea, her eyes on the clock. The moment the hands moved round to four she went into the hall and dialled the number of the hospital, holding her breath as the receptionist put her through to the ward.

'Miss Harvey?' the sister's voice was brisk and efficient. 'Yes, her operation was successful. A large kidney stone was removed. She's now back on the ward and recovering comfortably.'

'Oh, thank you. I'm so glad,' Fiona said, her voice trembling with relief. 'May I visit her this evening?'

'I'd rather you left it till tomorrow,' Sister said. 'She's still very groggy from the anaesthetic. I don't think you'd get much sense out of her and she needs rest. No doubt she'll be pleased to see you tomorrow though. Visiting from two till four.'

Fiona immediately rang Sally and gave her the news. When she replaced the receiver she found that she was shaking. 'Pull yourself together,' she told herself. 'Nanny's going to be all right so what's biting you?' But nevertheless the tears of relief spilled over to run down her cheeks.

She made herself a sandwich for supper, and then decided to go upstairs and pack the things she knew Nanny would want once she recovered from the operation. In the bedroom at the front of the cottage she began to open drawers. Nanny had always been a very private person and it felt like an intrusion, but she knew she must put together the list of things the sister had given her, plus other things she knew Nanny would want.

She found the essentials, clean nightdresses, a hairbrush, comb and hairpins. Nanny's dressing gown hung behind the door. It was the same blue one she had always had and as Fiona fingered the well-remembered soft material she recalled disturbed nights when she and Stephen had been feverish with childhood illnesses. It had always been a serene-faced Nanny who had come in to comfort them, her long plait down her back and wearing the same blue gown. She held it against her face now and breathed in the familiar smell of lavender and rosewater that would always remind her of Nanny Joan.

She collected toothbrush, soap, flannel and talcum powder from the bathroom then went back to the bedroom to find a sponge bag in which to put them. The dressing-table drawers seemed to hold everything and anything except what she was looking for, which was hardly surprising as Nanny hardly ever went away from Moon Cottage. Fiona told herself that it was high time they took her away for a holiday. Maybe when she was well enough . . .

She opened the bottom drawer to find that it was almost empty except for a large chocolate box with a picture of kittens on the lid. Fiona opened it. Inside was a bundle of letters tied with a faded ribbon. They looked as though they had been there a long time. Love letters? She put them aside. There were two tiny baby shoes — hers and Stephen's? There was also a bundle of diaries held together with an elastic band. The top one bore the year that Stephen had been born. Shuffling briefly through them Fiona saw that they covered the period that Nanny had spent at Saltmere St Peter.

Sitting on the floor she began to read Nanny's

record of Stephen's babyhood, his first baby laugh, his first words and faltering steps. But in the second diary everything changed. Fiona was soon aware that she was reading something not meant for her eyes, but she could not resist turning the pages. The entries became brief, in places they were written almost in a kind of shorthand. One entry read. '*Oh God help me!*' Another, '*If only it can really be as he says. Please God let it be.*' After that there were several blank pages and then, then she came to the one that was written on her own birthday. '*The most adorable baby girl born five a.m. today. She is to be called Fiona.*'

Fiona let the diary drop back into the box. What did it all mean? What had made Nanny so unhappy? Then, at the bottom of the box she noticed another envelope, a long brown one. It was unsealed and there was nothing written on the outside. Looking inside Fiona saw that it was a copy of Nanny's will. She sat for a long time with the document in her hand, turning it over and over, knowing that she was not meant to see it. She already felt guilty about reading the diaries. She should not betray Nanny's confidence by looking at her will. Just contemplating it felt like tempting fate. Nevertheless, as she slowly unfolded the document she saw with surprise that it was quite brief and could be read almost at a glance.

I bequeath the whole of my estate, the property known as Moon Cottage and its contents, all adjacent lands and outbuildings, implements, vehicles, livestock and moneys to Fiona Crowther, adopted daughter of Donald and Marcia Crowther, of Saltmere Manor, Saltmere St Peter, Suffolk.

Adopted daughter? For a long moment Fiona sat staring numbly at the words. What on earth could it mean? Then, pushing the will back into its envelope and closing the drawer she ran downstairs. Locking up the cottage she set off urgently for Saltmere St Peter.

★ ★ ★

'Why didn't you tell me that I was adopted?'

Fiona faced her parents across the dining table where they were finishing their evening meal. Donald stood up.

'Sit down, Fiona. You're obviously upset.'

'You *bet* I'm upset! But before I go any further, you might be interested to hear that Nanny Joan is in hospital. She had a major operation this afternoon to remove a kidney stone.'

'I'm sure we're sorry to hear that,' Marcia said coolly. 'But I don't see what . . . '

'I was packing some things to take in for her when I found a copy of her will,' Fiona interrupted. 'In it she names *me* as her sole beneficiary — Fiona Crowther, *adopted* daughter of Donald and Marcia Crowther, it says.' She sat down heavily, her legs suddenly too weak to support her. 'I think you owe me an explanation.' She looked from one to the other. 'And I need it *now* please.'

All the colour had left Marcia's face. She rose from the table and went out of the room without a word. Fiona looked at her father.

'Well — I suppose that leaves you,' she said.

Donald sighed. He got up and went to the sideboard where he poured two glasses of whisky. Coming back to the table he put one on the table in front of Fiona. 'Drink that,' he said. 'You look as though you need it.'

Fiona sipped the spirit and felt it sear her throat and warm her chilled blood. 'So, you and Mother adopted me. Don't you think it would have been kinder to have told me yourselves?' She took another sip of the whisky and looked up. 'Just as a matter of interest do you happen to know who my parents are?'

Donald tossed back his whisky in one draught then met her eyes. 'Joan Harvey is your mother,' he said. 'And I am your father, Fiona.' As her mouth dropped open in surprise he went on, 'I have no excuses and it's down to your mother's supreme act of generosity and forgiveness that I've had the privilege of seeing you grow from a beautiful child into a lovely young woman. We all owe everything to her. That is all I'm prepared to say at the moment. If you want the rest of the story you're going to have to ask Joan herself. It wouldn't be right for me to betray her trust.'

'I see. It doesn't matter about mine though!' Fiona stood up. 'Thank you for telling me.'

Donald stood and took a step towards her but she held up her hand to ward him off. 'No, don't! I need some time to think. All this has been a shock. I have to be by myself.'

'Don't go back to Fairfield tonight,' Donald implored. 'You're upset. You shouldn't drive.'

'I'm all right. Let me go, Dad.' She smiled wryly. 'Yes, ironically I can still call you that, can't I? Just let me go.'

She stood for a moment in the hall, her head spinning. A dozen conflicting emotions over-whelmed her. Suddenly her entire existence seemed to be in question, a huge tangle of lies and deceit surrounded her very being and she knew she needed time to unravel it before she would be able to assess how she felt about this shattering revelation. She was reaching for the door handle when a voice from the staircase made her turn.

'Fiona — please come upstairs. I think we need to talk.'

She was about to refuse when she saw Marcia's face. She looked deathly pale.

'I want to explain,' she said. 'It's high time as you have already said. Please.'

Fiona followed her silently up the stairs and into her bedroom. Marcia closed the door. 'Sit down,' she said. 'Please bear with me, Fiona. I have to say all this but it isn't easy. We were so wrong for not telling you.'

'Then why didn't you?'

'It was part of the agreement.'

'What agreement?'

'The one I made with your father and Joan Harvey. You mustn't blame them, Fiona. You mustn't lay all this at their door. I was just as

237

much to blame.' She took a deep breath and began.

'Stephen was just two weeks old when Joan came to take up her position as nanny. He was a beautiful child and she was so good with him. I was just very happy to hand him over to her — relieved that the humiliating business of pregnancy and birth was over. I was never a very maternal woman and I wanted to resume the busy social life I'd enjoyed before. Your father had always wanted more children, but Stephen's birth had been difficult and the doctors advised us that it would be unwise for me to have more children. I have to admit to you now that when I heard those words it was a profound relief.' She turned her head to look at Fiona. 'I made up for lost time as soon as I was well enough. I told myself I deserved it. I was away from home for weeks at a time. There were skiing jaunts to Switzerland, weekend house parties, long summer holidays in Cannes and shopping trips to Paris. Your father couldn't get away very often because of his work in the City and he must have been lonely. I confess to you now that I was selfish enough not to care. I was enjoying myself too much to consider him. I'd done my duty and given him the child he wanted so why should he complain? Donald loved his little son and while I was away he spent all his spare time in the nursery with him — and with Joan of course. She was a very attractive young woman in those days and gradually — over the months, they grew — close. I suppose what happened was inevitable.'

'It must have been a shock.'

'It was. The first I knew was when I discovered that Joan was pregnant with my husband's child.'

Fiona was silent. It was beginning to be clear to her now why her mother had always resented her. Marcia went on,

'At first I ranted and raved — demanded that she be sent packing, but your father was adamant. It was his child and he refused to turn his back. He promised that his affair with Joan would end if I agreed to adopt her child. But the agreement was to include her staying on and caring for you along with Stephen.'

'And you were happy with that?'

'No! Far from it at first, but when I saw that he meant what he said I knew I had little choice.' Marcia gave a little shrug. 'It was that or a divorce and I couldn't face the scandal. Since the war divorce is nothing, but in those days it made you a social outcast. But it was more — *much* more than that. Once I calmed down I realized how foolish I'd been. I loved Donald very much and I'd treated him shabbily. I saw how much my marriage, my son and my life here meant to me and I knew I couldn't bear to lose them.'

'You must have resented me so much,' Fiona said quietly.

'When you were first born I couldn't even bear to look at you,' Marcia said. 'I went to the nursery as little as possible and refused to allow you to be brought downstairs with Stephen in the evenings. But Donald was besotted with you. He had always wanted a daughter. He insisted on spending time with you every day and the only way he could do that was to go up to the nursery. I soon saw that although he had kept his word that the affair would be over, I was forcing him back into Joan's arms.'

In the pause that followed she reached out to touch Fiona's hand. 'You might find this hard to believe, but although I was obliged to let you into my life it wasn't long before I was enchanted by you too. You were an adorable baby and it would have taken a very hard-hearted woman not to grow fond of you. But I was always acutely aware that you weren't mine — afraid that one day Joan might want you back — that she would leave and insist on taking you with her. So I kept my distance and concentrated all my efforts on keeping my marriage intact.' She pressed Fiona's hand. 'I'm so sorry, Fiona, if I've appeared not to care for you. But believe me I did — I *do* think of you as my daughter and want the best for you — just as much as if you were mine.'

Fiona looked at the woman she had called 'mother' for the past twenty-six years. The hard lines of dissatisfaction around her mouth seemed to have melted into softness and her eyes were misty with remembered pain. She felt a stab of compassion. How difficult it must have been for Marcia to bring up her husband's lover's child as her own and still keep its mother as an employee in her own house.

'Does Stephen know about this?' she asked.

Marcia shook her head. 'No. You are at liberty to tell him of course, but . . . '

'But you'd rather I didn't.'

240

'For the moment at least.'

Fiona sighed. 'All this is going to take some time to sink in,' she said quietly.

'Of course it is. But can you at least forgive us for keeping you in the dark all these years?'

Fiona looked up with a wry smile. 'It seems to me that three people made great sacrifices for me. How could I not forgive them?'

Next afternoon Fiona went to the hospital to visit Nanny. She found her propped up in bed looking pale but much better. She bent and kissed her then began to unpack the case she had brought.

'You'll feel better in your own nightdress,' she said, 'And I've brought your dressing gown and slippers and all your toilet things.'

Nanny smiled. 'Thank you dear. I'm sorry to put you to all this trouble.'

'Of course it's no trouble.' Fiona pulled a chair up beside the bed. 'I brought you some flowers too. The nurse is putting them in water. And you're not to worry about things at home. Jerry Makepeace is seeing to everything and he sends you his regards and hopes you'll soon be well again. How are you feeling?'

'A bit sore, but a thousand times better than yesterday. I'm sure they'll let me out of here in a few days and then you can go back to . . . '

'No!' Fiona held up her hand. 'You're not even to think of it. I'm going to stay on for as long as you need me and look after you. After all you've done for me it's good to have a way of repaying you.'

'All that I've done?'

Fiona took her hand and bent close. 'Nanny

— I know,' she whispered. 'While I was looking for your things I found the box with all your mementos — and your will. I know I was wrong to look and I have to beg your forgiveness for that. But now that I know . . . '

'Oh my dear.' Nanny was biting her lip. 'This wasn't what I intended. Have you told anyone else?'

'I went straight home and demanded an explanation,' Fiona said. 'Dad told me the bare facts, but later Mother told me the full story.'

Nanny was shaking her head. 'I'm so sorry you had to find out like this,' she said. 'You weren't meant to know until I was gone.'

'I'm glad I know,' Fiona gripped her hand tightly. 'But I would like to hear your side of the story.'

Nanny lay back against the pillows, the colour slowly returning to her cheeks. 'I was twenty-eight when I first went to Saltmere Manor. I'd been engaged to a wonderful man who was killed in the Great War. The letters in the box are from him. I felt just as you did when Mark was killed, convinced I would never love again — never have the family we'd planned. She looked at Fiona. 'I thought that my life was over.'

Fiona drew her chair closer. 'Oh, Nanny.'

'Stephen was a joy. He was left completely in my charge. Your mother was a very popular socialite before he was born. She was beautiful and accomplished and as soon as she had regained her health and her slender figure she was eager to resume the whirl of society events she had given up. She was away a lot and Donald was lonely. He spent a lot of time with Stephen and me and — I'm ashamed to say that we fell in love.' She sighed. 'When I look back now I see that it was loneliness and our mutual love for Stephen that drew us together. Normally he would never have looked at someone like me.' She reached for the glass of water by the bed and took a sip. 'When I first discovered that I was pregnant I was shocked — at my wits' end wondering what to do. It was such a disgrace. I thought I would have to go away and the thought of having to leave my darling little Stephen and bringing shame on my parents broke my heart.'

'So what happened?'

'Donald took charge. He was very firm about it — insisted that he would stand by me and our child and see that we didn't suffer. He told Marcia and presented her with an ultimatum. He promised that his association with me would end on condition that she agreed to adopt my child so that he could bring it up as his own. He also insisted that she was to let me stay on afterwards and care for you.'

'I know. Mother told me.'

'It must have seemed like a terrible punishment to her and I believe she eventually agreed because deep down she loved your father very much. His confession made her see how much she had neglected him and I suspect she wasn't entirely innocent herself. There were several handsome young men who paid court to her. But she saw the error of her ways and that as a result she might lose her husband and their marriage. There was the scandal too. That would have been hard to bear.'

'It must have been so hard for her to trust him again.'

'Oh, he kept his promise,' Nanny said. 'From that day he made sure that he and I were never alone again. You were born in a small discreet private nursing home and immediately adopted to be brought up as a Crowther.'

'And no one else ever knew about this?'

'No one.'

'How could you bear to stay on?' Fiona asked.

'How could I bear to leave?' Nanny smiled wryly. 'It was my only chance to be with my daughter — with you.'

Fiona sat back with a sigh. 'I don't know if I could have done what she did — or what you did either.' Looking up she saw with concern that the colour had left Nanny's cheeks. She lay back against the pillows looking tired and drained. 'Nanny?' She touched her cheek. 'Nanny, are you all right?'

The ward sister hovered at the end of the bed. 'Now now, Miss Harvey,' she said, stern-faced. 'I think we've been overdoing it a little, haven't we?' She reached for Nanny's wrist, looking at her fob watch and shaking her head. 'Mmm. I think she's had enough for today, Miss Crowther. After all, it's early days after such a major operation. So if you wouldn't mind . . . '

'Of course.' Fiona stood up and bent to kiss Nanny's cheek. 'Rest now. I'll see you tomorrow,' she said, then leaning close she whispered, 'Thank you, darling Nanny — for telling me your story and for *everything*. I love you very, *very* much.'

13

Moon Cottage seemed very quiet without Nanny. Fiona rose early next morning and did the morning chores. At eight o'clock Jerry arrived to do the heavy work. She was just finishing her breakfast when the telephone rang.

'Hello. Moon Cottage Nursery.'

'Fee, it's me, Sally. How is Nanny?'

Fiona winced. 'Sally! I'm so sorry. I should have rung you last night. Rather a lot has happened and it went right out of my head. Nanny is fine. Her operation was successful and she's recovering well.'

'What a relief. Give her my love if you go to see her today,' Sally said. 'Stephen and I thought we'd come over on Sunday. I can't come before because of my spot at the club. Did you know that he's off to Cambridge at the weekend?'

'Is he — so soon?'

'Something about sharing some rooms and getting all his arrangements sorted out.'

'I see. We'll miss him.'

'I know. I'm trying not to think about it at the moment. Fee, I've taken two bookings for parties. I've talked to Annie and she's happy to help me. As they only want buffet food we thought we'd have a go by ourselves. Are you all right with that?'

'Of course, if you are.'

'I don't know how long you'll have to stay

there with Nanny, but I worry that we might lose the reputation we've built up if we keep turning business down.'

'I know. Me too.' Fiona bit her lip. 'I'm going to have to put my thinking cap on. There's no question of letting Nanny down of course but we'll have to think of something.'

'She wouldn't come back to Gower Street with us, would she?'

'I don't think so. I've got a local man helping out at the moment, but I know Nanny wouldn't want to be away from the place.'

'I suppose not. Don't worry, we'll think of something. See you on Sunday then.'

'I'm looking forward to seeing you both,' Fiona said. 'And I'll try to cook a Nanny Joan style Sunday lunch.'

'Ooh, lovely.' Sally laughed. 'Can't wait!'

★   ★   ★

Sally and Stephen arrived at Moon Cottage soon after midday on Sunday. It had been hard for Sally to get up early after her late night cabaret spot at the club, but she had made the effort and enjoyed the drive. It was a beautiful morning with a hint of autumn in the crisp early September air and as they drew up outside Moon Cottage Stephen turned to her.

'Well, here we are. I don't suppose I'll be seeing much of this place for a while.'

Or of me, Sally told herself inwardly. Aloud she said, 'I'm sure you'll make time for Nanny when you're home in the holidays — if no one else.'

He looked wistfully at her. 'I'm going to miss you terribly, Sally.' He took her face between his hands. 'Three years is a long time. Are you sure you want to wait that long?'

'We-ell,' she pursed her lips doubtfully. 'Maybe I might — if nothing better turns up.'

'Do you think it will?'

'Who knows?' She shrugged. 'We live in hope.'

'You little . . . ' He grasped her shoulders and shook her gently. 'If I thought for one moment that you meant that I'd . . . '

'Yes — you'd what?'

He kissed her by way of reply then sighed as he hugged her close. 'Oh, I love you very much, Sally Joy. I mean that. You do believe me don't you?'

'I believe you mean it right now this minute,' Sally whispered. 'Whether you will in six months' time is another matter,' she added to herself.

'Are you two going to stay out here all day?' Fiona rapped on the windscreen. 'I've been watching your abandoned behaviour from the window. Get out of there at once the pair of you!'

Laughing, they obeyed and followed her into the cottage where the table was laid in the kitchen and delicious aromas were coming from the Aga.

After lunch they went to visit Nanny in the hospital. They found her sitting up in bed wearing her pink bedjacket and looking much better. Her delight at seeing them brought colour to her cheeks and the old sparkle back into her eyes. Stephen and Sally had brought her flowers and chocolates, bought with their combined sweet rations. She shook her head.

'You really shouldn't spoil me like this. By the time I get out of here I shall require slimming pills!'

'I can't imagine you as a fat lady,' Stephen remarked. 'Which isn't surprising with all that hard work you do.'

She wanted to hear all their news and seemed relieved to hear that Sally and Annie had managed two bookings without Fiona.

'I've heard a lot about Annie,' she remarked. 'She sounds a positive treasure. I'm looking forward to meeting her.'

Back at the cottage Stephen had time only for a quick cup of tea before leaving for Cambridge.

'Something Nanny said this afternoon gave me an idea,' he said. 'She mentioned that she was looking forward to meeting Annie and it struck me that the two of them might hit it off rather well. How it would be if Annie came and stayed with Nanny for a while when she comes out of hospital? It would free Fee up to come home.' He looked at them. 'You could always pop down at weekends to keep an eye on her.'

Fiona looked thoughtful. 'It's certainly an idea,' she said. 'Of course we'd have to see if Annie liked the idea. Then we'd have to ask Mother's permission. Annie is her employee after all. But somehow I don't think she'd have any objections.'

'Annie could come and stay for a couple of days while you're still here to start with,' Sally said. 'Just so that they could get to know one another.'

Stephen looked at his watch and then apologetically at the girls. 'I hate to break up the party but it's time I started out,' he said. 'Are you sure you don't want me to take you home first. Sally?'

She shook her head. 'No. I'll stay the night here with Fee then catch the train back tomorrow.'

Fiona said goodbye to her brother then tactfully left Sally to walk with him to the car. When Stephen drove away she saw that Sally looked preoccupied as she walked back up the path.

'Goodbyes are hell, aren't they?'

Sally sighed. 'This one feels depressingly final,' she said. 'Stevie doesn't believe me but I think he'll soon grow out of me once his new life begins.'

'I'm sure you're wrong,' Fiona said. 'Tell you what — let's have another pot of tea and drown our sorrows.'

Sally watched as she busied herself around the kitchen. 'You said on the phone that a lot had happened,' she said. 'What did you mean?'

Fiona shrugged. 'Oh — just Nanny's illness and everything.'

'It was more than that though, wasn't it? I tried to ring you several times on the night she had her operation. Where were you?'

249

'I went to Saltmere St Peter to see Mother and Dad,' Fiona said, her back to Sally as she put the kettle on.

Sally's eyebrows rose. 'Did you — any particular reason?'

Fiona turned to look at her. It was uncanny sometimes how Sally could almost read her thoughts. 'Something pretty dramatic has happened as a matter of fact. I've longed to talk to someone about it but because of the circumstances there's no one I can tell.'

'There's me. Unless you feel you can't trust me.'

'Of course I can trust you but I'd have to ask you to swear not to tell Stephen.'

'Not if you don't want me to.' Sally frowned. 'It all sounds deadly serious.'

'It is.' Fiona sat down at the table. 'When I was getting some things together to take into the hospital for Nanny I found — well — evidence that I was adopted.'

'Adopted? Sally gasped. 'And you had no idea?'

'None at all. That was why I went to Saltmere St Peter. To get some answers from Mother and Dad.'

'And did you get any?'

'Yes. More than I could ever have imagined. Much more.' Fiona hesitated and Sally said,

'You can tell me — if you want to that is. I promise you it won't go any further than these four walls.'

Fiona paused. 'It's still so hard for me to take in. It seems that I was the outcome of an affair

250

that Dad had with . . . ' She took a deep breath. 'With Nanny Joan.'

Sally's mouth dropped open. 'Oh, Fee!'

'It's a long story,' Fiona said. 'Dad persuaded Mother to adopt me and have me brought up as their own — with Nanny staying on to look after Stevie and me.'

'Phew! That was a lot to ask of any wife.' Sally was thoughtful. She had been brought up to believe that the upper classes were beyond reproach, but it seemed that sometimes their morals were just as questionable as those of ordinary everyday folk. 'So Nanny is your real mother. Hearing that must have been a shock,' she said. 'How do you feel about it?'

Fiona shook her head. 'I'm still trying to come to terms with it to be honest. Poor Nanny, but poor Mother too. As for Dad — they both say he was lonely and unhappy at the time. Mother left him alone a lot after Stevie was born while she went off enjoying herself. It seems like a case of guilt all round and it could so easily have ended in tragedy. The thing is, the three of them have lived with it all these years. To me it's still new and — and shocking.'

Sally was silent for a moment, remembering the conversation she had had with Nanny recently when she mentioned being in love. 'At least your dad stood by you and your real mother,' she said. 'And at least you know who your parents are — and grew up with them around you, which is more than I did.'

Fiona reached out to touch her hand. 'We have even more in common than we realized.'

Sally nodded. 'Gran wrote. She's coming up to London in a couple of weeks. I'm hoping to get a few answers myself when I see her.'

'I owe Nanny so much,' Fiona said. 'What a secret to keep all these years. I keep trying to think of a way to make it up to her.'

'And I'm sure you will,' Sally said. 'But meantime we have to decide how she's going to be looked after without *Dinner At Eight* going to the wall.'

⋆　⋆　⋆

Annie was delighted at the prospect of spending some time in the country and meeting the famous Nanny Joan that she'd heard so much about. Fiona rang her mother and asked her permission to loan Annie to Joan. Marcia seemed a little taken aback, but agreed without argument as Fiona had predicted. The following Friday Fiona drove up to London to cook for a dinner party which had been a long-standing booking. And the following day she took Annie back to Fairfield with her to make ready for Nanny's discharge from hospital early the following week.

Alone at Gower Street the house felt empty. Sally missed Fiona and Annie very much and so far there had only been one hastily written postcard from Stephen. He seemed to be enjoying finding his way round Cambridge and meeting some of his fellow undergraduates. Sally pinned it up above her dressing table mirror at the *Pink Parrot*. To her it was a different world

252

— one where she was convinced she could never fit in.

When Friday evening came round she went off to the club, glad to have something to occupy her and take her mind off Stephen. After the ten-thirty cabaret there was a tap on her dressing room door and she opened it to find a familiar face smiling at her.

'*Jenny*! How lovely to see you. What are you doing here?'

'Max said it was all right to pop in and see you. Is that all right?'

'Of course. Come in.'

'Gerry and I saw your poster outside,' Jenny explained. 'And we decided we had to come and see you. You were great, Sally. I love your frock and your songs went down really well.'

'You're looking well,' Sally told her. 'Married life seems to agree with you.'

Jenny smiled. 'I can recommend it. Any news yet about you and Stephen?'

'No. He's gone to Cambridge now. I don't suppose I'll be seeing much of him in the future.'

'Why? Did you fall out?'

'No. It was never serious anyway.' Sally changed the subject. 'How was the honeymoon?'

'Oh, lovely,' Jenny said with a sigh. 'Bournemouth is such a lovely place, Sally. The weather was smashing and you should see the beach and the gardens. And the shops! As good as the West End.' She glanced at her watch. 'Better be going I suppose. I'm on an early shift in the morning. You won't forget where we live, will you, Sall? Mum'd love to

253

see you when you've got some spare time.'

'I won't forget,' Sally told her. 'Gran's coming up next week, so I daresay she'll be popping in on your mum.'

When Jenny had gone Sally sat down at her dressing table with a sigh. Seeing her old friend made her nostalgic for the old days when they'd been children. Sometimes lately she had the feeling that she hardly knew who she was or where she belonged any more.

'Are you decent? Can I come in?' Max put his head round the door.

'Yes, come in, Max.'

'Fancy sharing a spot of supper with me?' He drew up a chair and sat astride it, watching her as she repaired her make-up. 'You're looking a bit fed up tonight,' he said. 'I thought seeing Jenny might cheer you up.'

'Oh, it did. It was lovely to see her.'

'But not enough to put the smile back on your face, eh? Want to tell Uncle Max all about it?'

She sighed. 'I miss Stevie,' she admitted. 'And with Fee and Annie away too I feel a bit deserted.'

'Poor kid,' he said, reaching out to touch her hand. 'Tell you what, I've got some smoked salmon.' He tapped the side of his nose. 'Best Scottish. Ask no questions. How about I go down the kitchen and order us some sandwiches and a bottle of bubbly?'

Laughing, she agreed and he reappeared fifteen minutes later with a tray and ice bucket. As they were sharing the sandwiches and champagne Max asked if Ian had been around lately.

'Haven't seen him for weeks,' she said. 'Fee and he were getting along well, but something must have happened. She lost her fiancé in the war and I don't think she really ever got over it.'

'Pity. Got his head screwed on the right way, that lad. He's got the magic touch with engines and he's a good salesman too. That little business has really taken off since I took him on.' He shook his head. 'Pity about him and your mate, Fiona. Life's too short to pass up any opportunity to be happy.' He looked thoughtfully at her. 'Grab everything while you can. That's my motto.' He looked at her over the rim of his glass. 'So — you really stuck on this Stephen of yours, are you?'

She shrugged. 'I suppose you could say that. Not that I'm holding out too many hopes.'

'What's the snag? Bit of a playboy, is he?'

'No, it's just that he's out of my class. We come from very different backgrounds. It could never work.'

'Well — maybe you're right.' Max re-filled her glass. 'Personally I think he'd be a mug to let you go. Lovely, talented girl like you.'

'It was different when the war was on,' she said. 'We were all equal then. But now we're all finding our own level again. I'm OK as a girlfriend for Stevie. But I don't flatter myself that I've got what he'd need in a wife, 'specially when he's a barrister.'

'Barrister, eh?' Max shrugged. 'Still, you shouldn't worry. What's so special about being someone's missis? Plenty more fish in the sea.'

'That's not very helpful when you're in love.'

'You're just a kid. You'll get over it when someone else comes along.' He looked at his watch. 'Hey, look at the time. Better get up to the office. The cashier will be leaving off soon and I'll need to stash the takings away in the safe.' At the door he turned to her. 'Got a lift home tonight, have you?'

She shook her head. 'No. I'll get a cab.'

'Not on your nelly you won't! Just tip me the wink when you're ready and I'll run you home.' And without waiting for a reply he was gone.

After the midnight show Sally went back to the dressing room and changed. As she came out into the corridor Max was waiting for her.

'Car's out the front,' he told her. 'Have you home in no time.'

Sally settled back into the passenger seat of Max's comfortable car as they drove through the almost deserted streets.

'I still can't get used to seeing all the lights on again,' she remarked. There was now a blown-up photograph of her displayed outside the club. In it she was wearing the red dress. A photographer friend of Max's had taken it one evening as she worked. There was now a small neon sign too. It was pink and flashed on and off but Sally thought that the rudimentary bird on it looked even less like a parrot than the one on the previous sign.

Max was looking at her thoughtfully. 'You know, there's no need for you to go back up West at weekends really,' he said. 'There's the flat over the shop. It's empty and I've got no plans for letting it at the moment. You could always stay over there Friday and Saturday nights.'

'It's kind of you to think of it, Max. But I think I'd rather go home.'

'OK. But the offer's open if you change your mind.'

As Max drew up outside 28 Gower Street he turned to her. 'I reckon that bloke of yours wants his head testing.'

Sally laughed. 'What makes you say that?'

He slid an arm along the back of her seat. 'Lovely girl like you — wouldn't catch me going off to no Cambridge and leavin' you on your tod.'

'Why, do you think I'm not to be trusted?'

He chuckled. 'It's the blokes I wouldn't trust.' His dark eyes burned into hers and Sally felt for the door handle.

'It's late. I'd better be going. Thanks for the lift, Max.'

The arm that lay on the back of the seat suddenly dropped on to her shoulders and his hand cupped her shoulder to pull her close. Before she could stop him he was kissing her. She pushed him away.

'Max — don't.'

'Ah, give me a break, Sall,' he whispered. 'I've been wantin' to do that ever since I first set eyes on you at Jenny's wedding. I was always sweet on you when we were kids at school. What's a little kiss among old friends? We're two of a kind, you'n'me.'

'It's late. I have to go, Max.' She moved away

but he held on to her hand.

'No hard feelin's then? You know me, gel. I don't mean no harm.'

'No — 'course not.'

'An' I meant what I said about the flat over the shop. No strings mind. Remember that eh?'

'Yes — I will.'

'OK. See you next Saturday then — yes?'

'Yes. Goodnight, Max.'

On the pavement she watched with dismay as his car drove down the street and turned the corner. If he was going to start behaving like that she was going to have to abandon her cabaret at the *Pink Parrot*. And that would mean losing the money they were saving up to pay Donald back for the van. Oh, why did life have to be so complicated?

★   ★   ★

Fiona left Annie at Moon Cottage while she collected Nanny from the hospital.

'I can't wait to get home to my own bed,' Nanny remarked as they drove. 'I'm grateful to the hospital and all they did for me of course but there's no place like home.'

'You've got to promise me you won't try to do too much,' Fiona said. 'Annie's got strict instructions to watch you like a hawk. If you let me down I shall have to come back again to look after you.'

'Don't worry, I'll be fine. I'm looking forward to some nice long chats with Annie, and Jerry will make sure that everything's running as it

258

should. As for the market, I shall have to give that a miss for a few weeks.'

'No need. Jerry has the market sorted out,' Fiona told her. 'He and some of the other stallholders are going to man your stall between them, so no worries about wasted produce. And I'll be checking up on you remember, so you'd better behave yourself,' she added.

'I'm glad you're going back to London,' Nanny said. 'Oh, it's not that I won't miss you, because I will. But you do need to look after that business of yours, and you'll be able to catch up with that nice young man, Ian. He must be missing you.'

'Ian and I haven't seen each other for quite some time,' Fiona said.

'Oh — why is that?'

Fiona turned to look at her. 'We both decided that there wasn't any point.'

'What a terrible thing to say!' Nanny looked at her. 'Fiona. Stop the car a moment. I want to speak to you and what I have to say is between the two of us.'

With a resigned sigh Fiona pulled up at the side of the country road. 'All right. What have I done now?'

Nanny reached out and took her hand. 'It's more what you haven't done, dear. Now that you've discovered the truth about — what happened all those years ago I was hoping you might learn from it? Like you, I thought I could never feel deeply for any man again, let alone fall in love, but I was wrong. My trouble was that I fell in love with the wrong man and I had to pay the price.'

'Nanny — it must have been agony for you.'

'It was, all those years of having to let you believe you were someone else's child. It should never have happened. It wouldn't if I hadn't tried to shut myself off.'

'Shut yourself off.'

'I thought that by applying for a job in the country and engrossing myself in someone else's child I could escape from life and its temptations. I think you're making a similar mistake, Fiona, and it's asking for trouble. Fate always wins in the end no matter how hard we try to cheat her. You're still young. You should *live* life — accept what fate offers. If you don't she has a nasty habit of paying you back.'

Fiona smiled. 'I'm not sure I believe in all that fate stuff. Dear Nanny. It must have been so hard for you.'

'It was, so don't make me watch you relive it.' The older woman pressed her hand. 'You're fond of him, aren't you dear?'

Fiona nodded, tears pricking her eyes. 'Yes.'

'Then don't waste any more time. Get in touch with him — tell him you were wrong.'

'I — I'll think about it.'

'Don't think too long then dear. Promise me?'

'I promise, Nanny.'

★　★　★

By the time Sally got in it was after one o'clock and Fiona was already in bed. She had left a note on the kitchen table. It said, *Hello, Sally. It's good to be home, but I'm really tired so forgive me for not waiting up. See you at breakfast in the morning.*

With the house to themselves the girls breakfasted late in the kitchen next morning in their dressing gowns, catching up on the news as they ate.

'Nanny Joan and Annie seem to get along like a house on fire, thank goodness,' Fiona said. 'I feel quite confident leaving Nanny in her care. Annie won't let her do too much. They're a good match for each other when it comes to determination.' She buttered another slice of toast. 'How are things at the club?'

Sally sighed. 'Fine. Jenny popped in to see me last night. She looked fine and it was lovely to see her.' She paused. 'Trouble is, something rather worrying has cropped up.'

'What's that?'

'Max seems to be getting some strange ideas about us.'

'Us?'

'Him and me.'

'You mean he made a pass?'

'Yes.'

'Oh. I was afraid that might happen.'

'He's even offered me the flat above the shop so that I can stay over at weekends. I'm not quite sure what he has in mind.'

Fiona looked sceptical. 'Oh, I think I've got a pretty good idea.'

'I suppose I'll just have to play it by ear,' Sally said. 'If he gets too amorous I shall have to leave,

261

which would be a shame when we still owe the van money to your dad.'

'Sally — you don't have to put up with Max's unwanted attentions just because of the money,' Fiona said. 'You don't have to do anything you don't want to. In fact, thinking about it, Dad probably owes me a few favours after what he did.'

'Don't be too hard on him,' Sally said. 'It happened a long time ago after all. Your dad is a lovely man and he *is* still your father when all's said and done.'

'Mmm.' Fiona looked doubtful. 'I'm still having trouble even thinking of him as a philanderer, let alone forgiving him.'

'If he hadn't done what he did you probably wouldn't even be here,' Sally reminded her.

'Do you think that makes it any easier?'

'There's nothing you can do about it,' Sally said. 'And nothing's changed. You have three parents instead of the two most people have. In my case I only have one — one I've hardly ever set eyes on at that.'

'That reminds me, when is your grandmother due?'

'Wednesday,' Sally said. 'I promised to meet her train and take her out to lunch.' She smiled at Fiona over the rim of her teacup. 'Who knows, there could be some surprises in store for me.'

14

The coach from Southend was due in at Victoria at twelve o'clock and Sally was waiting to meet her grandmother when it drew in. It was almost two years since she and Gran had last met and Sally wondered whether she would have aged. But the elderly woman who stepped off the coach looked fit and well. Lizzie Joy's hair, once worn scraped back into a severe bun, had been cut and permed, and the smart green coat she wore was in the latest style with a jaunty hat to match. When she saw Sally waiting for her, her face lit up in a smile.

'Sall! Well now, you're a sight for sore eyes and no mistake.' She kissed her granddaughter and held her at arms' length. 'Let me look at you. You're as pretty as ever.' She frowned. 'A bit on the thin side for my liking though. You eatin' properly my gel?'

Sally laughed. ''Course I am, Gran. Fee and I work with food. Do you think we'd go short ourselves? But look at you. It's obvious you're doing well. How's Auntie Edna?'

'I'll tell you when I've got a cup of tea in front of me,' Gran said. 'I'm so dry I'm spittin' feathers!'

When they were seated opposite each other in a nearby café Sally repeated her question. 'How's the guesthouse? This was your first summer season, taking boarders wasn't it?'

Gran took a long draught of her tea and nodded with satisfaction. 'All the servicemen comin' home and wantin' a holiday — second honeymoon in some cases. Oh yes, we've done really well. Season's just about over now and Edna'n'me are planning to spend some of our profits on doin' the place up over the winter. We're gonna get a decorator in to smarten the place up and we're plannin' to have wash hand basins put in all the bedrooms.' She nodded proudly. 'Not many boardin' houses can offer that. Hot'n'cold runnin' water in all rooms. That'll look good in the adverts for next summer.'

'Sounds really posh, Gran. I'll have to come down and stay myself.'

'That you will, gel. It's been far too long. Edna does all the cookin' and she's a wonder. Never wastes a thing. Why throw away all your profits, she says. You should taste the shepherd's pie she makes from leftovers.'

Sally smiled to herself, wondering what Fiona would make of left-over shepherd's pie. 'Can't wait to taste it,' she said.

'I'm gonna take Ada back with me for a little holiday when she comes out of hospital,' Gran said. 'Now the season's over we've got plenty of room an' the sea air'll do her a power of good.' She looked at Sally. 'You said in your letter there were things you wanted to ask,' she said.

'Yes. I sent off to Somerset House for a copy of my birth certificate and there are a few things I'd like to know about my mum,' Sally said. 'You and Grandpa never spoke about her much.'

264

'Less said about 'er, the better, more's the pity,' Gran said disapprovingly. 'Come on then, cough up — what d'you want to know love?'

'Why did she leave me like that when I was a baby to start with? And who was my father? It says 'unknown' on the birth certificate.'

'Oh.' The smile left Gran's face. 'Now you're askin' gel. What difference do you think it'd make, knowin'? Sometimes it's best to let sleepin' dogs lie.'

'That's all very well,' Sally said. 'But I need to know who I am, Gran and why Mum just threw me aside like some old piece of rubbish.' She paused. 'I know that she was married but on the certificate her name was different from mine. Does that mean that her husband wasn't my dad?'

'Oh my dear Lord, you don't wanna know much, do you?' Gran sighed and looked around. 'Look, there ain't no privacy in this place. Can we go somewhere quieter?'

They deposited Gran's case in the Left Luggage and walked along the embankment. It was a warm and mellow autumn day and they chose a seat and sat to watch the busy river traffic for a while. Gran had been quiet as they walked and when at last she began to speak her face was solemn.

'Your mum was only seventeen when she got married. Your grandpa and me thought she was far too young, but she was always a wilful gel and she thought she knew best. Jim Mays was in the Merchant Navy. Ten years older than her. He was a sober enough young feller — for a sailor

265

— and we thought maybe someone older would be good for her, keep her in order like. Well, he used to be away at sea for months at a time. They lived down in Southampton and Ethel used to get fed up on her own, so she'd come home to stay with us for a while.' Gran paused and glanced at Sally. 'She used to go off out in the evenin's. Never said where she was goin' and your grandpa and me — we never asked no questions. Knew we'd get a flea in our ears if we did. She thought now she was married she could do as she liked. Well, she met this chap again. She'd known him from when they was kids at school. He was always talented with his music and when he left school he got a job with a dance band. Ethel met him at some dance or other where he was singin' with the band.'

'So what was his name?' Sally asked impatiently, but Gran shook her head.

'All in good time. Well, as I was sayin', Ethel met up with him again while she was home this particular time and they fell for each other, or so she said. Personally I reckon it was just his glamorous life that took her fancy. Anyway, next thing we knew, she'd fallen pregnant with you.'

'What happened, Gran?'

'Well, Ethel was terrified of Jim findin' out o'course. No way she could pass the baby off as his. He'd been away too long. She said he'd half kill her! There was never no question of this other feller stickin' around. He'd already made that clear. He 'ad big ideas. He was goin' places and he didn't intend to be lumbered with no hangers-on. Once he knew she was up the duff he took off sharpish, leavin' no address and Ethel was left to work things out as best she could.'

'Did her husband find out?'

'No. Ethel managed to keep the pregnancy from him in the early stages and he went back to sea before she started showin'. She came to us, had the baby — you — and when Jim was due in port again she went back home and left you with us.'

'And never even came back to see me?'

'She thought it best for all concerned if she stayed away. And I have to say that we was inclined to agree with her. Ethel was never what you'd call the motherly type.'

'That must have been very convenient for her,' Sally said bitterly. 'So was he — my — this chap — ever heard of again?'

'Oh, I should say so! He got spotted by some big agent up West soon afterwards and made quite a name for himself as a crooner. During the war he made a big comeback. He was hardly ever off the wireless and he went all over, entertainin' the troops an' that. All the gels used to queue up for his autograph, screamin' their heads off an' all that rubbish.'

Sally's curiosity was really aroused now. 'So — are you going to tell me his name or not?' she asked again.

'You're gonna be shocked.'

'I'm used to shocks.'

'And you're gonna have to promise me you won't make no trouble.'

'Not much point now anyway, is there?'

'That's right. Too much water's gone under

267

the bridge. There wouldn't be nothing to gain.'

'What — you think I'd try to cash in?'

'No, 'course not.

'So — who is he then?'

'You'll've heard of Johnny Starr.'

'Of course. Who hasn't?' Sally gasped. 'Wait a minute — are you saying Johnny Starr is *my* *father*? You're joking! We used to listen to his records all the time when we were at the factory.'

Gran nodded. 'Give him his due, he's got a smashin' voice. I reckon that's where you get it from.'

'Well, at least he gave me something!'

'His real name was Lenny Willetts,' Gran went on. 'His mum was one of our customers in the old days when we first had the shop. Never had two pennies to rub together — always after damaged fruit and what veg we had left at the end of the day, poor cow. Always up the pawn shop of a Monday mornin' with 'er Sunday coat. Lenny bought her a posh house over Stanmore way when he made his pile. I'll say that for him. He was good to his old mum.'

'Did he marry — have any children of his own?' Sally asked.

'Yes, I read a bit about him in the paper some years back. He married a dancer and they had a little boy, but he died of diphtheria.' She shook her head. 'Some might say it was a judgement on him.'

Sally shivered. 'Come on, Gran. It's time we made a move. It's beginning to get cold. We'll find somewhere to have lunch.'

But Gran shook her head. 'No love. Mary's

expectin' me — said she'd have a bite to eat ready.'

'Right then we'll go and pick up your case and I'll get you over to Bethnal Green.'

By the time they got back to the coach station Sally noticed that Gran was stiff. 'Come on, we'll get a cab,' she said.

Gran looked scandalized. 'No need for extravagance like that, gel. I can walk to the bus stop.'

Sally took her arm. 'Come on. I said we'd get a cab. You're tired.' On impulse she bent and kissed the older woman's cheek. 'Thanks, Gran — for telling me all that and for all you and Grandpa did for me over the years.'

Gran looked surprised. 'No need for no thanks, gel. You were the apple of your grandpa's eye. Mine too.' She smiled. 'You were the daughter we always wanted. Not unruly and awkward like your mum. No, it was her loss, not ours.' She glanced at Sally. 'But you won't go rakin' up the past now that you know, will you?'

'No, Gran. I just needed to know, that's all.'

★ ★ ★

Fiona had picked up the telephone and put it down again three times that morning without dialling Ian's number. Finally she forced her finger to dial the number but as she listened to it ringing out at the other end the same feeling of panic almost made her drop the receiver back on to its rest once again. She was seconds away from doing it when there was a sudden click at the other end and a voice said.

'Hello, Feldman Autos.'

She recognized his voice immediately and her mouth went dry. She swallowed hard. 'Oh, Ian — it — it's Fiona.'

There was a pause, then, 'Fee! How are you?'

'I'm fine thanks. You?'

'Fine too. What can I do for you?'

'Nothing really — I mean . . . ' She took a deep breath. 'I'm ringing because I'd really like to see you, Ian.'

'Is there something wrong with the van?'

'No! No, it's absolutely fine. I'd just like to — talk. If you want to, that is.'

'OK, where? And when?'

'You could come here. Or we could meet somewhere.'

He hesitated. 'Later today be all right?'

'Yes.'

'I close up here at six. If you could drive over and meet me we could go back to the flat. I'm on my own now that Stephen's gone.'

'Right. I'll see you at six then. 'Bye, Ian.'

' 'Bye.'

As she replaced the receiver her heart was beating fast. She wasn't sure what to make of the conversation. Ian had sounded guarded. But then he had every right to. It was her fault they had parted and she knew he had been hurt by her behaviour. She had refused to admit to herself how much she had missed him and now the thought of seeing him this evening set the butterflies fluttering in her stomach. She looked at her watch. Two o'clock. Four hours till their meeting. It was going to seem like an age. Suddenly she remembered that she hadn't had any lunch.

She had just made herself a sandwich when Sally came down the basement stairs.

'Hello. Having a late lunch.'

'Yes.'

'Is there enough for two?'

'Yes, and there's plenty of tea in the pot. I thought you were taking your grandmother to lunch.'

'I was, but Mary was expecting her so I took her straight to Bethnal Green.'

Fiona got up to fetch another cup and saucer from the dresser. 'Is she well? Did she tell you what you wanted to know?'

'She's fine.' Sally said. 'As for the answers — more or less. No skeletons in my cupboard. No old lag languishing in prison and no aristocratic father about to leave me his country estate either. It seems I'm just the working class cockney kid I've always been.'

Fiona smiled. 'Good. I wouldn't have you any other way.'

Sally looked at the pink spots in Fiona's cheeks. 'What've you been up to? You look like the cat who got the cream.'

Fiona bit her lip to stop the smile that threatened to spread across her face. 'I rang Ian. We're meeting this evening.'

Sally paused with a sandwich halfway to her mouth. '*Fee!* That's great. What made you change your mind?'

'It was Nanny. She gave me one of her pep

talks when I was driving her home from the hospital. It was nothing she hadn't said before but since I — well since I found out about my birth it put a different perspective on things. Nanny was engaged to a young man who was killed in the First World War. She said it was like history repeating itself and she didn't want me thinking as she did all those years ago — that life was over.'

'Good for Nanny. Well, good luck for this evening then.'

Fiona looked doubtful. 'I'm not pinning too many hopes on it,' she said. 'Ian might have had second thoughts after the way I treated him. He might not want to have anything to do with me any more.'

'If he felt like that he'd hardly have arranged to meet you, would he?'

'I'm hoping not.' Fiona leaned towards her. 'So — did you find out who your father was?'

Sally hesitated. She and Fee had always told each other everything, but somehow this was different. She wasn't proud of having two parents who wanted nothing to do with her. And when one of them turned out to be a celebrity it was something of a responsibility. She made a quick decision to keep it to herself, at least for now.

'No one I know,' she said truthfully. 'It seems I was a mistake my mum made while her husband was away at sea.' She smiled wryly. 'But at least she handed me over to Gran and Grandpa, so I suppose I have to be thankful for that. I'm the little bit of muck that got swept under the carpet.'

'Don't you dare say that!' Fiona said. 'Your mother missed out on a little gem when she walked away from you.'

'Gran said something similar.' Tears pricked Sally's eyes. 'Thanks, Fee. I'm so lucky to have a friend like you. And I do wish you all the best with Ian. You deserve it.'

★   ★   ★

Fiona found Feldman Autos without much trouble and parked the van on the forecourt. As she drew up her heart gave a jerk as she saw Ian locking up. He turned and saw her.

'Fiona!'

'Hello, Ian.'

He got into the passenger seat and looked at her. 'How are you? It's been a while.'

'I'm fine. I've been down in Fairfield quite a lot. Stevie probably told you Nanny's been in hospital.'

'He did. Please give her my best when you see her.'

She started the engine. 'Where to then?'

'Back to Edgware if that's all right with you. I'd like to have a wash and change. Then perhaps we could go out for a meal or something.'

'Sounds fine.'

'I'll be moving now that Stephen's gone,' he said as they drove. 'It's a bit of a nuisance travelling over from Edgware every day. There are a couple of rooms over the garage. Max said

273

I could have them for next to nothing if I care to do them up.'

'That's lucky.' Fiona found the drive to Edgware long and difficult. Their conversation was stilted and trivial — an exchange of news about their respective businesses and the weather — a discussion about the van. There was so much she was aching to say, but not like this — while she was driving. She needed to be face to face with Ian — to see his reaction.

At last they arrived and Ian produced his key and let them into the flat. He waved a hand towards the living room. 'Sorry about the state of the place. No one to share the chores with me now that Stephen's gone. Take a seat. I'll try not to be too long.'

'No, Ian — *wait!*' she could stand the delay no longer. 'Please don't go. I need to say something and I have to say it now while I still have the nerve.'

He stopped and turned to look at her. 'OK — go ahead. I'm listening.'

She took a step towards him. 'It's just — you were right when you said we shouldn't see each other again. Not with me behaving like some . . . ' She shook her head. 'I don't know — some ice maiden. I wouldn't let myself feel anything, Ian. Not after Mark was killed. But I was wrong and I know that now. Deep down I *did* feel something. I just wouldn't let myself admit it.' She swallowed hard. 'And I sent you away because of it. You have no idea how much I've regretted that. I'm so sorry, Ian. Can you forgive me?'

He reached out to pull her towards him. 'There's no question of forgiveness. You couldn't help the way you felt. I won't say I wasn't hurt and disappointed. It hasn't got any better over the weeks either. But hearing you say those things now makes up for a lot.'

'If only I hadn't been so selfish. You were hurt too, in a much worse way than me. And here I was, hurting you even more. I was so afraid to ring you — afraid you wouldn't want to see me again; afraid of hearing the truth about myself I suppose.' She looked at him. 'So you haven't — haven't given up on me?'

He smiled. 'What do you think?' He drew her close and kissed her. 'I love you, Fiona. I've already told you that. And the fact that you put me through hell and nothing's changed tells me for sure that it's for keeps.'

'Oh, Ian, I'm so sorry. What can I do to make it up to you?'

He looked into her eyes. 'Tell me what I want to hear to begin with.'

She looked up at him. 'I love you. I know now that I always have.'

'Are you sure you really mean that?'

She reached up to kiss him. 'Surer than I've ever been about anything.'

'I'm not dreaming this, am I?'

She laughed. 'You're not dreaming.'

'And if I were to ask you to marry me?'

'I'd *probably* say yes.'

'Only probably?'

'Well, you won't know unless you ask me, will you?'

He looked deep into her eyes. 'Fiona — will you marry me?'

She smiled. 'Don't you think we should wait for a while?'

'Wait — what for?'

'To be sure.'

'I *am* sure.' He held her close. 'I've never been more sure of anything, so don't think you're getting away from me again. What's it to be — yes or no?'

She laughed. 'It's yes, Ian. I'll marry you.'

He shook his head suddenly. 'Look at us! This is hardly the romantic proposal I've been fantasizing about. The two of us here in a messy flat that hasn't been cleaned for weeks, with me in all the dirt from the garage.'

'I don't care. It's romantic enough for me.'

'Don't you want to go out for a romantic candlelit meal?'

'I'd rather stay here with you, garage dirt and all.' She wound her arms around his neck. 'And who knows? If you were to play your cards right I might even help you tidy up in the morning.'

'Did I hear you say 'in the morning'?' He pulled her close. 'Now I know I'm dreaming.'

15

Marcia and Donald Crowther arrived the day before Stephen's investiture and immediately the whole house was in turmoil. Marcia could think of nothing but her new outfit, made especially for the occasion. She unpacked it and instructed Annie to press it carefully, then she put it on and asked Fiona's opinion as she paraded before the cheval mirror in her room. Peering critically at her reflection she pursed her lips.

'Tell me honestly, Fiona, is this colour too bland for my complexion?'

Fiona assured her that it was not.

'What about the length?' She asked, her head on one side. 'A touch too long?'

'Not at all. Skirts are definitely longer this season.'

'Well, if you're sure. Living in the country one loses touch with fashion.' Apparently satisfied she took out her diary and consulted it. 'Now — I've made hair appointments for both of us with Pierre of Bond Street,' she said. 'We're to be there at nine o'clock and he advises taking the hats we're to wear along with us so that he can create styles to suit the shape.' She turned to Fiona. 'Now, what about your outfit — are you going to try it on for me?' When Fiona returned Marcia sat on the bed to view her critically from all angles.

'Turn round for me. Mmm, you don't think

pale blue is a little too summery for October, do you?' she offered.

'No, I didn't want anything drab and the weather looks like holding,' Fiona said. 'And anyway, I've used up all my clothing coupons so it's this or nothing.'

'This is the most important day of your brother's life,' Marcia pointed out. 'We want him to be proud of his family, don't we?'

As usual the remark carried the suggestion that she was letting the side down. In the old days Fiona might have countered by suggesting that perhaps Marcia would prefer her not to go at all, but nowadays she was a little more diplomatic so she bit her tongue and said nothing.

Donald, who had just come into the room sized up the situation and stepped in with his usual diplomacy. 'Stephen will be the proudest man there,' he said. 'How could he fail to be with two such beautiful women at his side?' He smiled at Fiona. 'And the dress is charming my dear. Powder blue was always your colour. And the hat with the matching ribbon sets it off to perfection.' He turned to his wife. 'And you my love are the epitome of elegance in your cream silk as you very well know.'

Slightly appeased, Marcia viewed herself once more in the mirror. 'Mmm. Well, I'm sure I've done my best.' She pursed her lips. 'I wonder if people from *The Tatler* and *Country Life* will be there to photograph the occasion. I do hope so.' She looked at her husband. 'Did you book the table?'

'I did.' Donald smiled. 'Everything is laid on. Cocktails here for a few friends at five, then dinner for four later at the Savoy before we head back to Saltmere St Peter.' He looked at Fiona. 'You will be joining us for the weekend, won't you?'

Fiona shook her head. 'Not this time. I thought you might like to have Stephen all to yourselves.' She took a deep breath. 'Mother — Daddy, there's something I have to tell you.'

'Oh do you really have to go into it now?' Marcia said tetchily. 'I can't really think about anything but getting ready to go to the Palace and we've got our hair appointments first thing in the morning. Donald — now are you sure we'll be able to park the car nearby? I don't want to have to walk too far in these heels.'

Donald sighed. 'I've told you several times my dear. We've all been issued with special permits to park in The Mall. We'll start early and get as close to the Palace as we can.'

'I really want to talk to you. It's important.' Fiona put in. 'Very important. And as I can't join you for the weekend I'd really like to tell you now.'

'Why can't you join us?' Marcia asked.

'I'm having a celebration of my own.' Fiona held out her left hand on which a diamond and sapphire ring sparkled. 'I'm engaged,' she announced. 'To Ian.'

Marcia frowned. '*Ian*? Ian who?'

'Ian Jerome. Stephen's friend.'

Marcia looked shocked. 'The *used car* salesman?'

279

Fiona sighed. 'He's not just a salesman. He has a half share in the business.'

'He's still a used car salesman,' Marcia said. 'And anyway, what do you mean, you're engaged? Surely it's customary to ask your father's permission before proposing marriage?'

Donald shook his head. 'Fiona came of age long ago darling. Anyway, that kind of formality seems to have gone out of fashion since the war.'

'Well more's the pity if you ask me,' Marcia was still looking at herself in the mirror. 'Standards are falling much too fast if you ask me. The sooner we get back to normal, the better.'

'I had wondered if we could include Ian in our celebration dinner,' Fiona ventured. 'He and Stevie were in the RAF together. And Sally too. I'm sure he would appreciate having his friends to celebrate with him.'

Marcia swung round. 'Certainly *not*! This is one thing I'm going to have to insist on. This is a family occasion. I'm not having *any* outsiders spoiling it. Certainly not a used car salesman and a singing waitress!'

Fiona had to bite her tongue very hard to stop herself from protesting hotly at Marcia's insulting remark. She didn't want to get into a row at this particular time. Anyway, when Marcia was in this mood there was little point in arguing with her. She looked at her father who raised an eyebrow and gave an almost imperceptible shrug. Suddenly she knew why he had given in to his wife so frequently over the years. He owed

her a great deal and undoubtedly he had never
been allowed to forget it.

★ ★ ★

Downstairs in the basement Annie and Sally sat
at the table over a pot of tea.

'D'you reckon we'll get a good view?' Annie
said.

'I should think so,' Sally replied. 'It's not as if
it was a royal wedding or anything. It'll only be
friends and families I daresay.'

'I must say I thought they'd have invited you
to go along with them,' Annie said.

Sally shook her head. 'Stephen did ask me, but
I didn't want to intrude. It's a family occasion,
after all.'

Annie looked at her. 'I thought you and him
were goin' steady like.'

Sally smiled. 'We're only friends — through
Fee. Nothing more.' Changing the subject she
produced her little box Brownie camera. 'I
thought I'd take some snaps if we can get near
enough,' she said. 'A set for Nanny Joan to keep
as a souvenir.'

'That's a nice idea,' Annie said with a smile.
'Seems to me she had more to do with his
upbringing than his mum did. I bet she'd give
anything to be there and see him in his uniform
with his medal pinned on.' She looked at Sally.
'What are you wearing? Do you think my blue
coat would be all right?'

Sally smiled. 'Fine. You look very nice in it. I
think I'll just wear my navy suit. Anyway all eyes

281

will be on the people being decorated and their families, not us.'

'Do you think they'll get to shake hands with the King?'

'I expect Stephen will.'

Annie's eyes were dreamy. 'Oh, how lovely. It'll be a day he'll always remember, won't it?' she said.

★   ★   ★

On their way to the hairdresser's in the taxi Marcia turned to Fiona. 'Are you really determined to marry this Ian person? You seemed so sure that there'd never be anyone else for you after Mark was killed.'

'It's true. I did feel like that, but with Ian it's different. We both feel so lucky to have found each other. Ian was married very briefly during the war. He lost his wife and his parents in the same air raid.'

'And you're sure you're not on the rebound?'

'Not in the least. We love each other very much.'

Marcia gave a resigned little sigh. 'I suppose you'll be planning some hole in the corner registry office affair with a couple of road sweepers for witnesses.'

Fiona turned to look at her. 'Is that what you'd prefer?'

Marcia coloured. 'Of course not! A country wedding in the village church at Saltmere St Peter with all our friends present is what I've always visualized for my only daughter.

Even . . . ' She looked away. 'Even if you and I know that strictly speaking you're not.' She flicked a glance at Fiona. 'Have you told — Ian, by the way?'

Fiona didn't need to ask what about. 'I wanted to ask your permission first, though I do think it would be a mistake to start our marriage with secrets.'

'I suppose you intend to tell him — everything.'

'Unless you want me to keep some things back. Ian is very discreet. I know it would be strictly between ourselves.'

'So I should hope.' Marcia sighed. 'Then I suppose you had better tell him.'

'There's something else,' Fiona said. 'I'd like to ask you for a favour. Will you and Dad tell Stevie about me this weekend. I think he should know, don't you?'

'Your father has already decided to tell him,' Marcia said. 'You're right. It is time he knew. He'll be driving him back to Cambridge on Sunday evening. I think he plans to tell him then.' There was a pause and her hand came out to cover Fiona's. 'What we decided, all those years ago — keeping it a secret — we thought it was for the best at the time.'

'I know.'

'And I do appreciate your asking my permission to tell Ian,' she went on. 'It's very thoughtful of you. Whatever you might think, your father and I have always wanted the best for you. And for you to be happy.'

'I know that too, Mother.'

'You won't ever stop calling me that, will you?'

Fiona turned and was surprised and touched to see that there were tears in Marcia's eyes.

'Of course I won't,' she said softly.

★　★　★

There was quite a crowd outside the Palace gates to see the people come out. Annie was almost beside herself with excitement.

'Oh look, it says British Movietone News on that camera over there. That means they might be in the newsreel at the pictures. Fancy that! We'll have to go next week. And there are lots of other photographers — from the newspapers and magazines.' She waved an excited arm. 'Ooh look! Here they come!'

People had begun to emerge from the palace gates and Annie took Sally's arm and urged her forward for a better view.

'There they are!' she shouted. 'Oh, just look at Mr Stephen. Don't he look handsome in his uniform?'

Sally's heart was beating fast as she spotted Stephen walking out through the gates with his parents and Fiona. He did indeed look handsome and proud as the four of them posed for photographs. Annie nudged her.

'Go on then. Aren't you gonna take them snaps?'

Sally pushed the camera into Annie's hands. 'You take them,' she said. 'I'm not really very good with cameras.'

Annie looked at her briefly and saw the

brightness in her eyes and the slight trembling of her mouth. Quickly sizing up the situation she took the camera and pushed her way to the front of the crowd.

'Sir! Madam! Look this way please. Smile.' She clicked the shutter. 'There, that's lovely. One of Mr Stephen on his own, can I?'

When she returned to Sally's side she was breathless. 'There, it's done,' she said. 'I reckon I got some good ones for Nanny Joan. She will be pleased.'

Sally swallowed hard at the lump in her throat, which refused to go away. 'Thanks, Annie,' she said.

The older woman looked at her and laid a hand on her arm. 'Cheer up, lovey. I expect you'll see him before he goes back to Cambridge.'

⋆　⋆　⋆

The Crowthers had invited a select group of friends to the small cocktail party at Gower Street after the investiture. The girls had made the canapés themselves and Annie and Sally hurried home to change and serve them along with the drinks. As she circulated with her tray of cocktails Sally saw that Marcia's friend Muriel St John-Pickard was there with her husband and a tall blonde girl who, according to Fiona, was their niece. Her name was Angela and she had quite clearly set her sights on Stephen. She was monopolizing his attention, gazing up at him with huge blue

285

eyes and hanging on his every word.

Annie nudged her. 'I bet you feel like bumping into her with a tray of drinks,' she said with a wink.

Sally smiled. 'I don't think that would do me much good.'

Fiona edged her way through the crowd towards her. 'Sally, Stevie has asked Ian and me to go for a drink with him after this little shindig is over. I've just rung Ian and he's picking us up at the end of the road in an hour. Stevie wants you to come too. You will, won't you? You and he haven't had a chance to speak to each other what with all the fuss.'

Sally heart lifted. 'I'd love to. What time?'

'The minute the last of these people has gone. They're thinning out now. Look, give me your tray and go and change. We'll meet you in the hall later.'

When Sally was ready she went downstairs to find the others. In the hall three people were waiting: Fiona, Stephen — and Angela St John-Pickard. Her heart sank. Fiona had said nothing about the other girl joining them. Stephen's face lit up when he turned and saw her.

'Sally! Haven't had a minute to speak to you since I got home. How are you?'

'I'm fine. Congratulations, by the way.' She looked at the casual tweed jacket and grey flannel trousers he was wearing. 'I thought you'd be wearing your uniform.'

He pulled a face. 'Glad to get out of it. I just felt the need to relax for an hour or so.' He turned to the other girl. 'By the way, you haven't met Angela. She's a fresher at Cambridge like me — different college of course. She's reading English and history. Angela, this is Sally, Fiona's business partner.'

Sally turned to the girl. Everything about her screamed 'privilege' from her clothes and elegantly styled hair to her condescending expression. Sally took the limp white hand she offered.

'Pleased to meet you.'

Angela's lip curled in what could have been interpreted as a smile or a sneer. 'How do you do?' She turned to Stephen. 'Fiona's business partner, did you say? What *business* would that be?' Her voice held a note of faint disdain.

'Sally and I run a catering service,' Fiona put in.

'Oh, I *see*.' Angela nodded.

'Come on, Ian will be waiting,' Fiona opened the front door. 'We have to be back here by eight so we don't want to waste any time chatting.' As they walked down the steps on to the pavement she whispered to Sally, 'Sorry about her. Mother suggested that we take her along in front of her so I couldn't do anything about it.'

Ian was waiting with the Bentley at the corner of Gower Street and Euston Road. He greeted Stephen warmly and invited him into the passenger seat, leaving the three girls to pile into the back. Sally found herself sitting next to Angela and breathing in the overpowering scent of the expensive perfume that she seemed to have doused herself with.

'How did you two meet?' Angela asked, addressing the remark to Fiona.

'We worked in a munitions factory together during the war.'

'Did you? I was too young for war work,' Angela said. 'I was at boarding school for most of the war, down in Wales where the school was evacuated.'

'That's a shame. You missed a lot of valuable experience,' Fiona said. 'We had so much fun, didn't we. Sally? Wartime conditions give you a view of life that really broadens the mind.'

Angela shot a scathing glance in Sally's direction. '*Evidently.*'

Fiona leaned forward to look at Sally. 'Are you working this evening?' Sally nodded and she went on. 'Sally is a talented singer. She sings in a nightclub at weekends.'

'Really? How amusing.' Angela's lip curled again.

'She sings classical music too. She sang for us at a concert in the church at Saltmere St Peter a few months ago.'

'*Fascinating.* Actually Mrs Crowther has invited me to spend the weekend at The Manor.'

'Has she, when?'

'This weekend,' Angela said with satisfaction. 'As you couldn't go she thought it would be nice for Stephen to have company of his own age.'

The rest of the short journey was spent in silence as Sally and Fiona digested this piece of news, while Angela sat for the rest of the short journey with a smug, sphinx-like smile on her exquisite face.

They spent about an hour in a little pub off Euston Road. It was not a success. Fiona and Ian only had eyes for each other and Angela made sure that Stephen spoke to no one but her, bombarding him with questions about his RAF career and exchanging university gossip about people only the two of them knew, punctuating her comments with shrill little peals of laughter that set Sally's teeth on edge. At ten to eight they left the pub and piled back into the car for the journey back to Gower Street. This time Fiona got into the front with Ian and Stephen sat in the back between the two girls. Once more Angela monopolised his attention but under cover of darkness Stephen's hand found Sally's and squeezed it hard. Back at Gower Street Stephen took her hand and held her back as the others went upstairs.

'We've hardly seen each other at all. I'm sorry darling. There was nothing I could do about it, but I promise I'll make it up to you. Next time I get a weekend off we'll spend it together,' he promised.

'That would be nice.' Sally swallowed her disappointment. 'I know how hectic it's been for you this time. I understand.'

'I wish you were coming down to Saltmere St Peter with us,' he said.

'I do too but I have to do my cabaret at the club.' She nodded towards the staircase. 'You'll have Angela to keep you company. She's very attractive.'

He pulled a face. 'She's a bit much really, isn't

she? That laugh! I can't imagine why Ma has invited her.'

Sally could — all too easily. Angela was just the kind of match she wanted for her son. But she didn't say so.

'You'll have to take time off and come to Cambridge one weekend,' Stephen said. 'I could take you on a sightseeing tour and I'd love to show you off to all my chums.'

Sally wondered if he really would. If they were all like Angela there would be no common ground between them at all. It really was time she let go of her dream of sharing her life with Stephen. It was destined for heartbreak. She made herself smile. 'That would be lovely,' she said.

From somewhere above Marcia's impatient voice called, 'Stephen! What on earth are you *doing* darling? It really is time we were off.'

Stephen pulled her into the shadow of the staircase and kissed her swiftly. 'Goodbye darling. I'll see you soon — promise.' Then he was bounding up the stairs two at a time. 'All right, Ma. Keep your hair on. I'm here.'

★   ★   ★

Max's appearance with a tray of tempting supper snacks between the two cabaret spots at the *Pink Parrot* had become a regular occurrence. Tonight it was anchovies on toast and a bottle of Chablis. When his expected tap came on the door Sally was still in her dressing gown, feeling and looking down.

'How's my girl then?' Max set the tray down and looked at her. 'Your show went down a bomb tonight,' he said. 'I thought you'd've been over the moon but you don't look it.'

'Take no notice of me,' Sally said.

'Come on, what's up? Tell Uncle Maxie.'

'It was Stephen's investiture this morning,' she told him. 'Now everyone's gone off to celebrate for the weekend. It's a bit of a let-down.'

'You should've said.' He passed her a glass of wine. 'You could've had the weekend off.'

'Oh I wasn't included anyway,' she told him. 'I watched it all from the crowd outside the palace gates, then I went back to serve the cocktails.'

'I don't know why you bother with that lot,' Max said. 'They treat you like a skivvy. You've said yourself there's no future in it. All you're doing is giving yourself a lot unnecessary heartache.'

'I know, Max. You don't need to rub it in.'

'You're a lovely girl, Sally. Why hanker after a bloke who's wrong for you when you could have anyone you crooked your little finger at.'

'I don't want just *anyone*,' Sally snapped. 'Look, Max, can we talk about something else?'

'O'course we can love.' He passed her the plate of snacks. 'Here have something to eat. Life always looks a bit bleak on an empty belly.'

Sally took an anchovy toast and nibbled unenthusiastically at it.

'Here, I've got something that'll cheer you up,' He said suddenly. 'I've got a job for that catering service you and your mate run. What's it called — *Dinner For Eight*?'

'*At*,' Sally corrected. '*Dinner* At *Eight*.'

'Yeah, that's it. Well, as you know I've got a few mates in show business and they're organizing this benefit concert. It's in a theatre up West but they've asked me to do the party afterwards because some of 'em come from round here. Now, as you know I only have the bar here — don't do food, so I wondered if you and your mate.' He cocked his head on one side. 'What's 'er name?'

'Fiona.'

'Yeah — if you and Fiona could come and do a buffet or something.'

'When is it?' Sally opened her handbag and took out a notebook.

'Next weekend — Sunday.'

'That's short notice. I'll have to check when I get home and see if we're free.'

'OK. You do that and let me know, eh? I'll pay whatever the goin' rate is plus a bit on top for it bein' Sunday. OK?'

She smiled. 'OK.'

He returned her smile with obvious pleasure. 'There, that's better. I said it'd cheer you up.' He looked at her. 'Sall — you said everyone had gone off to celebrate for the weekend. Does that mean you're on your tod tonight?' She nodded. 'Well, you don't have to go back to an empty gaff,' he said reaching for her hand. 'There's always the flat. We could have a little celebration of our own after closing time.' He cupped her chin and kissed her. 'What d'you say darlin'? Go on, give it a try. No strings eh?'

'I can't, Max.'

'You can. You don't owe him nothing. D'you think your precious Steve turns his back on gels up there in Cambridge. Lives like a monk, does he? I don't think so.'

She shrugged. 'Maybe not.'

'No maybe about it. Come on, Sally, loosen up a bit. You'n'me, we're two of a kind. I know I could make you happy so why don't you give me a chance?'

'I don't think I'd be very good company tonight.'

'I'd be prepared to take a chance on that.' He took both her hands and pulled her to her feet. 'I like you in any mood at all, Sall. Come on, you know I'm potty about you, don't you?' He drew her gently into his arms and kissed her. At first she resisted, then the sheer seductiveness of being wanted thawed her and she responded, her mouth softening under his. When they drew apart he looked at her, his eyes dark with desire. 'What d'you say, Sall? Give it a go, eh? Just this once?'

'I don't know.'

'Just come. If you change your mind I'll take you home at once — promise.'

'Let me do the show, Max,' she begged. 'It's almost time and I have to get ready. I — I promise you I'll think about it.'

'OK then.' He let her go reluctantly. 'I'll see you after the cabaret.'

Max was sitting close to the stand as Sally sang her way through the second cabaret. His eyes never left her face. It occurred to her that he looked quite handsome in his dinner jacket, his dark hair slicked back and his eyes shining with desire. Sally's heart gave a lurch as she thought of his suggestion that she stay at the flat for the night. She hadn't agreed, but she had half promised. Clearly he would be disappointed if she refused now. What was she getting herself into? Why on earth hadn't she turned the suggestion down flat? She dallied with the thought of running away — changing quickly and escaping before he could catch her. He would be busy in the office, cashing up before the club closed. But if she did that she wouldn't be able to face him again. An honest refusal was the least she owed him.

In her dressing room as she changed into her street clothes all she could think about was Stephen. She longed so much to hear his voice. Suddenly it occurred to her that if she rang from the payphone in the corridor she could say goodnight to him before she faced Max.

In the corridor she inserted the coppers into the box and dialled, waiting impatiently as the number rang out. At last Marcia's voice answered. She sounded less than pleased.

'*Hello*. Who is it?'

'Oh — hello, Mrs Crowther. It's Sally. Can I speak to Stephen please?'

'Isn't this rather late to be calling?'

'Yes — yes, I suppose it is. I'm sorry.'

'Donald and I were in bed. And Stephen isn't here. He's gone out with Angela — to a party at a friend's house. They're not back yet and I've no idea when they will be so please don't ring back. Goodnight.'

'Goodnight, Mrs . . . ' There was a click as Marcia hung up abruptly. Sally swallowed the lump in her throat as she replaced the receiver. Max was right. They treated her with contempt. Marcia Crowther hated her and there was no way at all that she would ever allow her precious son to become involved with her. It was time she stopped reaching for the moon and accepted her own place in the world.

'All right darlin'?'

She turned to see Max coming down the corridor. She forced a smile. 'Fine.'

He followed her back inside the dressing room and closed the door. 'What's the verdict then?'

She swallowed hard. 'I — I'll stay, Max.'

He looked surprised. 'You sure?'

'Of course.'

He pulled her into his arms and kissed her hard. 'Oh my God, Sall. You don't know what this means to me.' He took her coat from her and wrapped it round her shoulders. 'Come on, I'll take you up there now. You can put our feet up for a bit while I lock up here. I'll bring some champers up with me.'

The flat was sparsely furnished but it had all the essentials. Sally found that there was plenty of hot water so she had a bath, hoping that it would soak some of the tension out of her. When Max appeared he had changed out of his dinner jacket into a sweater and flannels. He fetched glasses from the kitchen and opened the bottle of champagne with a loud pop, pouring the frothing wine and handing one glass to her.

'Here's to us, darlin'.' He touched his glass to hers. 'And what's to come.' He looked round the room. 'I know this isn't much of a place but I'm plannin' to have it decorated and get some new stuff in — furniture an' that.'

She sipped her drink. 'It's fine.' The bubbles tickled her nose and the astringent way it stung her throat made her feel even more nervous.

'It's private anyway. That's the main thing.' Max took her glass from her and put it down. Taking her hand he led her through to the bedroom. She stood passively as he gently removed her dressing gown, her arms at her sides as it fell to the floor. But when he bent to kiss her skin she shuddered. Taking it for a sign of passion Max slipped an arm under her knees and lifted her on to the bed.

'You're so lovely, Sall,' he murmured, his breath hot against her ear. 'I've wanted you ever since I saw you again at Jenny's wedding. I can hardly believe this is happening.'

As he stroked and kissed her she steeled herself to accept what was happening. Her whole being cried out for Stephen. But Stephen was with someone else, she reminded herself — at a party, enjoying himself — maybe even making love to Angela at this very minute. Stephen was soon going to forget that she ever existed. She must forget him too and this was as good a way as any.

Max's breathing became ragged as his excitement mounted and his lips were hot as they consumed hers. But all she could think of was the nights she had lain in Stephen's arms and what they had shared. Suddenly she knew she could not go through with it and she pulled away abruptly.

'*Max* — *no*! I'm sorry. I can't.' Tears slipped down her cheeks as she sat up and turned her back, reaching for her dressing gown.

Raising his head he looked at her. 'Christ! Don't do this to me, Sall.'

'I'm really sorry. I thought I could but it's no good. I can't.'

'What's wrong?' He reached out to touch her shoulder. 'It's still him, isn't it?'

'I'm sorry. I'm *sorry*.' She could hardly speak for the tears that tightened her throat. 'I know it's not fair, but it's no good.'

'It's OK, darlin', don't cry. You'll get over him and I'll be here to help you. I won't ask you to do anything until you're ready, I promise. I want you to want me as much as I want you.' He put his arms round her. 'Come here. It's OK, I'm not gonna get awkward. Just relax.'

As she sobbed against his shoulder the absurdity of the situation struck her. She felt humiliated and angry with herself. 'I should never have come,' she muttered.

He shook his head. 'It don't matter. Forget it. Look — something to think about. Why not move in here? I'll make this place nice for you — anything you want. You can choose. I've got some mates in the furniture business. All good stuff. No rubbish. Then we could be together every weekend.'

'I don't know.' Ever since Fiona and Ian had

297

got engaged she had been worried about what would happen after they were married. Would it be the end of *Dinner At Eight*? She would certainly have to move out of 28 Gower Street. And she felt she'd already lost Stephen. Could she really afford to lose another friend as well as her home and livelihood?

'Say yes, darlin',' Max whispered. 'On any terms you want. No strings. I'll wait for you, no matter how long it takes.'

She let out a shuddering sigh. 'OK then, Max, if that's what you want,' she whispered resignedly. 'If that's what you really want.'

16

It was almost a fortnight before Sally had a letter from Stephen. When it came it was brief, a few hurried lines. He made no mention of her visiting him in Cambridge or his weekend at Saltmere St Peter with Angela, which she took to be significant. His words of love at the end of the letter seemed to her like an afterthought.

Fiona had been delighted with the booking for the benefit concert after-show party at the *Pink Parrot* and now that the date was only a couple of days away the girls were busy planning the buffet menu and getting ahead with the preliminaries.

'Did Max say who the benefit concert was for?' Fiona asked. 'Is it anyone famous?'

'I've no idea,' Sally said. 'He just said there'd be about a hundred people. He's closing the club for the night specially.'

Fiona smiled. 'I'm quite looking forward to it. Meeting all those stars and show business people will be quite exciting, won't it?' Sally made no reply and Fiona looked at her. 'Are you all right, Sally? You've been looking a bit peaky lately.'

'I'm fine.'

'Nothing worrying you?'

'No.' She hesitated. 'I miss Stevie, that's all.'

'Have you heard from him?'

'Just one short letter. He seemed a bit distant.'

'There might be a reason for that,' Fiona said.

'I had a letter too — from Mother. When he went at home the weekend before last Dad took him aside and told him about me — you know, about my birth and Nanny Joan. Apparently he took it very badly.'

'I see.'

'I feel guilty about it because I told Mother I wanted him to know and I didn't feel it was my place to tell him. It didn't feel right that you and Ian knew and Stevie was still in the dark about it. He's always looked up to Dad so it must have come as a shock. Apparently he went out on a bender that night — came home in the small hours very drunk and left early next morning. Ian said he turned up on his doorstep on Sunday afternoon. Mother was furious, especially as she'd invited Angela St John-Pickard for the weekend. The poor girl took herself off home later on Sunday, absolutely disgusted.'

Inwardly Sally was filled with relief. 'I tried to ring Stevie that night,' she said. 'I had a sudden urge to speak to him. Your mother answered the phone. She said that he and Angela were out at some party or other.'

Fiona smiled wryly. 'Dear Mother. Always one for saving face.'

'Can you imagine how it made me feel? I almost . . . ' She broke off, biting her lip at the memory.

'Almost what?' Fiona looked concerned. 'Sally — there is something wrong, isn't there? Is it just Stevie or is it something else?'

'It's — several things really.'

'Like . . . ?'

'Well — I've been wondering what will happen to *Dinner At Eight* after you're married,' Sally said, voicing her fears. 'And naturally we can't stay on here at Gower Street much longer, can we? I mean, all the decorating and building work is done and Annie is here to look after things. After you've gone there'll be no reason for me to stay on.'

'Oh, you silly goose!' Fiona threw her arms round her and gave her a hug. 'Why didn't you say something before? Did you really think we'd have left you homeless and jobless? Am I that thoughtless?'

'No, but it's up to all of us to think for ourselves, isn't it?'

Fiona frowned. 'You must know I'd never leave you in the lurch after all we've been through together. What is it, darling? You haven't been yourself for days. Are you going to tell me?'

But Sally shrugged. There was no way on earth that she could ever tell Fiona that she had almost slept with Max. 'I told you — I'm fine — really. I've always known that there's no future for Stevie and me. It's just hard coming to terms with it, that's all.' She turned away before Fiona could contradict her. 'Actually I've had the offer of a flat.'

'Really, where?'

'There are some rooms above the club. Max has offered them to me.'

Fiona frowned. 'Is that a good idea?'

'What's *that* supposed to mean?'

'*Nothing*!' Fiona held up her hand. 'Don't be so touchy. It's just living on top of your work isn't always a good idea, that's all.'

'I won't be. We'll soon have paid off what we owe for the van and I plan to give up singing at the club.'

'Sally — you know you don't have to keep that cabaret job on if you're not happy. Now that Ian and I are together he's not going to care about the van payments.' Fiona reached out to touch her arm. 'Sall — look, don't take this the wrong way, but is Max — all right?'

'All right? In what way?'

'Is he on the level? Is all that he does legal?'

'I don't ask — none of my business really. I think he probably sails quite close to the wind at times and he has mates in all kinds of places, high and low. But I don't think he'd risk his licence by breaking the law.' She looked closely at Fiona. 'Why do you ask?'

'It's just that Ian has been a bit concerned lately about where some of the cars come from. They just seem to turn up out of the blue. Ian is never asked to look them over first.'

'Has he asked?'

'Of course, but Max just hedges. Ian is a partner in the business but he feels he's being kept in the dark. And some of the things Max asks him to do are against his better judgement.'

'In what way?'

'He's worried about the safety angle. Recently Max has asked him to patch up cars that have been written off. Weld two halves together — that kind of thing. He hates doing it. There's a heavy penalty for that kind of thing.'

'I see. No wonder he's worried.' Sally sighed.

'I don't quite know how but I'll see what I can find out.'

The girls arrived at the *Pink Parrot* at nine o'clock on Sunday evening to prepare for the party. Max met them and showed them to the kitchen. He had set up a long table close to the bar and Sally went through to the club, leaving Fiona to unpack the food in the kitchen.

Max stood in the doorway, watching Fiona as she worked. 'I'm thinking of having some catering arrangements here,' he told her. 'A lot of the punters fancy a bit of supper when they come in.' He winked at her. 'You don't fancy the job, do you?'

She shook her head. 'No, thank you. We've built up our own clientele now and our main service is that we go out to people's homes and cook.'

Max shrugged. 'Well, it was worth a try. S'matter of fact I've just taken on a new barman and he used to be in catering, so I daresay he'll be able to manage that side of things for me. I don't want nothing elaborate.'

Sally was setting the buffet table and unpacking plates and cutlery when a familiar voice made her start.

'Well, bugger me! If it ain't little Sally!'

Her heart plummeted as she looked up and came face to face with Alf Chandler. 'What are you doing here?' she asked.

'Work 'ere, don't I?' he said, pulling on a white bar jacket. 'This is my first night. I'm Max's new barman. Come to that, what's your excuse?'

'If it's any of your business my friend and I

run a catering business,' she told him. 'We're here to provide the buffet for the party.'

'Oh! Hoity-toity! Know yer way around the place well for someone who ain't been 'ere before, don't you?'

'I sing here some weekends too.'

'Oh yeah?' He smirked at her. 'What you mean is, you're his new bird!'

'No!'

'I'd like to know who is then. Something funny's goin' on. When he offered me this job he told me there was a flat to go with it. Now he tells me he wants the flat for his *secretary* — which is code for his latest bit of stuff. I'd like a few words with her — whoever she is — doin' me out of a nice little gaff!'

'Well, I wouldn't know anything about that,' Sally swallowed hard. She glanced up at him out of the corner of her eye. He was as greasy and unsavoury looking as ever and she shuddered at the memory of his big groping hands and suggestive remarks. 'How's Milly?' she asked pointedly.

He shrugged. 'Gawd knows, an' he won't split. I couldn't care less either way. She went back to 'er bleedin' mum.' He leaned across the bar, narrowing his beady little eyes at her. 'Come to think of it, it was soon after you slung yer 'ook. It weren't nothing to do with you, was it?'

'Hardly. I was very ill in hospital for weeks after I left the caff,' she told him. 'I was in no state to get my own back on anybody. Not that you didn't deserve it.'

He grinned unrepentantly. 'Well, you can't

blame a bloke for trying, can you?' He began polishing glasses, glancing thoughtfully at her. 'I suppose Max is a better proposition than I was.'

'That's a disgusting thing to say!'

'You do know he's married, don't you?'

'Really?' She tried hard to sound casual, her head averted as she smoothed the long white tablecloth into place.

'You *didn't* know!' His tone was triumphant. 'Yeah — got a kid as well. Married Leah Rosen, daughter of Manny Rosen — you know — chain of furriers and fashion shops. Loaded! Knew what he was doing there all right. Where d'you think he got the cash to buy this place? He keeps 'is respectable little private life well separate. Nice house out Stanmore way. Very posh!' Alf went on polishing glasses, his face a mask of resentment. 'Oh yes, Max likes to keep his life in separate boxes if you know what I mean. He has to. Manny'd do his nut if he knew Max was playin' away.'

'I don't know why you're telling me all this,' she said. 'It's none of my business — none of yours either. I'd be careful if I were you, slandering your boss.'

'Oh yeah? What are you gonna do about it then?' he sneered. 'Believe me, I got enough on Max Feldman to send him down for a good few years so a little bit of gossip about his private life ain't gonna bother him. Anyway, if I can't 'ave the flat I won't be stoppin' 'ere long anyway.'

'What do you mean, you've got enough on him?'

He tapped the side of his nose. 'Ah, wouldn't you like to know?'

'I know he likes to dabble in a lot of things,' she said. 'But there's nothing wrong with that, is there? He's a businessman.'

Alf laughed. 'That's a new name for it.'

'I know he has a used car garage for instance,' she said, her eyes intent on the napkins she was folding. 'There's money in that nowadays, isn't there? It's a very profitable business.'

'And a dodgy one!' He chuckled. 'There's more'n a few geezers still lookin' for some o'them so-called *used* cars!'

She looked up at him. 'You're not saying they're stolen?'

'I'm not sayin' anything' darlin'. I know which side my bread's buttered. Anyway, I got no proof.' He leaned across the bar again, leering at her. 'If you'd like to hear more about our beloved boss, why don't we meet up sometime? I could satisfy your curiosity.' He chuckled. 'In more ways than one!'

Sally felt sick. 'I'm busy,' she said. 'I've got to get on and I suggest you do the same.' She went off in the direction of the kitchen, his mocking laugh following her. Alf was a fool. He'd always been a loudmouth, but what he'd said had given her plenty of food for thought.

The hour that followed was busy as the girls set out the food and made the rest of their preparations. Sally was preoccupied, her head full of what she had heard. Was Alf just being vindictive or was he telling the truth about Max's marriage and illegal activities. Ian must certainly be warned as soon as possible. As for Max's marriage, she must find out if there was any truth in it.

It was half past ten when the party guests began to arrive. Sally and Fiona circulated with trays of champagne and cocktails, recognizing several well-known faces as they did so. On her way back to the bar to replenish her tray Sally was waylaid by Max.

'I want you to sing,' he said.

'Max! I can't, I'm too busy. You never said anything about a cabaret.'

'Nothing wrong with wantin' to show my girl off, is there?' He leaned forward to kiss her but she stepped backwards to avoid his lips. 'Come on darlin'. Look, you are gonna stay over tonight, yes?'

'No, Max.'

'Come on, I've been patient. You can't say I haven't.'

She was about to tell him she would not be staying over, tonight or any other night when she remembered that there were things she needed to know. She couldn't risk antagonizing him. 'It'll be too late by the time we've finished here and I can't leave all the clearing up and unpacking to Fee.'

Grudgingly, he acceded. 'OK then. Next week?'

'Actually, I'd like to come and see you before that,' she said. 'I'll give you a ring tomorrow. All right?'

He looked delighted. 'More'n all right darlin'. I'll be waitin' for your call.'

'You'd better give me your home number.'

For a moment he looked nonplussed, but he soon regained his composure. 'Ring me here at the club,' he said. 'I'm here more than anywhere.'

'All right, Max.'

'What about givin' us a couple of numbers now?' he suggested. 'You can go and change in your room. I'll clear it with your mate. Put the red dress on. It's my favourite.'

In her dressing room Sally changed and went up to the stand to talk to Dave Grant about what she was to sing. The pianist was in a mellow mood, having been treated to drinks by several of his old show business colleagues.

'Right old turn up for the book, this,' he said. 'Haven't seen some of these old faces for years — not since before the war. Most of 'em spent the war with ENSA like me. It's good to catch up.'

'Who is the benefit for anyway?' Sally asked. 'Max didn't say.'

Dave pointed to a group of people standing near the bar on the far side of the room. 'Over there, see?' he said. 'Washed-up crooner. Don't you recognize him, or was he before your time?'

Sally followed his pointing finger. A man stood in the centre of the crowd. He was tall with thinning dark hair, longish and curling over his collar. Although his looks had faded the face was still unmistakable. Sally had seen his picture on record sleeves and sheet music — in the Radio Times too. And she had heard him sing a thousand times. Her heart flipped.

'My God! It's Johnny Starr!' she said breathlessly. 'But why the benefit concert? He can't be that old.'

'Like I said — washed up,' Dave said. 'Voice has packed up — booze and fags and God knows what else. Since Sinatra started making it big over here no one buys Johnny Starr's records any more. I heard his agent and the recording company dropped him a while back.' He smiled. 'Still, by the look on your face it seems he can still wow the girls!' He sat down at the piano. 'OK then, want to start now? I'm ready when you are. Max looks busy so I'll introduce you, yeah?'

Somehow Sally got through her two numbers, her eyes returning to the man at the bar as though magnetized. When she had finished the applause was enthusiastic. Relieved that her ordeal was over she was just leaving the stand when she felt a hand on her arm.

'Did they say your name was Joy?'

She turned, her heart jumping when she saw who was speaking. 'Yes,' she said. 'Sally Joy.'

'Come and have a drink with me, Sally.' He took her hand and led her to one of the little booths on the far side of the club, away from the rest of the tables. It was what Max called 'seduction corner'. As Sally watched his unsteady progress to the bar for drinks she studied his appearance. He had the slightly raddled look of a habitual drinker and he had certainly had more than his fair share this evening. He returned and placed a glass of champagne in front of her.

'You've got a great voice, Sally,' he told her. His speech was slightly slurred.

'Thank you.'

'I knew a girl called Joy once,' he said, his eyes reminiscent. 'When we were kids. Met her again a few years later — married by then and very attractive. Made a bit of a pig of myself with her, I have to admit.' He peered at her through narrowed eyes. 'Matter of fact you look a bit like her.' He leaned forward and covered her hand with his. 'Listen sweetheart, if you like I could introduce you to a few of the people who matter, if you know what I mean. A voice like yours deserves a better shop window than this dump.'

She withdrew her hand gently. 'Thanks but I'm not interested.'

'Oh, but you should be. You could have a great future — maybe sing with one of the big bands to start with. I could get you a recording contract. You're pretty enough for the films too.' He moved across to sit beside her, slipping an arm around her shoulders and forcing her into the corner of the booth. 'If you were to stick with me you could really go places.' His eyes were bloodshot and slightly unfocussed as they looked into hers. Gently, she pushed him away.

'Look, I like singing but I'm not interested in making a career out of it,' she told him.

He looked slightly bemused. 'I don't think you know what's good for you. You could be making big money. Listen sweetie, you do know who I am, don't you?'

'Yes, *Mr Willetts*. I know who you are!'

He was so shocked that he let go of her and

moved back. Sally stood up and pushed past him, heading for her dressing room. As she passed the stand Dave leaned down to her, a big grin on his face.

'Try to give you the old routine, did he?' he said. 'By the looks of it you told him where to stick it. Good for you, gel. I bet he's led a few poor kids up the garden path in his time with that line.'

'He's drunk,' Sally said. Her heart was thudding and she was having trouble stopping the tears from welling up in her eyes.

Dave looked at her with concern. 'Hey! You all right kid?'

'I'm fine thanks, Dave,' she said. 'Got to go and change now — work to do.'

In her dressing room she closed the door and sat down in front of the mirror, letting her tears flow. So that was the man who had fathered her. Dave had labelled him a washed-up crooner, but he was a womanizer and a drunk too. He could be no more than forty-five and yet his career and probably his life too, were finished, thrown away by self-indulgence and debauchery. She had missed nothing by not knowing him. She dried her eyes and changed out of her evening dress, collecting her tray of drinks from the kitchen and rejoining Fiona in the club.

Later she heard that Johnny Starr had been taken home in a cab, practically paralytic. She felt as though a chapter of her life had been closed forever.

It was next morning at breakfast that she told Fiona and Annie what had happened the previous evening. Oddly enough, after the initial shock of meeting her father had abated she felt nothing but relief. Clearly he had no idea of her existence and would not have wanted to know her anyway. Oddly enough she found that fact liberating. At last she was free of the spectre of her nameless father.

'I met my father for the first time last night,' she announced over the toast and marmalade. Her statement riveted Fiona and Annie's attention. They stared at her.

'Your father?'

'For the first time?'

'Yes. Johnny Starr.'

'The singer? Him on the wireless?' Annie's mouth dropped open. 'You're kidding!'

'My mother had a brief affair with him,' Sally explained. 'She didn't want her husband to find out so she didn't tell him. My grandparents brought me up. I've always been curious and now I've met him I realize I missed nothing.'

'Did you tell him who you are?' Fiona asked.

'No.' Sally shook her head. 'He wouldn't have wanted to know, and I could see straight away that he wasn't the kind of father I'd have wanted. He even tried to — to proposition me. He was disgustingly drunk.'

'Oh, Sally!' Fiona put an arm around her shoulders. 'How awful for you.'

'Maybe you should have told him,' Annie said. 'There must be lots of people who never knew their sons and daughters and long to meet them. How do you know he isn't one of them?'

'You'd have to meet him yourself to know

312

that,' Sally said. 'I shouldn't think he's ever had a thought for anyone but himself. Anyway, I'm not sure that what you say is true.'

'Oh, it is,' Annie said, her eyes far away. 'I had a baby once.' She looked up to meet the girls' shocked eyes. 'I was only a kid at the time — sixteen. I was so ignorant that I was five months gone before I realized. My dad hit the roof — said I had to let it go for adoption or get chucked out. He was born in this convent place, my baby. I got no sympathy from the nuns I can tell you. I called him Peter, my little boy. When he was six weeks old I had to hand him over. I'd had him with me all that time.' Tears filled her eyes and began to trickle down her cheeks at the memory. 'Breast fed him and cuddled him, sang him to sleep — got up to him when he cried in the night. The day they took him from me he smiled at me for the first time. There hasn't been a day since that I haven't thought about him. Wondered where he finished up. Did he have a nice mum and dad? Was he loved as much as I loved him? I used to dream that one day he'd come and find me, but I gave up dreaming of that a long time ago.'

'Oh, Annie.' Fiona took her hand. 'It might still happen.'

The older woman looked up, shaking her head. 'No. Not now. He'd be a grown man by now — forty-odd. Probably got a wife and kids of his own. Sometimes I wonder if maybe he was killed in the war like so many others. I suppose I'll never know.' She looked at Sally. 'So don't you never think that people don't remember the babies they gave up.'

'He didn't give me up. He never even knew I existed,' Sally said.

Annie nodded. 'Perhaps he was lucky then.' She got up and went out of the room. Sally and Fiona looked at each other.

'She's right,' Fiona said. 'At least you and I know who our parents are. We know our origins. It's more than some people ever have.'

Later that morning Sally took the telephone directory for Middlesex up to her room and looked for the name Feldman. There were quite a few of them, but sure enough there was a Mrs L Feldman at a Stanmore address. It was a long shot but she had to find out for sure if she was Max's wife.

At the library she asked to see the electoral register for the Stanmore district. Taking it to a table in the reading section she looked through the Feldmans again. There it was — Feldman — (Max David), followed by Feldman — (Leah Rachel). Both at the same address, 148 St Cecilia's Avenue.

In a telephone box she dialled the number of the club and asked to speak to Max. The voice that answered sounded suspiciously like Alf's so she didn't give her name. A few minutes later Max answered.

'Good morning. Pink Parrot at your service.' He sounded in a good mood.

'Max, it's me, Sally. Can we meet?'

''Course we can darlin'. How about I see you at the flat around three o'clock? We can have the afternoon together.'

'I'd rather just come to the club if that's all right,' she said. 'I can't stay long.'

'Oh, that's a shame. When then?'

'Now.'

'Well, I don't know about now.'

'It's important, Max. I need to see you.'

'OK then, but it better be good. I've got a lot on today.'

'I promise not to take up too much of your time.'

The club was looking as it always did in daytime, slightly scruffy, littered with the detritus of last night's revelry. The cleaners were still working and she was relieved to see that Alf was not behind the bar. Max wasn't smiling as he greeted her.

'Better come through to the office.' He led the way and closed the door behind them, turning to face her. 'So — what's so important it can't wait then?'

She came straight out with it. 'When were you going to get round to telling me you were married, Max?'

His eyebrows shot up. '*Married* — me? Who said? That'll be the day!'

'So you're saying that Leah isn't your wife? Why is she living at the same address as you then?'

'Didn't it occur to you she might be my sister?'

'You never had a sister called Leah, Max. I was at school with you, remember? I know she's your wife — and that there's a child as well.'

He shrugged. 'So what then? We've got one of

them what'd'yer call it — open marriages. She goes her way and I go mine.'

'So she wouldn't mind knowing about me then — the way you've asked me to move into the flat and be with you at weekends?'

He narrowed his eyes. 'Are you threatening me?'

'According to you it wouldn't be a problem.'

'What d'you want, Sally? Just spit it out.'

'I want you to give Ian Jerome his money back.'

'You what?' His mouth dropped open in surprise and then he laughed. 'You bein' funny or what? Why the hell should I do that? Did he send you?'

'No. No one knows I'm here, but they will if you don't do as I ask. I know all about your illegal dealings with the cars, Max. You're making Ian an accessory. He could go to prison because of you.'

'Tell who the hell you like!' he blustered. 'You can't prove a thing.'

'Not about the cars, perhaps. I could go to see Leah though,' she said. 'Or maybe your father-in-law would be even more interested in me. Mr Rosen, isn't it? The one with all the shops.'

At last she could see that she'd got to him. He visibly paled. Manny Rosen was well known for his business connections, his influence and his wealth. Upsetting him would be a really bad mistake.

'What d'you want me to do then. Sack your mate Ian? I'm sure he'd be pleased to know

316

you'd got him the sack.'

'You can't sack a business partner,' she told him. 'Just tell him you're winding the business up and do yourself a favour at the same time. Give him back his investment, and maybe a little bit extra for the risks you've made him take,' she added. 'Oh, and make it cash.'

He laughed. '*Huh*! He'll be lucky. And if I refuse — what then?'

She stood up. 'I don't make empty threats, Max. If I don't hear that you've done what I ask by tomorrow evening I'll go to your father-in-law. Do it and I'll keep my mouth shut.' She walked to the door. 'I mean it. I think you'll find what I'm asking you to do is cheap at the price. Oh, and by the way, I won't be singing at the club any more.'

'Like hell you won't! Get out of here. And don't bloody come back.'

'I hope I never have to.'

He moved in front of the door, barring her way. 'Just one thing. Who's been shootin' their mouth off?'

She faced him defiantly. 'You know better than to ask that, Max. But if you want a bit of advice, don't upset people who know things about you. It's not very clever. Now, will you let me pass please?'

He stayed where he was. 'You're a fool to yourself, Sally. I could have helped you a lot. There was a lot of interest in you last night. Several people asked who you were and if you'd be interested in furthering your singing career. I was gonna offer to be your manager. You'n me — we could have made a lot of money together. I could've made you into a big success.'

'I'm not interested in your kind of success, Max. I won't be seeing you again. Let me go now. If you keep your side of the bargain I promise to keep mine.'

He stood aside but as she made to walk through the door he grasped her arm in a painful grip and pulled her to him, his mouth tight and his eyes black with anger. 'If it was anyone else but you, Sally . . . '

'But it *is* me, Max.' She met his eyes levelly, though inside her stomach lurched. 'And you know I mean what I say.'

For a moment he held on to her, clearly weighing up his options. Then he let her go abruptly. 'OK, have it your way. Off you go and enjoy your dull little catering career. I thought you had more about you than this, but you're just a stupid little tart like all the others. Too dim to know what you're missing.'

'Oh, I know what I'm missing all right.'

For a moment his eyes flashed menacingly, then he shrugged. 'Have a nice life, Sally,' he mocked. 'See you around.'

As she walked up the stairs and out into the street she had to force herself not to run. Her knees felt like jelly and she was trembling. Max could have done anything. She had seen a darker side of him this morning. He could have turned really nasty — beaten her up

318

even. She knew now that he was capable of it. But she had managed to convince him that she was serious. Thanks to Alf Chandler's dissatisfaction and his loose mouth she'd had Max over a barrel. He had no choice now but to keep his side of the bargain.

17

Late the following afternoon Sally and Fiona were in the kitchen, preparing the food for a dinner party booking when there was a ring at the front door bell. Annie went to answer it and a moment later Ian appeared at the top of the basement stairs.

'I hope I'm not disturbing you.'

Fiona looked up in alarm. 'Ian! Are you all right? Is anything wrong?'

He began to descend the stairs. 'Well, it's hard to say really. My main problem at the moment is that I appear to be homeless. I hope it's all right but all my worldly goods are in a bag upstairs in the hall.'

'Of course it's all right.' Fiona pulled out a chair. 'Come and sit down and tell us all about it.'

'I'll put the kettle on,' Sally said. Her heart was beating fast. Ever since she had left the club yesterday she had convinced herself that Max would call her bluff. Now it seemed he had taken her at her word.

'I really didn't know what else to do,' Ian was saying. 'It'll only be for a couple of nights — till I find somewhere else.'

'Don't be silly. You're welcome to stay as long as you want.'

He looked at the table, laden with dishes and bags of prepared vegetables. 'Look, I can see you're busy. It's an imposition.'

Fiona cleared a space for the tray of tea Sally carried through from the scullery. 'Look — just stop apologizing and tell us what's happened, will you? We've got ages yet. Sally always likes to be well ahead, don't you, Sall?'

Sally looked from one to the other. 'Would you like me to make myself scarce? Is it private?'

'God, no!' Ian said. 'In fact I have a hunch you might already know something about this.'

'About *what*?' Fiona asked. 'You're driving me mad!'

Ian took a sip of the tea Sally had poured for him. 'Well, Max Feldman arrived unexpectedly this afternoon with a briefcase full of banknotes and announced that he was winding up the business due to unforeseen circumstances. No explanation — nothing. He said he was sorry for the inconvenience. He said he was paying me back what I'd put into the business and that he wanted me out immediately.' He took another sip of his tea. 'I wish he'd told me sooner. I'd only just given up the flat to move into the rooms above the garage — which is why I'm homeless.'

'And the money — did you get all of it back?' Fiona asked.

'Yes. He said he'd added payment for the cars I took with me and a bonus by way of compensation for the short notice. When I counted it the bonus amounted to a couple of hundred, so I suppose I can't grumble.'

'Sounds like hush money to me,' Fiona said. 'You were getting concerned that there might be some funny business going on, weren't you?'

Ian nodded. 'I can't say I'm sorry to be out of it. The trouble is of course that I'm back to square one — out of work. On the dole.' He smiled wryly at Fiona. 'Not much of a prospect as a bridegroom, am I? And there we were planning a Christmas wedding.'

Fiona reached across and kissed him. 'You're not to say any such thing,' she told him. 'You're a skilled mechanic. You'll be snapped up in no time. Maybe you can even buy into another business.'

He sighed. 'Not unless an opportunity comes up quickly. What I got back from Max looks like a lot but it won't last long. I had hoped it'd go towards our new home together.' He looked up at her apologetically. 'Sorry darling.'

'You're better out of Max's business,' Sally put in. 'I heard he was into some very dubious deals.'

Ian looked at her. 'So you did know?'

'In a way,' she admitted. 'Max's new barman is a man I used to work for. Max had let him down and he was disgruntled about it. He — hinted — well more than hinted at certain things. I was scared you might get into serious trouble along with him if someone blew the whistle so I asked Max to pay you back and let you go. I felt responsible as it was me who put you in the way of it in the first place. I'm sorry it's put you out of a job, but I think it was best in the long run.'

'Oh, I agree completely,' Ian said. 'I told Fee that I wasn't happy about some of the things Max was asking me to do. Some of the cars were death traps and once or twice I flatly refused to touch them. He wasn't best pleased, but he never pressed the point. Just took the cars away — probably to someone with fewer principles.'

'Have you heard from Stevie since he left?' Fiona asked. 'Do you know if he's all right?'

Sally had been longing to ask the same question. 'I suppose he's gone back to Cambridge,' she said.

Ian shook his head. 'He only stayed with me a couple of nights. I went back upstairs one evening and found he'd gone. He just left a note to say thanks and that he'd be in touch. His car had gone from the back of the garage and I haven't heard from him since.'

Fiona sighed. 'Did he mention anything to you about the row he'd had at home?'

Ian hesitated, glancing at Sally and Fiona put in, 'Sally knows everything. I insisted that my parents told Stevie too. It seemed unfair, keeping him in the dark about it.'

Ian sighed. 'He did tell me. He seemed very cut up about it. I'm afraid he's pretty bitter. He was very quiet and subdued while he was with me and I've no idea where he went when he left me. I rang his digs in Cambridge but the chap who answered said he hadn't returned.'

Fiona looked worried. 'If he isn't there then where is he?'

'I expect he needs some time to think,' Ian said.

'But it's been over a week. What about his work? He'll be missing important lectures.'

Sally touched Fiona's arm. 'Fee — the time's getting on. Would you like me to go upstairs and get changed while you finish the packing up here?'

Fiona nodded. 'Yes please, Sall. I'll start loading the van.' She looked at Ian. 'We'll talk later, when we get back.'

Upstairs as Sally changed in her room her heart was heavy. Where could Stephen be? Why hadn't he turned to her when he was unhappy? Clearly it was over between them if he didn't feel he could trust her enough for that.

In the van as they drove to their evening booking Fiona looked at her. 'Are you going to tell me just what really happened between you and Max?' she asked. 'There's a bit more to this than you've admitted, isn't there?'

Sally hesitated then decided she had to come clean. 'Max made a pass at me,' she said. 'It was the night of Stephen's investiture. You'd all gone off to celebrate and I was feeling really down. He wanted me to move into the flat above the club so that we could — be together every weekend.' She glanced at Fiona. 'I almost — *almost* gave in, Fee. There — I've told you now. It's been on my conscience ever since. I feel so ashamed and I wouldn't blame you if you said you wanted nothing more to do with me.'

'Oh Sally.' Fiona took one hand off the wheel to touch Sally's arm. 'You must have felt so left out that day. I wanted you to celebrate with us — Ian too, but you know what Mother's like. She insisted it was to be family only.'

'It wasn't just that,' Sally went on. 'It was Stevie. Ever since he went to Cambridge I've felt him slipping away from me. That day it felt like the end of the road and just for a moment it felt good to be wanted — even by Max.'

'Poor Sally. Why didn't you say something?'

'You don't know the half of it yet. On the night of the benefit concert I discovered that Max's new barman was Alf Chandler.'

'Chandler? Not that horrible man you worked for at the Cosy Café?' Fiona looked horrified.

'Yes. I almost had a fit when I saw him. He said that Max had offered him the flat along with the job, but he'd since backtracked and said that it wasn't available after all as he was letting someone else have it.'

'I take it he meant you.'

Sally nodded. 'Alf s wife has left him and he wanted the flat. The worst of it was that he suspected I was the would-be tenant. He was very resentful and just *happened* to let slip that Max was married. He also hinted that he was into stolen cars among other dishonest practices. After what you'd told me I put two and two together. I couldn't risk Ian going to prison and your life being ruined for something he was completely innocent of. I was furious that he'd tried to seduce me when I was feeling low too, so I . . . '

Fiona stared at her wide-eyed. 'Are you telling me you *blackmailed* him?'

'I suppose I did. Come to think of it, it isn't the first time I've had to threaten to tell someone's wife he was up to no good. It's what I did to Alf.'

For a moment they stared at each other, then Fiona began to laugh. '*Sally*! You're priceless! I don't know how you dared! Didn't you realize how dangerous it was, threatening a man like Max Feldman?'

'I knew him when he was a snotty-nosed little kid in scruffy hand-me-down clothes,' Sally said. 'Somehow you can't be seriously scared of someone like that.'

'But you should have been.' Fiona wasn't laughing now. 'To think you took a risk like that for Ian and me. You're a good friend, Sally — the best. Don't ever think I don't appreciate you.'

They had reached their destination now and as Fiona drew up outside. Sally said, 'Fee, what are we going to do about Stevie? Where can he be? We have to find him.'

'I've been thinking about that. None of us is doing anything tomorrow. I think we should go and see Nanny Joan. If he needed someone to talk to it's more likely to have been her than anyone else.'

'But if he was angry with your father won't he be angry with her too?'

'Not if I know Stevie. Anyway, we need some more supplies so I think that's what we'll do,' Fiona said. 'If he isn't there, we needn't worry her. If he is — well, we'll meet that if and when we come to it.' She opened the van door. 'But right now, we'd better get cracking with this dinner party before the hostess starts panicking.'

* * *

The following morning was bright and clear, more like spring than autumn. Ian had kept the

Bentley and the three of them travelled down to Fairfield in it.

'At least I'll still be able to hire myself out for weddings with this old girl,' Ian remarked as he drove. 'She's my one asset and I have to say that she does look a treat with her bodywork polished up and white ribbons tied to her bonnet.'

Moon Cottage looked serene in the golden autumn sunlight. The little front garden was littered with leaves and Nanny Joan was busy sweeping them into heaps as they drew up outside the gate. She wore an old pair of khaki trousers and a chunky cardigan, her hair scraped back and tightly plaited. As they got out of the car she looked up, shading her eyes against the light then threw down her broom with an exclamation.

'*Well*! Why didn't you let me know you were coming?'

Fiona hugged her. 'Sorry, Nanny. It was a spur of the moment decision. I hope you don't mind.'

'Mind? Of course I don't. It's always a pleasure to see you — all of you. I only wish you hadn't caught me looking like a tramp, but there — can't be helped. Come in and I'll put the kettle on.'

They followed her into the kitchen, which, as always was warm and cosy. Barney the cat, looked up at them his green eyes narrowing with disdain and jumped down from the rocking chair to disappear upstairs.

'Poor Barney, we've chased him away,' Sally said, sitting down on the catwarmed cushion.

Fiona was busying herself getting cups down

from the dresser and fetching milk from the pantry. 'We thought your Bramley apples should be ready by now,' she said. 'And maybe there are some Brussels sprouts and cauliflowers too. We've got two dinner parties booked for this coming weekend.' She came face to face with Nanny as she carried the teapot to the Aga.

'And you were wondering if I'd heard anything from Stephen,' Nanny added quietly. 'I daresay you've been worried about him.' She turned to pour boiling water into the pot. 'He's here. Turned up out of the blue just like you.' She glanced at Sally and Ian, then back at Fiona. 'I take it all of you are aware of the — what shall I call it — the family secret?'

'Yes, they know,' Fiona told her. 'I needed to tell my best friend and Ian and I are going to be married so he's almost family anyway.'

'I heard, and I'm delighted for both of you.' Nanny set the teapot on the tray with the cups. 'Stephen was shocked by his father's revelation. It hurt him deeply. I don't know where he'd been before he turned up here, but he looked terrible; unshaven and crumpled. It wouldn't surprise me if he'd been sleeping in the car. But a good meal and a comfortable bed soon put him right. That and a good talk.' She smiled. 'We've done plenty of that — really burned the midnight oil. I think he's straightened his mind out now.' She looked at Sally. 'He's out in the apple shed at the moment,' she said. 'And I think he'd rather like to see you.'

Sally hesitated. 'But surely — Fee . . . '

'Yes, obviously he'll want to talk to Fiona,'

Nanny said. 'But trust me, Sally, it's you he needs right at this moment.' Sally got up and walked towards the door, her heart beating fast. 'Bring him in with you when you come back,' Nanny called. 'I'll see what I can rustle up for lunch.'

She found him in the apple shed as Nanny had said, sorting the keeping apples and wrapping them for winter storage. He had his back to her as she opened the door.

'I'm putting the Bramleys on this side and the Coxes on the other. Is that all right?' When she didn't answer he turned and his face lit up with delighted surprise when he saw her. '*Sally!*' He covered the space between them in one stride and grasped her to him, holding her so tightly that she could scarcely breathe. 'Oh, if you only knew how much I've wanted to hold you like this,' he whispered against her cheek. 'I love you so much, Sally.'

'I love you too, Stevie.' Tears were trickling down her cheeks now.

He drew back his head to look at her, wiping the tears away with his thumbs. 'Hey! Don't cry darling. I've got so much to tell you.'

'I know — about Fiona — your father and Nanny.'

'I know you do. I'm not talking about that. Yes, I was shocked and hurt that my father could have behaved so badly, betraying Ma and taking advantage of a vulnerable employee. But Nanny, bless her, has sorted my head out now and I've come to some kind of understanding of it. She's made me see that Dad did his best to make amends to all of us and that something good came out of it for us all in the end. I might never have known I had a half-sister, or been lucky enough to be brought up by Nanny Joan, so I have to be grateful for those two things at least.' He looked down at her and she saw the new lines of anguish etched around his mouth and eyes. 'Listen — I've been doing a lot of thinking,' he went on. 'I've decided not to go back to Cambridge. I don't want to study law.'

She stared at him. '*Stevie*! You can't give it up. It's what you've always wanted.'

'No! It's what *they've* always wanted. My mother and Dad. Maybe if there hadn't been a war, things might have worked out to plan. But I'm a different person because of it. You grow up very fast in a war. I've seen and done things I could never even have dreamed of, seen good men die before they'd had time to live — watched great cities burn to ashes.' He looked down at her. 'It puts things in perspective, Sally. It lets you see what's important and what isn't.'

'So what are you going to do?'

'I miss flying more than I ever thought possible, so I'm going to try for a job with an airline,' he told her. 'Civil flying. It's the coming thing. People are going to want holidays abroad again and now they'll want to fly. It shouldn't be too hard to get a job with my service record.'

'What about your parents?'

'I went to see them last weekend,' he told her. 'I told them what I've just told you. I said I'd give up any right of inheritance if necessary but I intended to go my own way from now on. I

330

should have done it long ago.'

'Were they upset?'

'Not as much as I'd expected. Maybe they half expected it. After I told them what I had in mind, they agreed. Not that they really had any choice because I would have done it with or without their blessing. Dad made just one stipulation. He suggested that I keep the money he had set aside for my Cambridge education. At first I refused but he insisted, so I had another idea. I'm going to ask Ian to give up that partnership he's in. I don't like the sound of that Feldman character. I'm going to ask him to throw in his lot with me. We could set up a car hire business and Ian could run it while I fly.' Sally was laughing and he looked puzzled. 'What? Is it such a daft idea?'

'No. It's wonderful! It's just that Ian has already given up his partnership with Max,' she said. 'Your instinct about Max was right all along. It's a long story and I'll tell you later along with everything else I have to tell you, but it's my guess that Ian's going to be thrilled with your idea.' She took his hand. 'Let's go and tell him. He's here now — and so is Fee. She's been so worried about you. Come and . . . '

'Sally — *wait!*' He pulled her back. 'I've got something important to ask you first. I have to know your answer before we go in. Will you marry me?'

The breath caught in her throat. She longed to say yes, but there was still a shadow of doubt in her mind. 'Oh, Stevie, are you sure — *really* sure?'

'*I'm* sure, but the question is, are you? You've always had this hang-up about your background being different from mine. Well, now you know that it isn't all that different after all.'

'You've had such a disturbing time these past couple of weeks. Your emotions must be all over the place. Maybe you should think about it a bit longer.'

'Believe me, I've thought of little else since I went to Cambridge. I've missed you so much, Sally. I want us to be together — for always. No matter what.'

'But your parents — they had such plans for you.'

'My parents have no right to tell me what to do or who to marry,' he said. 'If one good thing has come out of this it is that it's made me realize that I don't have to please them any more by living up to their so-called *principles*, based largely on social snobbery. All that trivial nonsense belongs in the past. I stopped being their boy when I risked my life for my country. Now I think I've earned the right to live my own life and to choose the girl I want to share the rest of my life with.' He drew her close and kissed her deeply. 'So what's the answer, Sally? Are you willing to take on a risky proposition like me?'

'Yes!' She wound her arms around his neck and kissed him. 'Yes, yes — *yes!*' she said between kisses.

He laughed. 'One yes is quite enough, but go on saying it anyway. I've dreamed of hearing you say it.' He smiled down at her. 'Do you remember quoting a poem to me once? It was when you were talking about the blitz and how it had changed things. I've never forgotten.'

'The Land of Lost Content,' she said. '*The happy highways where I went and cannot come again.*'

'That's right.' He held her close and rested his chin on the top of her head. 'Well, I've found my happy highway,' he said softly. 'And now we can walk it together — all the way.'

We do hope that you have enjoyed reading this large print book.

Did you know that all of our titles are available for purchase?

We publish a wide range of high quality large print books including:
Romances, Mysteries, Classics
General Fiction
Non Fiction and Westerns

Special interest titles available in large print are:
The Little Oxford Dictionary
Music Book
Song Book
Hymn Book
Service Book

Also available from us courtesy of Oxford University Press:
Young Readers' Dictionary
(large print edition)
Young Readers' Thesaurus
(large print edition)

For further information or a free brochure, please contact us at:
Ulverscroft Large Print Books Ltd.,
The Green, Bradgate Road, Anstey,
Leicester, LE7 7FU, England.
Tel: (00 44) 0116 236 4325
Fax: (00 44) 0116 234 0205

Other titles published by
The House of Ulverscroft:

ALL THAT I AM

Jeanne Whitmee

After her doctor father's death in the Great
War, Abigail Banks, a photographer, returns
to her childhood home of Eastmere. There,
Abby is reunited with her childhood friend,
Sophie, and welcomed back by the poor
Johnson family, who have never forgotten her
father's kindness. But she also meets with
hostility in the form of the hot-headed
Patrick Johnson. Setting up a studio in the
town, Abby finds herself encountering cor-
ruption and greed among those with
influence. But she finds allies in the editor of
the local paper and young Doctor William
Maybury. Many battles lie ahead for Abby
and she and Patrick are often destined to
cross swords . . .

PRIDE OF PEACOCKS

Jeanne Whitmee

Rose, an illegitimate child abandoned by her mother and brought up by a resentful aunt in an East End pub, joins the Women's Land Army when war breaks out. She looks forward to life in the country, where she can find the sense of belonging for which she yearns. But on her arrival at Peacock's Farm she is sadly disappointed; the farm is run down, its owner a bitter alcoholic who clearly resents her presence. Determined to make the best of things, Rose gradually convinces Bill Peacock that she can help to make the farm a profitable business again. But the future holds deceit and heartbreak and there are life-changing decisions for Rose to make before she can find true happiness.

KING'S WALK

Jeanne Whitmee

King's Walk is a row of semi-detached houses built by Albert King, whose family occupies Cedar Lodge, the big house on the corner. But the war changes the lives of all who live there, whether they are working or upper class. Albert's widow, Theresa, has one son reported 'missing in action' and the other about to marry 'beneath him'. For the religious Sands family the morals of their adopted daughter bring shame. Then there is Clarice, footloose when her grandson leaves to do his National Service, who accepts a job in service at Cedar Lodge. But it is very different from pre-war days and now it will be Clarice who makes the rules . . .

BELLADONNA

Jeanne Whitmee

Hurt and betrayed, fifteen-year-old Bryony
Luscombe knows instinctively that her love
for Paul Blythe, heir to Brashfield Hall, is
worthless. Brought up by a local wise woman
in a small fishing village, Bryony's history is a
whispered secret, but one which is destined
to lift her from poverty. Hounded from the
village on suspicion of witchcraft, Bryony is
forced to seek help from a most unwelcome
source. An ambitious entrepreneur, Max
Randal persuades Bryony to place her trust in
him. But Max has other motives and secrets
of his own, and Bryony cannot afford to
compromise her pride, independence — and
possibly her heart — again.